MY BROTHER'S KEEPER

By

M. D. NUTH

MY BROTHER'S KEEPER

By

M.D. NUTH

Published by
Crimson Cloak Publishing

Publisher's Publication in Data
Nuth, M.D.
My Brother's Keeper
1.Fiction 2. Literary

ISBN 13: 978-1-68160-773-3

ISBN 10: 1-68160-773-5

Edited by Kate McCracken and Denna Holm.
Cover by Carly McCracken and Matt Nuth

Too often we rely on those we should not
and sacrifice those we need.

—Simon Cartwright

PROLOGUE

Sometimes a sacrifice is required.
—Anders Cartwright

We are falling. There are bumps, some large, some small, along the way down, but these are only futile attempts by our small airplane to save itself. The noise is deafening; the engines groan and wail as they struggle for life. Our fuselage is under attack by the rain, each drop a bullet that hammers into the steel and aluminum on the way downward. The plane shudders under the vibration of the wings as they cut through the wind. And then…

There is no warning, just an ear-deafening bang and Ess' body slams into my left side with excruciating force, sending me crushing to the right into the first mate's shoulder. He is sitting against the bulkhead; there is nowhere for him to go as his head smashes hard into the wood and steel frame. It hits not with a dull thud but with a sound more akin to the crack of a baseball bat striking a homerun. There is a final and terrible sound of fracturing and tearing metal as the nose of the plane slaps downward. At that moment, the brave Douglas DC-3 moans and dies a quick and merciful death.

It is too dark to see. We are blind in the blackness. I blink my eyes, trying to get a sense as to what has just happened. The dark is disconcerting. There is no movement in the plane and I have no idea how long it has been since it came to a rest. Can I be the only survivor? How cruel would God be? It would not be fair to be alone. I shiver with cold and my body hurts. The banging water bullets have quieted, and the straining of the propellers is gone. Now, the only noise is the whistling breeze and the gentle patter of rain as it sheds over the outside hull of our downed aircraft. Where the metal skin has torn from its rivets, water streams into the cabin poring over me. I am drenched.

I close my eyes again, trying to calm myself to the pain, but it doesn't help. I am damaged. I don't know how badly. I fear I am lost and alone.

CHAPTER 1
Why?

I am Anders, Andy to everybody except my brother and the accountants who write my paycheck every two weeks. To them I will always be Anders.

I'm not alone. I've been thrown into this nightmare flight with five others. Only two, Simon and Shelly, did I know before we boarded the plane. It's fair to say that Simon has been an acquaintance of mine for years. I will not suggest we are friends, but let's say we share a common past. He is my brother and has been with me constantly since our parents died more than a decade ago. I suspect he will always be with me. I have become his reluctant caregiver.

I love my brother, but I don't like him. He tires me with his never-ending detail and his compelling need to explain things. True, he is knowledgeable—like an encyclopedia—a repository of information that nobody needs or wants to hear. He makes observations then follows them with directives. It's odd that he can't grasp why I ignore his ideas. He is incapable of receiving coaching or feedback, and he doesn't respect the authority of position. To him, authority should be the result of being right, not arbitrary assignment of a title, and since he is always right, he believes he is the authority. I think it's fair to describe our relationship as trying.

Shelly is my love, even though I doubt she knows it. I call her Ess, for short, which she hates but has learned to accept. We met just after our respective news agencies transplanted us to Singapore to cover the Chino-Japanese War. I wanted her from the first moment I spotted her at a gala at the famous Raffles Hotel. She is amazing: long legs, auburn hair, emerald eyes, perfect skin, smart, successful. Our lives were one of endless press meetings and interviews as we competed to make up fantastic stories for our respective news agencies. I say "make up" because nobody wanted to read the boring stuff of reality, so we embellished … everything.

The rapid Japanese expansion through East Asia didn't need embellishment to make it interesting and compelling to my editor and readers. The risk was real, the violence and viciousness of the warring Imperial Army was hard to overstate. Personally, I wish it had been one of my journalistic fabrications, but the reports of terror and death being waged on those conquered as the Japanese march southwards has become indisputable. Even if the stories were nothing more than the pure fabrication by other inventive minds, I have no intention of remaining in Singapore to test their substance. They are too frightening.

When I first meet our pilot, Captain Robert, and his crew of one—a large, wiry, worn-out man who looks to be missing the majority of his front teeth—they are leaning with their backs against the trailing edge of the wing next to the cargo door, smoking cigarettes. I privately dub the large toothless one "Toothless Joe" even though he is introduced as First Mate Thompson. I suppose it reflects a character deficiency in me that I invariably find it necessary to make light of the physical deficiencies of others. It makes me feel superior.

Upon first climbing the five steep steps to the lone door providing access to the craft, I can see this plane is significantly different from what I had flown when leaving Hong Kong. They are both DC-3s, but this craft is obviously not intended for passengers. The door is at least twice as wide as the passenger versions, and even though there are seats, these are hard and can be folded up to provide more room for cargo. Instead of facing forward bolted to the floor, they are situated sideways, bolted to the frame of the fuselage.

As I climb the narrow steps to board the plane, I cannot help but smile to myself at the name I have placed on First Mate Thompson as he barks, "You sit on this side. Them blankets on the floor are for you." He gestures toward a pile of stained, folded cargo blankets that are stacked opposite the cargo door. The floor is covered in dirt and dust. I don't think it's seen a broom since the plane began to fly. The filthy inside is a striking contrast to the glistening, spotless silver exterior of the proud craft. Toothless continues, "It'll be damn cold when we get up to altitude."

I choke back a laugh when Toothless struggles to pronounce his words without the benefit of front teeth.

Captain Robert, dressed in tan dungarees, thick chambray shirt, leather jacket, baseball cap, and work boots, fit exactly with my stereotypical image of a rough, tough pilot. Although dutifully respectful, recognizing we are paying customers, he makes it clear that our money is to pay for the transportation and a couple bottles of beer once we are airborne, nothing more. The beer came from a small steel cooler lashed to the pan of the co-pilot's seat well within reach of the pilot. At least the co-pilot's seat serves a purpose. No one is occupying it for our flight. If Captain Robert passes out, we'll be destined to drop into the ocean, a quick end to our lives—a scary proposition, but not as frightening as the horrors that could befall those who remain in the path of the Japanese.

Two additional passengers were already seated inside the cabin when we arrived, bringing our luckless gang this morning to seven. These two passengers are merely shadows until my eyes adjust to the relative darkness inside the plane.

The first fellow traveler appears to have had way too much fun the previous evening and is now sleeping with his head craned back against the hard aluminum frame lining the fuselage. His name is Preston James, a twenty-something-year-old brat with whom I had become acquainted over the past two years and come to dislike completely. He is still dressed in his black formal wear, but his shirt tails are untucked, and his bow tie untied. He's missing the top button from his collar, and the previously starched, brilliant white shirt is now stained with sweat, drink, and vomit. Preston is from a family of some means back in New York. He's spent the past two years in Singapore learning how to drink, flaunt money, and become an all-around jerk. I would rather he stayed in Singapore. I can't help thinking that losing him to the war would be a net gain for the world. I have no doubt his parents would be happy to be rid of him, too. A little mourning of his death seems preferable to dealing with the continuous publicity challenges his foolish acts bring his family.

The second passenger is dressed in the dark gray suit and red tie of a successful banker. Below his seat and behind his feet, I can make out what appears to be an expensive, tooled-leather valise. In his lap he holds a large briefcase, the kind that opens from the top by unfolding two leather flaps and that can be easily locked. It is the kind I was accustomed to seeing accountants and attorneys use to cart around client files and legal documents. Expecting him to be stuffy, I am surprised when he rises from his seat to introduce himself to Ess and me as Bradley Simmons, "But just call me Brad." To me, he looks more like a Bradley—I think I will continue to call him Bradley. He is not the banker I expected, but rather an import-export entrepreneur who relocated from the States several years ago. From his brief introduction I gather he'd been moderately successful in his business and was using the war as provocation to wrap things up and return to his home for the first time in almost twenty years. Most of the cargo on the plane is his. The portion that is not his was handed over to Captain Robert as payment for his passage on this plane. The cargo consists of wooden cases filled with bottles of scotch along with several unmarked corrugated cardboard boxes. Apparently, Bradley also thought it infinitely better to run than become a prisoner of war.

It's a huge relief for everyone when we finally lift off from this dangerous land.

"Whoa, it looks like this is going to be a fun one," Captain Robert shouts over his shoulder to no one as he reaches across to pull another beer out of the cooler. "Can you see this baby? She's a beaut."

The drone of the twin engines makes it impossible to hear anything unless it is shouted. As such, everyone has given up any hope of conversation to pass the time. Instead, we pilgrims resign ourselves to isolation by closing our eyes, using the constant noise to hypnotize ourselves into a sleep-like trance. Sleep is impossible since the thinly padded folding jump seats quickly became incredibly uncomfortable to even the most experienced of travelers. They might be practical for a plane designed to haul cargo, but not a good match for the butt, especially for hours of continuous flight. I had spent the last ten minutes standing to allow blood circulation to recover in my legs and buttocks when the captain's voice startles me back to earth, figuratively, in that we are flying almost 8,000 feet above sea level.

He yells, "I'm going to take us up to about 12,000 feet to see if we can get over the worst of it, but it's going to be a fun ride. Nothing that this babe hasn't seen before, though. So, don't fret."

I fall into my seat and watch the captain pull back on his wheel and push forward on a couple levers in the center console. We can almost feel the strain on the engines as the plane noses up in search of clear skies. Unfortunately, the storm clouds are huge and thick. I cannot see how climbing over them is going to be an option. As the airplane strains to gain altitude, the dark of the storm overtakes us. Looking out the windows across from me, I see dark mist eerily moving by, as in slow motion, cloaking us in nighttime even though it is still only midafternoon. Although Captain Robert sounds confident in his plane, I have no such faith. One might consider me a fatalist, but really, I'm just a pragmatist, and at this time it looks to me as though the storm has infinitely more anger than our little DC-3 is prepared to handle. Okay, sometimes pragmatism and fatalism align.

Toothless Joe shakes my arm and motions indiscriminately toward Ess and Simon, both seated to my left. "Best make sure you all are belted in tight." He looks across the cabin to the remaining two passengers. "That goes for you, too, else yer likely to get something broke when the storm starts playin' catch with us."

Bradley elbows Preston awake, nodding to Toothless as he straps in. Preston still appears sick as he fumbles with the harness to loosely tie himself to the seat. I want to tell Bradley he should help Preston but choose not to say anything. If Preston gets hurt that's his problem.

While we get ourselves tied in, Toothless jumps from his seat to ensure the cargo netting is tightly bound and the straps are correctly ratcheted to the floor. I guess any shifting of the cargo weight would doom the plane's stability. Once Toothless is comfortable the cargo is secure, he pauses to grab Preston's loose harness, cinching it tight, leaving the man pinned against the back of his seat. Toothless falls back into his own seat, but not before he leans over the co-pilot's chair to close the beer cooler and latch it tight. I'm shocked he can still smile as he straightens up and tightens his own belt and harness. It's almost as though he is looking forward to this. "Let's hope these bottles don't get too broken up. It'll make the rest of the flight awful long."

No sooner are the words out of Toothless Joe's mouth than the bottom drops out of our little world, quite literally. Our bodies push up against the harnesses as the plane goes into a brief free fall, no more than a second or two, and then crushing us back into the seats, knocking the wind out of each of us as the plane regains its footing on the pillow of air below its wings. From across the cabin, Brad's face grins stupidly at me and Ess. Preston has vomited again on his already soiled shirt.

I have no doubt Ess was unnerved by the sudden jolt. I reach to grasp her hand … to what? Provide comfort? Hell, I, too, feel pure panic. Had I taken advantage of the free beer, I would have pissed myself right then and there. Not much of an example of a knight in shining armor for Ess. Apparently, this is no big deal for the experienced crew of two. Toothless Joe's eyes are closed, and he seems strangely at peace. No doubt he's been through this type of weather before. Captain Robert appears to be enjoying himself thoroughly as he sings the cowboy hit song "Tumbling

Tumbleweeds" at the top of his voice, as if taunting the wind and rain as it plays with his plane. The thrill of the adventure has him completely enthralled and thrilled.

I can't do anything but stare straight ahead at the duo across from me. Not wanting to look to the side, I can only imagine what Ess' face must look like at this moment, tense and stressed with the recognition and certainty her life is going to suddenly end. I can also imagine Simon's face, in striking contrast, displaying no fear, merely an interest in understanding how far the plane had fallen before beginning to climb to its original altitude. In a way, I'm always jealous of Simon and his natural state of being disconnected from the emotions that fill us normal folk with fear and anger. If Simon could feel, he might also be jealous of others for their ability to experience pure joy and love. If he noticed he was different from others, or if he ever wondered what it would be like to be me, he'd never let it be shown or known.

The plane's engines increase in pitch and volume as Captain Robert juices them to correct their flight. With noticeable effort, they sluggishly respond to the increased throttle, pulling the craft up from the fall to gain altitude and speed once again. As a completely outrageous and nervous reaction, I laugh loudly, suddenly recalling that, as a kid, I'd happily paid for this type of thrill on the Cyclone roller coaster at Coney Island. I can handle this.

Toothless leans as far forward as his straps allow and turns to us. "Yer okay with that one? Hang on tight, we might have a whole bunch of these as we go dancin' through them clouds." While talking, he is reaching into his breast pocket to pull out a cigarette along with his Zippo lighter. He calmly lights up a smoke.

As the toothless one exhales his first cloud of blue smoke, the captain sticks his head through the cabin door opening and yells, "It's going to be a pisser for a while. This storm is too big to fly over, so we'll be going through it. Once we are through, we should be landing shortly in Semarang in Java to refuel. We'll have a little time to catch some sleep and check out the plane before we head east to Kupang. For now, make sure everything is stowed tight. I don't need things flying around up here."

Excluding the outside noise, the cabin becomes deathly quiet. In the dim lighting afforded by the wire encaged bulbs attached to the ceiling, I see the faces of Preston and Bradley, which had, up until several moments ago, been filled with excited anticipation. They are no longer smiling, but show the countenances of one sentenced and damned, resigned to the fact that their life can or will be taken shortly. Their only hope is that death will be quick, painless, and merciful. My fellow travelers busy themselves retightening their already tight belts, as if this activity will somehow help take the plane through the storm. This effort just means that each of them will feel every jolt the plane experiences, every bump transferred directly to their bones, leaving them bruised and sore tomorrow.

Toothless Joe sits quietly, his hands crossed over his chest, loosely gripping his harness, his eyes darting from side to side as the cigarette dangles from the corner of his mouth, its glowing tip rising and falling as his lips twitch with the stress. I find myself copying his actions, sans the cigarette. I could have used one of those smokes to calm myself. In contrast, Simon is the picture of serenity, eyes closed and just the hint of a smile turning up at the corners of his lips. He is either genuinely enjoying the stress or he has no comprehension of the danger facing this small crew. I think it is the latter. God only knows what goes on in Simon's head in times like these.

The rain hits first. It comes with short warning waves, sounding like nothing more than a couple snare drum riffs, quiet and all but gone before they even start. Then all hell breaks loose. The noise is ear-splitting as we enter the belly of the storm, like the overpowering, steel-on-steel, monstrous cacophony of a train speeding by. The previously harmless droplets have turned into an onslaught of deadly water bullets hitting against the aluminum skin of the plane at more than two hundred miles per hour. I wait for the skin of the plane to be severed from the frame, leaving us falling miles to our death.

Undaunted, Captain Robert keeps the engines revving against the onslaught of water just to keep altitude and speed, all the while bellowing out "…tumbling tumbleweeds…" I should take comfort in his singing. It must mean he is still delighted in fighting with the storm. If he is having fun, how bad can it be? Now, if he stops singing, that's the time for our butts to pinch—

He stops singing.

I turn to my left, looking at Toothless. His eyes stare out the windows into the blackness of the storm. He is motionless as his cigarette smolders, but the trail of smoke makes zigzags in the air as the plane jerks right and left and up and down.

The windows of the cockpit are useless as the dark, wind, and rain smear any vision. The captain is flying blind. The only relief from the darkness comes from massive flashes of lightning as gigantic electric bolts cross the sky above us. They appear as massive cracks, allowing blinding light into a black world that heal up as soon as they appear. The instantaneous crashing of thunder signals how close they are. The lack of any visual guidance makes it impossible to distinguish sky from sea.

Captain Robert drains a beer down his gullet and discards the bottle, tossing it backwards to the tail of the plane. I am afraid his empties will become deadly missiles as our little plane bounces in the air. The captain has one hand on his wheel and the other is moving continuously between the levers on his console as the plane goes up, down, and sideways in a game of toss with the storm. From his frantic movement and the whining of the engines, I can only presume the contest he started with the storm is one the captain and the plane are losing.

Directly across from me, Preston appears to have passed out—lucky for him. His head lifelessly wobbles with each movement of the plane, and then his neck stiffens for a moment and his eyes flutter open, as if to check if he is still on the plane. He raises his arm to wipe the drying vomit from his mouth with his sleeve, then he closes his eyes once again, descending into the fog of unconsciousness. It is as if his brain merely kicks him awake just enough to register that he is still alive and then sends him back off to a dreamless, alcohol-induced sleep. He is as hopeless and disgusting in his unconscious state as he is when conscious. I pray that maybe, if we are lucky, the plane will jerk just right and snap Preston's neck, forever ridding him from our lives. We could leave his body at the next stop and at least be rid of the stench of his vomit and stale liquor. If my harness would have allowed, I would have reached across to beat him until he came awake just so he would experience the same fear I feel at this moment.

Bradley looks to be cool and controlled. He has wrapped a blanket over his legs and chest, sitting quietly in a world of his own, completely oblivious to the danger facing the occupants of this flight. He continues to grasp his briefcase, holding it in his lap. The only action that belies our predicament is his nervous glances back to his boxes, as if they are the most precious things on this plane. I think it's not that the cargo is so valuable, but that his freight is the biggest danger for the flight. If any of it were to break loose from the straps holding it in place, we would likely be crushed when the wind provides another quick jolt to the plane. Even if the cargo doesn't smash us, if it were to shift just a bit, it might be heavy enough to kill any hope of Captain Robert keeping the plane in flight. Our trip would end abruptly somewhere in the Java Sea below us.

Toothless is obviously not as confident as he was just several minutes earlier. As soon as Captain Robert stops singing, he starts praying, not exactly the thing one wants to see from the first mate to instill confidence. He has his hands clinched together up under his chin. His eyes are tightly closed while he rocks to and fro with the constant rhythm of a clock pendulum in its futile effort to control time. In this case, the time being kept is not the countdown to a safe landing in the Javan city of Semarang, but, I fear, a drop into a black sea.

Ess stares at me with a look that is somewhere between pleading and accusing. I can fully understand either perspective, but I am ill prepared to respond. Can't she see I'm as powerless as her on this flight to hell, so the pleading is useless. I can't will the wings to stay on the plane or the engines to remain attached to the wings. I can't promise we'll be safe. I have no idea of what to expect if we get struck by one of those bolts of lightning that seem to be the only things capable of cutting through the deathly darkness of the squall.

I quietly pick my feet up off the floor. Why, for God's sake? My subconscious is thinking that somehow this small act will somehow insulate me from the hundred-million or so volts conducting through the metal floor and keep me from being fired to a crisp. People have told me that lightning is not a concern in a flying airplane, but I'm willing to wager that those same people probably have not flown through this type of storm. I don't suggest to anyone else that they pick up their feet.

Simon has his feet firmly planted on the floor.

Although I understand the accusing look showing in Ess's eyes, it is not fair. Does she think I am somehow blessed with divine knowledge that should have warned me our escape would be foolish? I talked her into this trip as an escape from a real threat and inadvertently dropped her into the teeth of real danger. At this point, I would have to agree that the Japanese Imperial Army seems relatively less intimidating now than it did this morning.

Ess had not wanted to go. She was convinced the London Times would make sure she returned to London long before the first Japanese incursion occurred, but she trusted me, and now this trust looks completely misplaced. It's not to say that the Japanese threat is not real. They had already invaded Malaya and were moving aggressively eastward and southward. In Simon's estimation, Singapore was doomed, and neither the New York nor London Times had done diddly-squat to prepare for our evacuation. We had acted rashly, but our choices were all bad. Perhaps waiting to get fare on a ship would have been safer, yet Simon was convinced the British Fleet was hardly capable of defending the commercial ocean vessels in the region. No, Ess, Simon and I had been trapped. It was too late to be saved.

This was our last chance for escape.

CHAPTER 2
Are we all right?

My first recollection after waking is that of quiet. The light is dim, and the air is stifling hot. My body aches. The pain is intense as I turn my head side to side. Oddly, I am soaked and feel chilled even though heat is radiating from the metal skin of the DC-3. The plane seems to have come to rest slightly elevated on the side where Bradly and Preston sit, leaning just enough toward me and Ess to allow several inches of water to gather below our seats, immersing my feet in a now foul-smelling concoction of dirt, dust, water, oil, and sacrificed scotch from the cargo that failed to survive the landing. Despite the travesty of the loss of exceptional scotch, I should be thankful the alcohol will kill any infection borne in the filthy, pooled water.

From the look of the torn and dented membrane of the DC-3 I have no idea how we survived. The crash landing may have hurt me, but it killed the plane. As near as I can see, the previous night's flight participants remain harnessed in their seats. It is still outside of the subtle noise of dripping water. I don't see any signs of life. I listen for the sound of breathing. Please, God, let me not be the only one who survived; I cannot bear being alone.

I hear nothing, but I have that odd sensation when one knows they are being watched. It's funny how silence can make one see and feel things that are not real. Raising my hands to my chest, I grasp the harness and release the buckle. I clinch my hands into fists around the straps a moment and then release them, letting them fall to my lap as I relax while leaning my head back to rest against the interior metal skin of the plane. Twisting my body to the right so as not to move my neck, I catch Toothless in my peripheral vision. He is blinking his eyes as a child might do when awakened from a deep sleep. Two dried streams of blood, the first from a gash on the right side of his forehead, has made a path outlining his eyebrow, sweeping around his eye down to his jaw just below his ear. The second originates from the same cut but makes a detour getting lost in his ear and hair before continuing its downward trek to reconnect with the first stream. The blood has left his shirt stained a brownish red. He whispers to me, as if to not disturb the dead, "You, okay?"

I tentatively nod. Barely catching myself to not blurt out 'Toothless,' I remember the first mate's real name. "Thompson, I think so. You?"

"I'm okay." With this, Toothless also unbuckles his harness, then closes his eyes and leans against the cracked bulkhead. I imagine the crack in the bulkhead was a result of Toothless Joe's noggin' slamming into it and was the cause of the bloody rivulets. Toothless must have a ridiculously hard head, at least hard enough to win a battle with the quarter inch plywood that divides the cargo hold from the pilot's cabin.

Toothless looks to me and then nods toward the cockpit. "It don't look like Cap'n Robert is okay, though. He looks pretty dead."

In the dim lighting it is difficult to see, but there is no movement beyond the bulkhead and no sound from the pilot's seat. At first, I can see nothing but what appears to be branches and tree leaves; there ought not to be branches and tree leaves. It is as if a garden has taken root in the cockpit. As my eyes adjust to the darkness, I can make out leaves which are attached to a thick branch that has poked through the left windshield and embedded itself in Captain Robert's chest. There is no blood, so I guess the tree did not impale him, but it certainly did crush him. The paradox is almost humorous in that this beautiful growth with soft, billowy leaves managed to beat him to death with a single, hard punch. What did they say, 'beauty kills?' Apparently so.

His head is slightly leaning forward and to the right, as if he has just fallen asleep. I half expect him to wake with a start and ask for a little help to clear the cockpit of vegetation. It is not until I see his broken arms that the force of last night's crash becomes truly apparent to me. Instantly, as the plane hit land, the steering wheel had bent towards the control panel as muscle fought steel. The bones and muscles that had been tensed in Captain Robert's arms as he gripped the wheel were destroyed. His thumbs were dislocated and both arms were now draped over the wheel, bending downward at a point between wrist and elbow where no joint is supposed to exist. His hands had been crushed by the impact, not just broken; they had been compressed into the arms and were now bent backward in a way not intended by nature. Still, no blood. The smell of urine and beer, yes, but no blood. Last night's storm would have counted Captain Robert as a quick, clean kill. Although I can't see his face from my seat, I imagine he is smiling in a last act of defiance in his losing battle.

We would miss Captain Robert. With his death our chance of survival may have died just a little, too.

Toothless moves into the cockpit and reaches across the good captain's body to retrieve something from the captain's left side, or perhaps from under his leather jacket. As he turns back toward me, I catch a glimpse of what the mate had been groping for, a black revolver, maybe ten inches in length. I have seen this type of gun before, a .38 Special, a very effective and reliable weapon, and one that could prove critical if we are to survive.

I lean forward and slide off the jump seat, falling to my knees and turn to face Ess. She did not deserve this and perhaps it would have been best if she had not survived the crash. Her death would have saved me from having to see that *'Why did you do this to me?'* look every day from now on. Her living will just remind her of the isolation unfairly forced upon her by me, and means I will be striving for forgiveness every day until we are rescued. This will be hell. I may as well get prepared to ask for forgiveness. Ess' chest is gently rising and falling, breathing calmly and quietly, as if in a deep and peaceful sleep. If Toothless weren't so close, I might reach up to cover her mouth with one hand, gently pinch off the supply of air through her nose with the other, to save her from experiencing what I fear awaits us when we exit the plane. There are no sounds of people outside, no sirens from ambulances, no bars attempting to pry open the door. We are alone.

I gently lean forward and place my hands on the sides of her face. “Ess. Ess.”

Her body shudders briefly and her eyes fly open. She cries out. I keep my hands pinned to the sides of her face so as not to let her head move too much in case her neck had been hurt in the crash. Her eyes calm as she recognizes me. “Are we alright?”

“Well, that depends.”

“What do you mean?”

“If you are asking if you and I are okay, then, yes, we are all right. That said, not all of us are. Captain Robert is anything but right. He’s dead. First Mate Thompson seems fine, and I don’t have any idea about the rest of us, yet.”

In the dim lighting I don’t notice the pent-up fear reflected in Ess’ face until she panics and begins to wildly pull at her harness, grappling for the release and freedom from the all-too-fresh memories of her fall from the sky.

“Dammit. Someone get these damned straps off me. I’ve got to get out of here. I can’t breathe.” Her hands are all motion. I fight her to get the harness unhitched. As soon as the belts release their grip on her, she falls from the seat to the floor, and she begins crawling to where she thinks the lone door should be. She reaches the door and begins struggling to find the release handle. Giving up quickly she resorts to merely pounding on the door with her fists until, in exhaustion, she slides to the floor, whimpering. “Let me out, please let me out.”

I crawl to her, past where Preston and Bradley remain seated, and I pull her away from the door to allow me to engage the lever, still on my knees, and open the door. Surprisingly, the door opens effortlessly, allowing light to flood into what had begun to feel like a prison cell. While crawling toward Ess, I didn't notice that Simon's seat was already vacant. He has already escaped the confines of the plane. He is outside sitting in the sand with his legs outstretched, facing the sun. He is placid, as if he were on vacation in a tropical paradise. Staring from the door, I realize I shouldn't be surprised that Simon let himself out of the plane without checking on any of his fellow travelers. It wasn't that he did not care about others, he just never thought about anyone else. Just Simon being Simon.

Rather than joining my brother outside, I turn away and, without even the slightest verbal acknowledgement, return to the belly of the craft. Even with the light of freedom in her face, Ess still finds it impossible to gain her feet and walk outside. Instead, she has crawled back into the hull and has her back propped up against the undamaged crates of cargo.

I hear new groans as Toothless unhitches Bradley from his lifesaving belts. Preston, too, is awake and, surprisingly, looks fine. In fact, he looks better than he has the entire trip. Inebriation allowed him to bounce through the previous evening without injury or fear. The fog of his drunken stupor and the resulting hangover are now long gone. It looks as though his only needs are food, water, and a shower, and not necessarily in that order. Bradley, on the other hand, has not fared as well. Not only has he received a nasty gash from bouncing off the bulkhead, he looks to have dislocated his left shoulder from the same collision. With Toothless Joe's impact, the toothless wonder won. In Bradley's case, the wooden bulkhead was the obvious victor.

Toothless gingerly pulls Bradley up from his seat, holding his left arm still. But instead of assisting him in his walk to the door, he abruptly pushes Bradley with one hand while simultaneously pulling on his left elbow with the other. I hear the sickening "crunch" as the arm pops back into its socket. Coinciding with the crunch, Bradley's body goes limp; it's lights out as he falls unconscious. Toothless catches the limp Bradley and lowers his frame to the floor without any further damage. He mutters, "He'll thank me for that when he wakes up." He then moves to gather up

Preston, who has already freed himself from his harness and is now kneeling between the pilot and copilot seats, staring at Captain Robert.

Preston shakes his head, commenting to himself, “Now ain’t that a bitch? He saves us, but then he ends up biting the big one.” Then, turning back to the cabin, he says, “Hey, Mate. You are the First Mate, right? You know how to get the radio working?”

Toothless Joe merely stares at Preston, shakes his head, walks back to the hatch, and disappears out into the sunlight.

CHAPTER 3
His

It is time to do something, anything. I have been lying here in the sand for how long? I do not know, but the sun has burned the skin on my neck and arms and is now on its downward trek to extinguish itself in the sea for the evening. I push myself up out of the sand with my hands to a kneeling position and brush the sand off my shirt and arms. To my right, I notice that Bradley, Preston, and Toothless have disappeared; I can only assume they are the source of the banging I hear emanating from inside the plane. Simon and Ess are silently sitting on a large fallen tree trunk not more than twenty feet from the only door of the plane. Ess is ignoring Simon. I am not surprised; he is not fun to be with even under normal conditions. But I am surprised he is not boring her with a dissertation as to what caused the plane to fall from the sky last night. He would have a very reasonable explanation, as if it matters to anyone.

Although being shipwrecked is bad, it could have been worse had the plane nestled up against the large fallen tree on which Ess now sits. It would have blocked the only doorway making us captives in the DC-3 until we could break through the cockpit's side windows. Even then, Ess would have been the only one of us small enough to fit through the opening. How ironic would that have been, survive the crash only to die of thirst or hunger or heat? Well, little blessings. *It looks like it is time to get to work.* I say to myself.

As I walk back to our de-facto camp, I am struck by the beauty of our new home. Even though yesterday's storm threw wood and debris all over my beach (yes, I claim ownership of it), the view is striking; the vibrant colors of the sea and rain forest are amazing. Under different circumstances I would have been thrilled to spend time here with Ess. Given our current circumstances, I can't wait to leave.

I stick my head in through the hatchway. To my left, Bradley is working with his uninjured arm to free his cargo from the straps and netting that had prevented it from being broken to pieces yesterday. He was making little headway. To my right, Preston and Toothless struggle to free Captain Robert from the hold of the tree branch. Preston is wielding the plane's fire axe in a useless attempt to chop away at the tree branch. He is finding the long-handled axe completely ineffective in the constrained confines of the cockpit. There is no room to swing the heavy tool to generate any power. He should give up with the axe to try another option. Toothless sits cross-legged behind the captain's seat and is struggling to remove the seat back with an old rusty wrench and a pair of pliers. At least he has a chance to release Robert's corpse.

I return my attention to Bradley and climb over the crates and boxes to release the cargo straps opposite from him. With one arm, he's useless. "Just sit down, I'll get these. It's not a job for a one-handed man," I suggest, merely trying to help.

Bradley scowls at me. It is a look I would never have equated to this quiet, almost professorial man. "Bugger off. I don't need any fucking help to take care of my stuff. And, by the way, it is my stuff. I don't want you and the Preston kid…" He nods to the cockpit. "…drinking up any of my inventory."

"Bradley, don't be an ass. Between you and me, you have few potential customers for your inventory now so don't piss us off. Oh, and by the way, we'll be paying you in IOUs or seashells, whichever you prefer." I continue working to release the straps freeing up the boxes. Bradley continues to work his side to no avail, unwilling to acknowledge his limitation.

Within minutes I have the cargo free and toss my end of the straps towards Bradley. "Done. Now what do you want to do with it?" I direct the question to the individual who, in my estimation, just displaced Preston as the real asshole on this flight.

Bradley turns toward me as he ponders the question. "You know, I haven't a clue." He sits back against the curved wall of the plane and weeps. I have little sympathy for the crying man.

Not knowing how to respond, I stoop, pick up a crate and start towards the door with the intent of depositing it onto the sand just beyond the fallen tree outside. "Mine," he whispers as I step through the hatchway. I ignore him.

Ess joins me as we go back into the plane for another load. We decide to remove only the cargo that is in wooden crates, which means all the scotch is coming outside. What will remain inside is a small mountain of corrugated cardboard cartons, soaked with rainwater. And inside these cartons, who knows? The other things that we leave inside are a toolbox, two duffle bags belonging to the Captain and First Mate, Bradley's valise and locked briefcase, and two suitcases belonging to Ess and me. I throw both Simon's and my clothes into one of the cases; we didn't need much. Preston has no luggage, but I suspect he does carry a fat wallet in his tux pocket.

We really have little choice but to leave the drenched cartons inside. I doubt we could pick them up without spilling the contents when the waterlogged sides rupture; better to leave these stacked in the cargo bay. Interestingly, although Bradley bitches about me and Preston drinking his scotch, he appears infinitely more concerned with the cargo that remains inside the plane in the water-soaked boxes. When I reach to pull open a flap to inspect what might be inside, he goes ballistic. "Get the hell away from that. It's mine and I'll take care of it. Even with my dislocated shoulder, I'll beat the shit out of you if I catch you sneaking into my boxes."

I smile and feign fear as I back away with my hands up. Bradley has a good fifty pounds on me, and it's not muscle. Combine that with his additional twenty years of age and a bum wing, I don't consider him much of a threat. I will leave his precious boxes to him.

It takes more effort than I expect to unload the crates. They are small but heavy, and I'm sore, tired, and hungry. By the time we stack fifty or so of them in the sand we are completely exhausted and sweating. We need water, we all do, and we need it soon or we will start feeling the effects of dehydration: dry mouth, headaches, dizziness, and lack of energy.

As we sit to rest, me on a crate, Ess on the fallen tree trunk, Toothless and Preston exit the plane. They must have the same realization; we are in dire need of drinking water. Both are holding open bottles of warm beer from the remaining stash of bottles that managed to safely ride out the crash in Captain Robert's cooler. Preston smiles and says, "If you want something to drink, there are still bottles in the cooler waiting for us. It is surprising they survived, but I guess the ice helped keep them from breaking each other. By the way, don't drain the water from the melted ice. The first mate here thinks we are going to need it to drink."

Toothless walks over to one of the crates filled with scotch and pries off the cover with his pliers. "These will do fine." He pulls out one of the squared bottles, uncorks the bottle and begins pouring the contents onto the sand just as Bradley sticks his head out through the hatch.

"What the hell? It is one thing to steal my scotch, but just to pour it out. What are you thinking?"

Toothless Joe, undaunted, replies, "What am I thinking? I am thinking that I'm going to use these bottles first thing in the morning to go and get some fresh water and save our goddamn necks. That's what the hell I'm thinking." Then as a parting shot, "And, by the way, these are from our share of the cargo, Captain Robert's and mine. So why don't you just say thank you, First Mate Thompson, sir, and fuck off." With that, Toothless reaches down and grabs two more bottles, emptying them each after taking a swig to 'test' their contents, and then recorks them empty. He continues drinking and dumping until he has a pile of empty bottles. "Damn good scotch, I guess, but then again, anything that doesn't burn too much going down and gets me drunk is good in my book. In fact, getting me drunk is exactly what I plan to do now. I need some shut eye." Toothless grabs another bottle and disappears into the body of the dead airplane.

With the sun dipping low into the horizon, it is getting noticeably darker. We file in behind Toothless as baby ducks might trail their mother and close the door behind us. We sleep sitting up in the same seats we occupied the night before, except for Toothless Joe. He folds himself into one of two hammocks attached to the plane's aluminum frame in the aft section of the cargo hold. The second empty hammock was for Captain Robert. It remains empty tonight.

CHAPTER 4
I Need a Drink

Day two—

The first hint of morning comes with dim sunlight filtering through the still, almost lugubrious haze of fog. It throws the interior of the DC-3 into grey shadow. Sleep has been fitful at best. I assume it was the same for all of us. My back aches from sitting. My neck is stiff. And in my discomfort, it is tough looking forward to the challenges a new day presents us. I close my eyes, hoping this is a dream, that this tragedy will disappear from my memory soon after I wake. The increasing light, the smell, and the very sound of the individuals breathing so close pull me back into reality.

I attempt to stand, and I mean "attempt," because I can't straighten my back. Sitting up all night has stiffened me, folded me over at the waist. My legs are numb from a lack of blood circulation. Vertebrae crack and pop as I slowly push my head painfully toward the ceiling. Pushing my arms and shoulders backward provides almost instant, albeit temporary, relief from the soreness. Each of my co-habitants are beginning to stir in the shadows. They will be as exhausted as me; the night has not provided any real rest. Well, except for Toothless Joe. He still sleeps soundly, snoring quietly, lying on his back with a half-empty bottle of scotch nestled between his elbow and body.

Pushing open the cabin door, I allow the gray, early-morning light to flood into our sleeping compartment.

"Shut the door, man. Let me sleep," growls Toothless Joe.

"Nope. Time to wake up." I step out the door onto the sand in my bare feet. It is still cool, wet, and soothing from the evening mist. It will become hot shortly and burn our feet. I need to dig out another pair of shoes from my suitcase.

Ess, Bradley, Preston, and then, finally, Simon file out after me. Ess is no longer the vibrant young woman who boarded the plane in Singapore. New, dark shadows are under her eyes, accentuated by the vestiges of makeup that has run, making tracks down her cheeks, cheeks now hollow and grey. Her normally full, red lips are thin and cracked. She moves off into the woods alone. As I move to follow her, she holds up her open palm toward me as a stop sign.

"No, I have to pee," she says.

I take the opportunity to relieve myself, too, and disappear around the tail of the plane to piss. I try to urinate but can't. The lack of fluid has me dehydrated.

Returning to the plane, I step into the cockpit, silently excusing myself for encroaching on the dead captain's domain. I don't think he minds. I reach into the cooler with both hands, pushing aside the bottles of beer to cup water that had been ice yesterday, but now is lukewarm, to my mouth. I suck it in and return for another scoop. A voice freezes me before I can pull the water to my mouth.

"Stop. That's got to be for all of us," Toothless growls from his perch in the hammock.

The rope billet rocks back and forth until his two long, hairless legs fall over the edge of the canvas, followed by the rest of his body. He tosses the half empty bottle back into his bed and stumbles around the cargo, making his way toward me. He pushes me hard to the side, propelling me into the murderous tree branch and Captain Robert's dead lap before dipping his own hands into the water to quench his thirst.

He looks at me as he wipes the dripping water from his face with his sleeve. "We're gonna die without the water. Don't take more'n your share or I'll make sure you don't take any more. Got it?"

I nod without saying anything. Toothless is obviously still more than a little drunk. No reason to push him. I slide by him to exit the cockpit, leaving him alone with the water. I have no idea if he will take more than his share, but I don't want to fight with him now. Embarrassed, I realize I have lost an important battle with Toothless Joe. I can almost see his face stuck in the cooler, smiling. He has established himself as the big dog, the one who calls all the shots. *Screw you, Toothless Joe.* I kick aside the blankets that litter the floor, making my way to the cargo hatch.

Outside I find Ess has finally returned from the jungle. I wonder if she had any more luck than me. Probably not, none of us have had much to drink over the past day and a half. She is sitting on the log next to Simon and doesn't even acknowledge me. She just stares out to the sea, a seemingly endless pool of turquoise interrupted occasionally by deep, emerald-green islands. Simon sits at her side as quiet as a sentinel. I take a seat on the log to her other side. Bradley and Preston have plopped themselves into the sand, leaning their backs against the plane's fuselage. They appear to be dozing. They didn't get any restful sleep last night either. We're all tired, thirsty, and hungry. I fear we will all die.

In contrast, Toothless bounces from the plane. He turns to me, pointing to the pile of empty bottles. "You think you can carry those bottles in the cargo netting without busting them? We'll need to bring back water if we can find any."

"Sure, why not? You want me to come along?" I ask.

Toothless looks at me and waits, almost looking through me. "That depends. You want to be useful or not? I'll need some help carrying enough water for all of us. So, get up off yer ass and let's go." Before heading into the trees, Toothless calls back over his shoulder, "The rest of you figure out how to get Captain Robert out of his seat without making a mess."

I wrap the bottles in the netting and without speaking, take off after Toothless through the thick vegetation. Simon trails behind. It would have been easier to leave Simon, but it's probably best to keep him close to make sure he doesn't start roaming.

Toothless makes aggressive headway despite the dense growth. It is a challenge to keep up. I guess Toothless knows exactly what he is looking for. Simon and I are just intent on following close so we don't get lost or bitten by a snake, spider, or God knows what else might be waiting for us in the jungle. Toothless may be older, but years of hard work have prepared him better for the physical challenges of the jungle than I ever will be.

Finally, he breaks his silence. "You know we are probably going to die here. Ain't no way anyone saw us go down, and I don't suspect these waters get fished too often by the locals … too far from a main island. By the way, this island looks to be too damn small to even serve up a spring of fresh water. And if that's the case, we'll be dead soon enough."

Although I should appreciate Toothless Joe's frankness, I don't. "If you think we're going to die here, then why don't you just head back to camp and jump into Bradley's scotch and drink yourself into oblivion. No reason wasting your time out here looking for water if there isn't any to be had."

Toothless surprises me. He reaches into his breast pocket and pulls out a couple of cigarettes. He pokes one between his lips then flicks the other to me. With his other hand he shakes open his Zippo and lights his cigarette while nodding to me to come closer. He lights mine.

"Forget it. Let's go find us some water," he grumbles.

"You sure?"

Toothless smiles and barks, "Sure, I'm sure. Because we might get lucky, and this gives me an excuse to get away from Bradley. I can't stand being next to that guy. The last thing I need is to have him chirping at me again that I'm drinking his fucking scotch."

Toothless falls silent as he turns to resume his trek into the jungle. He begins talking again. "You know, the Cap'n carried Bradley's cargo for years and made a damn good livin' off it. Too good. I knew we would eventually be sorry. Bradley knew there was going to be rough weather on this route, but he made us fly anyway. In his mind, it's his money so he gets to call the shots. Since the Cap'n flew, I guess he was right. Well, maybe he used to call the shots. But not now.

"Just so you know, you need to be careful with Bradley. I think he has us carry stuff that's a lot more valuable than scotch, a hell of a lot more. Cap'n never said, but I bet that cargo would get us killed if anyone ever wanted to check our manifest a little closer. No, I don't like the guy. So, let's just enjoy our hike and hope we find something to drink on this little sea pimple of an island."

"So, Bradley's a prick." I respond. "I gathered that from when Ess and I helped unload the scotch, but I don't see him as being particularly threatening."

"Don't trust him. He's the only reason Cap'n started carry'n his pistol anytime we ran his cargo. He said it was only a matter of time until his stuff got us into hot water. He tried to talk me into getting a gun, too, but no way. You see that suit he's wearing? I'll bet he's packing a .45 in a holster under his armpit. I tried to get it when I popped his arm back into its socket, but when he passed out, it was all I could do to catch him. I don't know if he's in cahoots with the Preston kid, so I didn't want to frisk him right there with Preston next to me."

For me this whole conversation is troubling and sounding more like a confession. First, it now looks as though we, at least Simon, Ess, and I, might never be leaving the island, and secondly, it sounds as though this is a group of fellows I should have avoided from the start.

"Look, Thompson, so you and Robert's got us spun up with a really bad guy. We really don't want to get involved, so you need to take care of the problem. I'm just trying to take care of my own.

We're in enough trouble without getting involved with whatever dealings you have with Bradley."

Toothless stops and turns to me. "Screw you and your little girlfriend. You're here, so you're involved. You'll need to choose between me and Bradley eventually. You understand?" Toothless turns back in the direction we've been marching and doubles his pace, making it a struggle for Simon and me to keep up.

He leads us crisscrossing the island twice before admitting defeat and heads back to the north beach that has become our newly adopted home. Although we failed to find a fresh spring, our effort was not a complete loss; we were lucky enough to find a couple murky pools of water. And by the look of the animal prints surrounding them in the mud, we learned a couple of things. First, we had "friends" on the island. By the looks of the prints, they looked to be pigs. Secondly, those muddy pools were likely our only fresh water source. Although the water did not taste of salt, I cannot imagine myself drinking it. Toothless laughs at me and challenges, "You'll be dying for a sip of this before long."

Simon shakes his head and whispers, "Dysentery."

Looking up to the sky, I can see the boiling sun is being overwhelmed by afternoon storm clouds. Hopefully, the storm will not be as severe as yesterday's and will deliver us some life-giving clean water. The storm that was a killer yesterday might very well be our savior today.

Ess and Bradley were thinking the same thought while our trio was traipsing through the jungle in search of water. As Toothless, Simon, and I exit the green of the forest, we see that Ess and Bradley had pulled the cooler from the cockpit and placed it where the wing attached to the fuselage to gather the rainwater as it sheds down the membrane of the plane. Just beyond the makeshift camp, they lay out scraps of aluminum deformed enough to possibly hold some more rain, keeping the precious liquid from percolating into the sand or running off into the sea.

With any luck they will be able to capture enough water to last us until the next rain.

Preston is in the same spot he'd occupied when we left. I wonder if he even moved from his seat except to grab a bottle of scotch. His partying habits in Singapore had, evidently, followed him here. In a slurred speech he greets us as we walk into camp. "Yo, the world-trav'lers return. You pricks left me with the dead Cap'n. You know, he started to stink bad. I can't get the smell off me."

He took another pull from the bottle before I could grab it from him. "Good way to die, Preston. You haven't had any water or food. You are a fool."

"Oh, screw you." He reaches helplessly toward the bottle I had just taken. "If I drink, I can't smell the dead Cap'n. I gotta get the smell off me. Gotta."

Toothless kneels beside Preston and grabs him by his filthy dress shift. "Get over it. So, where is he? Where have you taken him?"

I assume he is referring to Captain Robert. Preston stares blankly back at Toothless, as if he is having difficulty comprehending his question, but then waves his hand toward the south along the beach. Preston was not too smart even when sober. As a drunk, he truly shows off his complete lack of any higher intelligence, incapable of grasping the simplest direction or conversation. Preston is one of those few destined to coast through life based on privilege, not ability. After seeing him in Singapore, acting the part of the ass in party after party, I doubt that Preston would have been invited to any of the black-tie functions to which he had become accustomed had it not been for the acceptance that came from generations of wealth. He was the product of old money and power, now representing the decline of a family that had, quite frankly, peaked a couple of generations earlier. Preston was just the continuation of the further decline. It seems to me the only question left for the family is whether Preston would chew through the family's remaining fortune or would he rally to preserve enough of their wealth and prestige to pass it on to another generation of inbred brats.

"I can't do this now," Preston blubbers. "Gotta sleep. Gotta get this smell off me. I can't stand the stink."

And he does stink. He smells of that sweet, pungent stink of death. The smell reminds me of my first flat in Hong Kong. A rat—and the rats were huge in Hong Kong—had gnawed a hole through the bottom of the seat cushion of my sofa. I guess I killed the rodent when I plopped down onto my only comfortable piece of furniture to take a nap. In the battle of rat verses one hundred-eighty pounds of journalist, the journalist won, kind of. Sure, I killed the rat, but it was a kill I would have gladly foregone. Unfortunately, at the time, I never even knew there had been a battle, let alone a casualty, not until several days later. Returning from an overnight assignment, I was greeted by the overwhelming odor of death even before opening my front door. The stink was huge and penetrating. When I walked into the flat, the heat and humidity gave the smell dimension. I could feel it pushing back against me as I swam into the room, looking for the source.

It took several trips into the apartment, interrupted by quick exits to the outside to grasp a couple gulps of fresh air before I was successful in finding the source of the stench. Even after I found the dead rat and removed it from the sofa, it had been almost impossible to rid the apartment of the foul smell. Eventually, I discarded the sofa and started a habit of burning incense. Even then, it took days before one could walk into the flat without retching.

CHAPTER 5
Dead Weight

I assume the inside of the plane stinks of Captain Robert even though Preston and Bradley removed his body while Simon and I scoured the island in search of water with Toothless. Although I plan to sleep within the confines and the relative safety of the DC-3, if it smells anything like Preston, I will brave the outside in the elements. Even if the plane's interior doesn't reek, I can't imagine allowing Preston to sleep inside with the rest of us. He is like my old couch and needs to be relegated to the outside until the stench wears off. I doubt any of my friends here on this island, outside of Preston, will argue with me.

Stepping into the plane, it is obvious something has died in here. That same overwhelming sweet odor of rot is present, maybe not overwhelming, but certainly present. The stink is at its strongest in the cockpit, but still not terrible. Thankfully, most of the smell is dominated by the peaty odor of the tree that still occupies the pilot's seat. If the door of the plane remains open, I expect the sweet, sour odor of the dead, decomposing Captain Robert will be nothing more than a memory by this evening. The only reminder being the stench that still stubbornly clings to Preston. His stench is much worse than just that of death. He has managed to combine the stink of Captain Robert's decomposition with vomit, stale beer, scotch, and a sour BO. The odor leaches from his pores and permeates his clothes. Perhaps we should dispose of Preston along with Captain Robert. He already smells of the dead.

*

Toothless walked down the beach, following the wake of sand created by Preston dragging Captain Robert's body to its next home. Toothless wanted to check the captain's pockets for anything of value. In particular, he wanted to rescue the pistol's holster and any bullets, but most important would be the good captain's Zippo. Fire would be critical for survival, and he didn't want his lighter to be their only source.

Secondly, Toothless was intent on making sure that the home chosen by Preston would be appropriate as a final resting place for the captain. He imagined that Preston had merely dragged the body far enough to be out of sight, but not far enough to avoid creating a problem tomorrow or the next day. Decomposing flesh would be an invitation to animals and bugs that would not be welcome to camp. He figured it was best to keep the scavengers as far away from camp as possible. As he rounded the beach bending towards the south, it became apparent that Preston was typical lazy Preston. He had dragged the good captain's body only as far as necessary to get it out of view from the plane. What could one expect from someone that had lived his life feeling as though he was entitled to all the benefits afforded him by his family's name, never having to do any physical work more strenuous than swimming at the club or pulling a cork from a bottle of bubbly?

Staring at the body in disgust, the first mate took at least some consolation that Preston had been too lazy to remove the straps that he had wrapped under the arms of Captain Robert. He picked up the straps, thankful he didn't need to touch Captain Robert, to drag the body to a more appropriate location further away from camp. Wrapping the cargo straps around his chest, Toothless pulled the rapidly decaying body down the beach, leaving a shallow white trench occasionally stained with body fluid wiped off by the grinding sand. It proved difficult to get any realistic footing in the fine grit, making the work almost impossible.

Realizing that his energy was waning quickly, Toothless decided to forgo dragging the captain any further through the sand, electing, rather, to pull him into the water. Although he intended to release the swollen body to the seas in hopes that fish would quickly pick the bones clean of flesh, the bloated body easily floated on the water's surface, enabling him to pull the body down the beach as easily as a child pulls a toy boat on a string.

Toothless found the cool water lapping against his legs refreshing as he floated Captain Robert away from their camp until he reached a small lagoon on the very southern tip of the island. He pulled the body up onto the sand and dragged it several feet into the jungle. Toothless figured he had taken the body just about as far from the camp as possible. He needed to rest before returning. Leaning against a small tree, he took a moment to collect his thoughts.

"Cap'n, you and I been together a long time. It ain't right to leave you here, but I don't have any choice. I suspect I might end up lying here, too, before long. We are in a hell of a pickle," he says.

Toothless pulled the straps from under the body—no telling if they would need these in the future—and covered the body with some sand and branches before heading back into the water, dragging the straps behind him, hoping the sea water would wash away the smell, and headed back to the north side of the island and camp.

CHAPTER 6
What's the Big Deal?

I lay down to take a short nap; I am exhausted and in need of food and water. Simon is being Simon. For some reason he believes he can catch dinner for us, reusing a couple empty scotch cases as traps in the shallow water surrounding our beach. He has selected a section of relatively calm water that is shaded by a couple large trees leaning out over the water and has placed his boxes on their sides, so the open crate top remains partially submerged. I am tempted to interrupt him, recognizing the futility of his effort, but what good would it do? When has he ever listened to my suggestions? What did he think? That the fish were just going to swim into his boxes?

I am shocked when he calmly tilts the two boxes upright, successfully trapping his live prizes. Ess lets out a squeal and gives him a hug. Simon says nothing, but he smiles. I know he would never purposely harm me, but I can't help but think he is trying to embarrass me. I will need to catch him in private to tell him that I don't appreciate what he is doing. For now, I will just lay here silently, watch, and let him enjoy himself.

Simon picks up one crate, Ess the other, and they slosh through the water back to the beach. They are greeted by the expectant and excited Bradley and Preston. Ess smiles and states that she is so hungry she could eat the crabs raw, but she quickly acknowledges that would not be a good idea. Simon just nods in agreement. He is enjoying Ess' attention.

Bradley grabs Preston by the shirt sleeve. "Then it is up to us to get a fire going, son. Let's get a move on. You look in the jungle for some dead branches that look like they could burn, and I will pull apart a couple of crates to use them as kindling."

Preston rolls his eyes in exasperation, realizing that this task once again means physical work. To his credit, he turns to the trees and begins walking, only briefly stopping to take a long draw from one of the bottles Toothless and I had filled with the brackish water.

Just as he disappears into the growth, Ess calls out to Preston, "Bring back some long green branches, too." Then, looking to Simon, "We can use them to cook the crabs over the fire."

Simon just nods again.

Ess shakes her head and responds loudly to his nod, "You know, I don't understand how you can be so silent at times. You're not a mute, so talk."

Her mood seems to have turned instantaneously from happy to confrontational. It doesn't make sense to me, but the stress is wearing on her. She turns abruptly away from Simon.

In defense of Ess, I can't understand why my brother seems to refuse or is incapable of normal communication. Ess leaves Simon and moves off toward the plane in search of a lighter to start the fire. I'll bet she could also use a smoke, so her search mission will likely begin and end with her digging through her purse that was now thrown in the back of the plane beyond Bradley's cargo. I have no doubt the gray-blue smoke of a cigarette will calm her before she returns to light the campfire.

I can't help myself, but I chuckle at Simon's loss. He just stands there silently with his hands straight down to his sides. I want to yell at him, *God, at least try to act normal. Relax, put your hands in your pockets, or at least make some response more than that stupid nod. Say something!* I turn my head from Simon and fall into a deep sleep.

There is a push on my shoulder. I pretend to be asleep, fearful that if I open my eyes, I will find myself face to face with an animal prodding me to determine how tasty I might be. Okay, it's a stupid thought. If a wild animal is hungry, my lying still just makes me easy to catch and an easy meal. I feel the touch again, but this time it is followed by a grasp of my shirt and a persistent shaking. I open my eyes to the dark of the evening and Simon's face is only inches from my own. There is a wonderful aroma of wood burning and meat cooking. The sun has disappeared into the water on the horizon and the temperature has noticeably fallen to a more comfortable range.

Simon whispers, "We need to consume at least twelve hundred calories a day to remain healthy."

Thank you, Simon, for that tidbit of data. Rolling over to my belly, I push myself up from the sand and walk over to the fire to sit beside Ess. Simon is left in the dark just beyond the glow of light.

Ess hands me a crab that is skewered on a green branch and smiles. "Bon appétit, mon amour."

I shouldn't be angry, but I am because I saw her all but flirting with Simon earlier.

I forgive her and act as if it had never occurred. "Thank you. You are apparently as good a cook as you are a huntress."

Around the fire we are gathered: Toothless to my right, Bradley to Ess's left and Preston off to himself, directly across the fire from me. Preston still reeks of death, so I understand why he sits alone. Everyone is quiet as they pick the last pieces of flesh from the crab shells. They are eating quickly as if they had not eaten for days. It has been a day and a half since we had breakfast in Singapore, so we are famished. Also, one might consider our dinner a race with weather. Along with the fall of the sun into the sea, the clear sky has been replaced with black clouds promising a storm, and hopefully, a shower of life-giving water. A northerly breeze is picking up, threatening our fire. It will soon be extinguished by wind or rain.

I can't wait for the rain. I can feel the cracked skin when I run my tongue over my parched lips. Without water the cracks will soon break open and ooze blood. Preston made an error in judgement by drinking the water Toothless and I had brought back from the heart of our island. He is now sick. Even above the campfire's crackling, we can hear his stomach making rude noises as it fights against the water borne bacteria now living in his intestine. He drops his cleaned crab shell and jogs into the woods to relieve himself.

Toothless comments to no one in particular, "That's the third time since I've been back. He can't have anything more to crap out."

Ess and Bradley look concerned. I chuckle. Simon sits in the shadows simply shaking his head.

Rain makes an unmistakable noise as it hits the sea. It starts as a hum and quickly grows to a roar reminding me of a massive ovation of people clapping as it approaches our island. In a crescendo of noise, the storm climaxes in the crash of lightning, grounding itself in the sea or on one of the other small islands to our north. I am shocked at the power even before the first large droplet of water hits me. The rain grows from a single drop to a cascade of millions in a matter of seconds as we race for the door of the plane and the comparative protection inside.

Rain is already streaming in through cracks in the fuselage. I cup my hands to gather it to my parched lips. We all do. Simon remains outside. I imagine him standing with his mouth open, face to the sky, as he sucks in the fresh drops directly from the source. Then, he quietly slips inside, smiling. I can't recall when I have seen him show any emotion, but this storm certainly has him excited. Men need excitement; this is good for him. I am glad to see that something has finally been awakened in that desert of Simon's mind.

There is a pounding on the door. It's Preston. He's been caught by the storm with his pants down, quite literally.

I must scream to be heard over the storm, "You need to stay out there and shower off some of that stink before you come inside."

It comes across as a joke, but I realize I'm not joking. I mean it. He's not coming in here smelling of death. As far as I am concerned, he will spend tonight outside. I look at the other faces in the plane. Although I can barely recognize them in the dark, and even though they are silent, I can sense they agree with me. No one rises to open the door to Preston. We are sure he will be safe outside. Hell, he is lucky to not be cooped up in the dark, humid, hot interior of the DC-3.

The noise is intimidating, albeit not so much as last night. The pounding of rain against the metal skin is back and as loud as ever, but tonight it doesn't generate fear. Instead, we are thankful. We know that this will leave us with a supply of water that should sustain us for a while.

We make ourselves as comfortable as possible for the long night of storm. Toothless has returned aft to his hammock. Tonight, Bradley moves to the rear to occupy the second hammock. He doesn't ask the first mate for permission. I lay the thin canvas chair padding across the moderately flat surface created by three seat pans on the right side of the fuselage to make my bed. Ess lays likewise on seats attached to the other side of the plane. Her eyes glint in the dark as she looks at me.

Simon has taken up occupancy in the cockpit. He has elected to sleep sitting up awkwardly in the co-pilot's seat with his legs curled to the side and his head leaning against the window. I'm sure he is taking comfort in the relative coolness of the glass and the soft sound of large water droplets drumming on the tree leaves of the forest. The nose of the plane is completely insulated from the storm by the same jungle growth that killed Captain Robert. Even though Simon's legs can't spread out, I am jealous. He has managed to escape the pounding of rain while gaining a modest solitude.

CHAPTER 7
Night Out

Preston resigned himself to riding out the storm outside of the friendly confines of the grounded plane. He hated being locked out of the plane for the night, but it was for the best. He was still experiencing severe stomach cramps and the accompanying diarrhea. He would have needed to be outside much of the night in any case just to relieve himself.

Using his hands as shovels, he scooped out sand below the tail's right horizontal elevator to carve out enough room into which he could crawl and escape the stinging, wind-blown rain. His alternative was to sleep in the forest under the cover of trees. True, the growth would block most of the storm's ferocity, but it meant taking his chances with whatever creatures that live in the jungle. He shuddered at visions of snakes, or worse, spiders that would be in the shadows waiting for him. He had no desire to be awakened by a large arachnid creeping across his face. Even if the spider was harmless, the fear would kill him; his heart would just shock and explode. No thanks. He took solace knowing the cubbyhole he had hollowed out would protect him from wind and rain and, hopefully, the creepy critters of the night would keep to the jungle.

After crawling under the tail section, Preston thought this might not be so bad. He was protected from the drenching rain by the tail elevator and the heavy wet sand protected him from the blowing wind. The elevator was more than large enough to allow him to stretch out his five-foot, ten-inch frame while keeping him shielded from the storm. The only real problems were that it was difficult to climb out of his sand nest quickly if he needed to crap and the sand couldn't possibly percolate the torrential rain at a pace fast enough to keep from pooling under him. If he experienced another bout of diarrhea, this pool of water would be wretched. He would be like sleeping in a septic tank. He chuckled to himself that in the morning he could wash the shit off his skin and clothes, but his shit smell embedded in the sand would accost the noses of the assholes that had locked him from the plane when they exited in the morning. It would serve as a constant reminder to them of how poorly they had treated him.

The wind was already beginning to wane, and he had no doubt the rainfall would slow shortly. All would be well, except … Preston first felt the sensation starting on his leg, nothing painful, but a gentle tugging, as if something were gripping his pants. The clouds still covered the stars and moon, so he had difficulty seeing the source of the sensation. His imagination ran rampant. He felt legs gripping and crawling and he knew the spiders from the forest had come looking for a meal. He envisioned them wrapping him in webbing before sucking out his life with their fangs.

He kicked wildly as he struggled to escape from his sand nest. What had seemed a sanctuary had now turned into a horror chamber. He frantically swept his hands down over his legs, hoping to dislodge whatever had attached itself. He couldn't think of what his hands would be throwing off or he would be too petrified to act. He rolled out from under the tail fin and hopped onto the top of the elevator with his back glued to the plane's outer shell. Thankfully, the wind calmed, and the rain lost its sting. He would spend the remainder of the night up here.

As the rain stopped and the clouds lost their grip on the moon and starlight, Preston could now see black dots moving across the white sand. There were hundreds of the black dots. He could just barely make out the legs that propelled these little beasts. Moving in darting motions, he was shocked that the island could be the home to so many spiders. Most looked to be larger than his hand. Only these were not spiders. They were crabs coming up for their nightly feeding on any protein that had been left on the beach. Had he not been awakened, Preston imagined that he would have been part of that protein meal. Better to stay up here on the tail fin. The glossy aluminum would provide no purchase for their shell-clad claws. He slid down to his side, pulling his legs up close to his body in hopes of catching some bit of sleep before the sun started to rise from the sea.

CHAPTER 8
BFF? Never.

Day three—

The sun has pulled itself up out of the sea and thrown its light through the few windows that extend beyond the growth of the jungle. It would only be minutes before its full power and brightness would wake everyone sleeping within the safety of the plane's aluminum shell. Then the sun's constant beating on the metal will heat up the interior making the relative safety inside oppressive. Time to get up.

Simon hums quietly in the cockpit. This is odd. I can't recall him humming since our parents had taken us to see the New York Philharmonic years ago. That night the orchestra performed Beethoven's 9th Symphony and I had to put up with him humming the theme from the second movement for months. He was humming that same theme now, as if the staccato of this movement was somehow symbolic of our predicament. It was an introduction to adventure and excitement. I knew that this melody would now embed itself in my brain for days. Thank you, Simon. Thank you, Beethoven. I throw my shoe against the bulkhead to shut him up. Bang.

"What the hell was that?" stammered Bradley.

Toothless doesn't move, and Ess merely opens her eyes to gaze across the gulf of the fuselage at me as I sit up.

"Bradley, it's nothing. I was just trying to turn off the classical music," I say.

"What the-" he started to reply, but I cut him off saying, "Never mind." Bradley looks at me as if trying to decide if he should push the conversation further. Then as if in surrender, he rolls his feet out from the hammock onto the floor and lays his elbows on his knees and his face in his hands. He is quiet.

Ess sits up and with a smile says, "So, who wants to go out on the town tonight? Oh, too tired still? Well, let's at least go out to dinner at Raffles, dear. It will be charming. And so daring, you know, with the Japanese bearing down on us and all."

Ess could be sarcastic as hell, and it was not one of her better qualities. If I weren't so tired and guilt ridden, I would slap some sense into her. I can't believe she never grasped the horrors that were to befall those who chose not to leave Singapore.

I stand up, stretch, and walk to the door. I'm half concerned about what to expect when I open it, embarrassed by my actions last night when I insisted Preston not be allowed inside with the rest of us. Although I didn't notice it then, Ess had been appalled by my action. Now her face shows it and her countenance is one of rebuke. But last night, it didn't seem to bother her. She didn't insist he be allowed in.

I hope Preston is okay. What I did was wrong, and to be perfectly honest, I do not recall why I was such a jerk, or why the rest in our little group let me get away with it. Nobody really likes the spoiled man-boy.

I push open the door to let out the stale air and let in the cool morning from outside. Preston's back is to me, and he looks to be lying asleep on the elevator section of the tail. His pants are stained brown, either from dirt or shit; I am not sure, but the smell of feces is strong. A stream of brown also has stained the aluminum, so I assume his diarrhea has not yet completely run its course. I step outside and shake him lightly to check that he is still alive and breathing. He turns over and sits up to face me. Outside of being soaked and having little red bite marks all over his hands and face from mosquitos that swarm as soon as the sun loses its hold over the earth and the fleas that seemingly materialize out of nowhere once the sand warms from the gentle kiss of the sun the following morning, he looks no worse off. He does look tired and beaten, as though he has not slept for days. He has deep bags under his bloodshot eyes and his face appears deflated, as if there is no flesh beneath his skin. He is just beginning to experience the ravages of dehydration from his diarrhea. The scotch was not the way to rehydration.

He attempts to spit at me, but is unsuccessful at generating anything more than a couple droplets. "Never again, you hear. Just between you and me, you lock me out again and treat me like a dog, you're dead. You got it?" His voice is coarse and dry, like sandpaper and sounds as though each word uttered scratches from his throat with pain.

I want to stare at him in defiance and tell him to *fuck himself*, but I just nod.

"Good, then we have an understanding." He curls up in response to cramping and shits himself again.

I am repulsed at his action. He doesn't even try to make it to the privacy of the jungle to relieve himself. Watery shit is seeping out between his legs running down the slope of the tail into the sand below. "Well, at least you don't stink of death now. Now you just stink like shit. Wash the crap off you and maybe you won't need to sleep outside."

Preston swings his legs around, sliding off the tail piece to turn his entire body toward me. At the same time, he raises his fist as if to punch. I flinch.

"Just like I thought," he snarls. "A real bigshot until you are confronted. You can kiss my ass. By the way, you better watch your little girl in there. I might just want to dip my noodle in her. Bet she'll like it, too."

Just as I am getting ready to launch myself at the spoiled brat, Toothless hops out through the hatch and says, "What's going on?

God, don't we have enough problems without you two going at it. Cut it out or I'll end it." With this he pulls back his shirt to show us the handle of Captain Robert's .38 sticking out above his pants' belt. "I'll use it, too, if I need to. I got nothin' to lose."

I snarl at Toothless Joe. "Don't think you're tough just because you were the first mate on a one-person crew. Big fucking deal, go ahead and pretend you're tough, but to me you are not First Mate Thompson. No, you are just an old, worn-out toothless piece of shit hiding behind a gun. I have my own name for you, 'Toothless Joe.' You were Toothless from the first time I saw you and you will be until you die."

I can't believe that fucker pulls the pistol out and raps me across the mouth. I taste blood and spit out a tooth he has broken off.

"Now who's 'Toothless'?" he says, and laughs at me. Preston laughs, too, then cramps up.

Toothless raises the pistol as if to strike Preston, then shakes his head and sticks the gun back under his belt and pulls his shirt down to cover it.

I grab a bottle of scotch and take a pull into my mouth, not to drink, but to wash away the blood. It burns like hell.

Bradley steps out of the plane, followed by Ess. "We need to empty some more scotch bottles for the water we saved last night. It worked, didn't it?" He looks to Ess as she kneels to check our most important source of water, the beer cooler.

The cooler is completely full and already mosquitos have found this little source of fresh water to deposit their eggs. Ess waves them off and then scoops her hands into the chest, pulling the water to her mouth. She gulps greedily as if she had not had anything to drink in days, two days to be factual.

She says to no one in particular, "Give me a bottle so we can get this stored away before the mosquitos ruin it."

Preston grabs a couple of the bottles that contained the water we had found the previous day and drains them onto the sand.

"Wash those out with a little scotch or we'll all be shitting ourselves by noon," says Toothless. He cracks open a new case to retrieve another, as of yet, unopened bottle. He pulls the foil back from the neck to twist off the cap. After taking a healthy draw, he looks around to us and asks, "Anyone want a swig?"

Although I love a good scotch, seven in the morning is a little early for me to drink, so I decline, as does Ess. Even Preston passes at the opportunity to begin imbibing this early. Shockingly, Bradley walks over to Toothless Joe, smiles, grabs the offered bottle and takes several healthy gulps. After handing the bottle back to Toothless, he returns to his perch in the shadow of the plane. Toothless Joe doesn't bother to go into the plane to extend Simon the offer. I suspect Toothless thinks Simon to be a teetotaler. He is. I've never seen him take a drink of anything stronger than Coca Cola.

Toothless pours a couple ounces of the whiskey into each bottle before replacing their caps. "Shake those up well. We want the alcohol to kill whatever was in that water."

Preston shakes up the bottles before re-emptying them onto the beach. "You sure this is going to kill whatever got into me?" he asks Toothless Joe.

"Hell, alcohol kills all sorts of stuff. I think we'll be fine. By the way, not that I want to support your alcoholism, but it might be good for you to take a swig into your belly. Maybe even rub it on those nasty bites to make sure they don't get infected."

"Maybe we should leave a little in each bottle when we fill them with water," I suggest. "We already have mosquitos landing on the water. The alcohol ought to kill whatever may have already been introduced to our run-off"

"Sounds good," supports Bradley. It is beginning to look as though Preston is not the only castaway that has issues with drinking. Bradley is already on his way to being drunk and the sun has yet to be in the sky more than an hour.

Toothless nods and proceeds to pour a little of the whiskey into each bottle before passing them on to Ess for filling. After the bottles are full, we gather up the aluminum scraps we had laid out the day before to capture more rainwater. These had not been as useful in the harvesting effort. The wind had been strong enough to blow the top of the water out of the shallow troughs, leaving only immaterial amounts to be gathered. We pour what we can save into the cooler, dump in a little of the whiskey and close the cover of the cooler in hope that it will keep the insects from fouling our precious water supply.

CHAPTER 9
Fucking Simon

Simon is back out in the water with his cartons capturing unsuspecting crabs for our meal. He has improved his harvest by throwing in the shells from our dinner last night. The little cannibalistic bastards are swarming for their shot to grab a morsel of meat from their former family members. It is terrible watching them crawl over each other to pull at the discarded shells. They swarm like ants devouring any dead carcass, maybe not as frenetic, but certainly as ferocious in their eating.

I decide to take a short nap in the back of the plane. I doubt Toothless will take exception to me grabbing a little snooze in his hammock. My back is killing me from lying across the hard jump seats last night. Granted the seats have canvas padding, but it is less than useless. I could never get comfortable enough to sleep. After the first hour, I was ready to move to the floor. It couldn't have been much harder and at least then I could roll over without fear of falling off the chair. Tonight, I'll opt for the floor or trade Simon for his seat in the cockpit.

I climb over the remaining cardboard boxes in the hold to get to the hammocks. I don't think Bradley will care too much if my weight results in a little damage to his cargo. At this time, I think it is highly unlikely the cargo will ever be leaving this island, and if it does, we probably won't be going with it. After just one day, I am already resigned to the idea that we are going to die here, having earned a life sentence merely by running away from, rather than confronting, evil.

I wake in a sweat. The inside of this plane has become unbearably stifling. Even though the sun only has access to the rear third of the plane, it has made its power known by turning the entire fuselage into an oven and I feel as though I am being cooked. I roll out of the hammock, clamber over the cardboard boxes, and fall out through the doorway onto the soft sand. My body is coated in greasy sweat and the fine grit sticks to me. I grab a bottle of water and begin to gulp it down.

It is not until I have drained almost half the bottle that I take notice of the rest of my tribe. They have started another cook fire and have been actively roasting and eating crabs captured by Simon. He is quietly pulling little strings of white meat from the shelled leg of a creature that had been scrambling to eat one of his own only a couple hours earlier. The creature is just an ugly, shiny, large sea spider, but I guess it tastes good. I can tell from Simon's face he enjoys being the big hunter for our clan. He's fed us twice now. I should not be envious, but I am. I can't help but see the admiration in Ess' face as she looks at Simon. That look should be for me. Maybe after I rest some more, I'll have a private talk with Simon. If he tries to steal away Ess, I'll stop him.

*

Bradley leans back against the fuselage. In his right hand, he holds a bottle of scotch, in the other, the one dangling from his bruised shoulder, a half-eaten crab. I guess getting the bottle to his lips is more important than the food.

Toothless asks, "So, Bradley, we've handled your cargo runs from England to India, to Singapore, up and down from Hong Kong, and all the way to Brisbane. What are you going to do now?"

"Didn't the good cap'n tell you?" Bradley slurred. "I have been taking chances with my cargo forever. Now it looks as though I have tried my luck too long. Anyway, I was going to stop with this trip. Hell, you and the cap'n were going to need to change your flights and my success depended on your old routes. The Japs have screwed up everything." He pauses to toss the empty shell of the crab he's been nibbling on up and back over his head in hopes that it would clear the plane on which he leaned. His eyes were staring out to the sea, not looking at anyone or anything, as if just contemplating what would happen next.

"You know, when I left my home in the States, I swore I would not return until I was rich. It was my way of sticking it to my dad and my brother. Hell, my whole family. They had their idea as to how a businessman was to act and I had my idea; they weren't the same. I think my way has been a hell of a lot more profitable." He paused in thought before continuing, "I have more money than they ever dreamed of and now it doesn't look like I am going to get to spend any of it, let alone wave it in my family's face. I've been waiting fifteen years to show up at the home of my dear brother, Lattimore, to make him acknowledge me as the success I am. Shit, he is probably still living in our old hometown in Colorado. He has no sense of adventure. Well, I'll bet I carry more cash around in my wallet than he has in his entire savings, so it sure would be nice to get off this island alive so I can show him that I am the big fish now." Bradley fell quiet again, looking off into space, as if imagining the moment when he would walk into his family's old house and rub his money in their faces.

"So, what does your family do?" Toothless asks.

Bradley is shaken out of his private, imaginary world, looking startled, as if Toothless had woken him from sleep. "How should I know? I'm not even sure if Dad's alive. You know, maybe it's best that I never go back after all."

Bradley's eyes return to a blank stare. This time the focus is gone. I almost thought the man had died. But no; the scotch had introduced his brain to a drunken slumber but forgot to tell his eyelids. His head slumps forward and his eyes stare blindly at the sand.

Toothless rolls over to his hands and knees to push himself up out the sand. "I'm going to head back into the forest to see if I can find something else to eat besides crab. Maybe a bird or some eggs or fruit. Anybody know anything about plants?"

He looks to Ess as if expecting her to volunteer some expertise on the subject and join him on his hunt. She ignores him, choosing to avert her gaze toward the ground. For her, the First Mate is a dangerous man, uncouth and one to be avoided. Toothless stands and approaches her but is cut off by Simon. The two glare at each other for a moment, then Simon silently walks into the forest. I follow him. Of course, if anyone in our group knew what we could eat without dying, it would be Simon. Toothless shrugs and follows us. Ess, not wanting to be left behind, follows behind the First Mate, leaving Preston alone with the sleeping Bradley.

CHAPTER 10
Take That

"So, you drunken prick," Preston says to the passed-out Bradley, "What have you got hidden away in all those boxes? 'Look,' you say? Well, if you insist." Preston hopped up from his perch in the sand and pushed Bradley to the side to enter the darkness of the cargo bay.

Picking a box that was already falling apart from water damage, he placed his foot against its side and pushed. Voilà, instant access to the contents inside. Two small cellophane wrapped bags filled with what looked to be a sticky, dark brown gum fell out through the tear onto the floor.

"So, what you been hiding here, you rich hick? I bet this is something I could really get into." Preston grabbed the two bags and slipped them into his tuxedo jacket pocket and then turned the box around so that one would not see the torn cardboard.

"Now, let's see what's in the rest of these," he says as he pushed on the side of another water damaged box to tear open a window. Like the first, it was filled with little bags filled with the same gooey stuff. With the third box it was the same. "What the hell?" Preston had smoked opium before, but he had never seen so much packed away in one place. It must be worth a fortune, and now it would all go to waste.

Preston then climbed over the cartons to grab Bradley's valise. "And what might you be hiding in here?" he whispered as he pushed the spring-loaded buttons to release the latches. They were locked and wouldn't budge. "Screw this," he cursed as he crashed the case against the wall, breaking it open. Although the locks did not give, the wood that housed the locks did. The case fell open, spewing Bradley's clothes onto the floor along with a razor and a can of lamp oil. Wrapped in the clothes was a small, intricately tooled, silver oil lamp and a long, thin, ornately carved wooden pipe with a blue and white ceramic bowl. The pipe and the lamp would have been beautiful from purely an artistic perspective had their purpose not been for vaporizing opium. For Preston, anything beyond a purely utilitarian design was a waste … or Bradley had more money than he had expected, a lot more.

"Bradley, aren't you full of surprises?" he says as he then pulled out the leather briefcase that had spent most of the flight nestled tightly in Bradley's arms. Preston wanted to see what could be so important. He tore at the leather flaps until the latch gave and dumped the contents, a .45 caliber pistol, a couple boxes of bullets, pieces of old mail and several file folders, onto the floor just as the drunken Bradley stuck his head through the hatch to see what was making the commotion.

"What the hell," he screamed as he dove for the .45. "You are so fucking dead!"

For Preston's sake it was good that the anger alone was not capable of sobering Bradley; he crashed to the floor, knocking away the gun. Bradley could only look from his prone position as Preston knelt to pick up the gun and point it at Bradley's head. He pulled back the slide to cock the weapon and push a round into the barrel.

"Bang, you're dead," he says and pulled the trigger. The recoil almost knocked the gun from his hand, and the explosion was deafening. Bradley didn't notice as the bullet left a small dot about the size of a dime between his eyes and a hole the size of one of his opium bags out the back of his head. Bradley never heard the noise.

*

I don't recall noticing the constant noise of the jungle until it is gone. That is now. With the sound of a single gunshot, the vibrant diversity of sound, the chatter of birds and the buzzing of insects goes silent. Even the gentle whispering of the breeze brushing through branches and leaves seems to disappear out of fear, or maybe respect for the newly dead. The change seems to be lost on Simon as he continues foraging on his hands and knees through the verdant growth that carpets the forest, an apparent abundant food source we had previously ignored. He is intent on harvesting what he refers to as Lacy Java Fern, or technically, "Microsorum pteropus that grows aggressively amongst fallen, decomposing trees." Thank you, Simon, for the brief lesson in botany. In our case, the decomposing trees are almost invisible, having been replaced by new growth.

The ringing thunder of the gunshot and its instant impact in the forest is not lost on Ess. She stops gathering the fern and looks to the sky, as if trying to get a sense from where the sound had emanated. I know where it came from, so does Simon, so we continue pulling up the ferns that will soon provide us a refreshing lunch.

Toothless Joe, leaning against a tree, apparently unwilling to get down on his knees to work with the rest of us, lets out a quiet whistle and chuckles, "I guess Preston pissed off Bradley."

"You don't think he would have shot Preston, do you?" asks Ess, her face showing serious concern. I know her concern is a sham, but she needs to show that she is somehow more human, more sensitive, than the rest of us.

"I doubt it, but if Preston got into his stash, he'd be mighty upset. Hell, who knows, maybe so?" replies Toothless Joe.

I assume the stash to which Toothless refers must be the cargo that still sits in the cargo hold. I straighten up from my knees. "Toothless Joe, you need to get that gun. It's not safe having someone shooting when they get pissed."

"Yeah, but I got me some defense, too." Toothless pulls out his revolver to let us all see it.

*

Preston grabbed Bradley's feet and dragged him out of the plane, depositing him in the sand just outside the door before returning inside to see what other presents Bradley had left for him. He picked up the briefcase, intending to throw it out the door when he heard the quiet thump of something more in the case bumping against the leather walls. He opened the case that appeared empty save the brown silk lining. He reached in to pull at the lining to see if something had been squirreled away behind the material. The bottom of the briefcase lifted out easily to expose five stacks of white bank notes from the Bank of England. Bradley was indeed full of surprises. These bank notes were unique in that their denomination was huge. Even though he came from a well-to-do family, he could not recall ever holding so much money at one time. Here, sitting in his lap, were four packs of fifty £500 notes and a fifth pack of £100 notes. In all, Bradley had been hauling around £110,000 in cash, a huge sum of money. Preston tossed the money packets back into the briefcase and replaced the false bottom. He hid the case under a couple of the opium-laden boxes that still filled the cargo hold. As a castaway, money served little purpose for him. If they escaped this island the money could set him up to cut his ties with his family. He could be free.

Now the cache of opium; that was different. Opium had been a friend and constant companion throughout his time in Singapore and Hong Kong. When he wasn't drinking, he was patronizing opium dens. With his first drag on a pipe, he was hooked. He loved how the drug-laced smoke placed his mind in a fog, slowly cloaking all his troubles and concerns until they were gone. In truth, he recognized that some might not consider his troubles substantial, at least in comparison to a commoner, but to him they were huge. He spent more time than he could recollect using the drug and alcohol to forget his family and their threats to cut him off from their funds.

Alone in the middle of the Java Sea, it seemed almost serendipitous to be stranded with a mountain of the drug, more than he could smoke in several lifetimes. He could just lie here and let the time go by. Let his new-found 'friends' collect food and water; he would just enjoy the time. He was confident they would not let him die.

CHAPTER 11
Smoked?

We have been hugely successful in our foraging exercise. Beyond the ferns, Simon found us mushrooms that he assured were edible and nutritious if they were cooked. I trust him, but I think that I'll let him eat them first. I think he likes Ess too much and in his convoluted mind, he might be thinking of ways to get rid of me. I can't trust him.

We carry our harvest in makeshift sacks that are nothing more than pant legs tied together from a couple pairs of dress slacks I had hurriedly thrown into my suitcase in Singapore. It now seems so long ago. We bring the sacks back to camp as though they are precious cargo. In one respect, I guess they are. What's inside will sustain us for another day or two. The crab is good, but none of us are looking forward to another meal of the ugly arthropods today. We are quiet and anxious; we have heard no further man-made noise since the gun shot more than an hour ago. Nobody speaks.

I am the first to exit the forest onto the beach a couple hundred feet south of our camp. Looking north, away from the sun, I can see Preston sitting in the sand, leaning his back against the plane. He appears to be sleeping. Beside him lies Bradley. Neither of them bothers to get up to see if we need help. In fact, they fail to acknowledge our return at all. I walk toward camp with Toothless following directly behind me. Ess and Simon bring up the rear.

As I get near, Preston begins to laugh, at least I think it's a laugh. He doesn't open his eyes, but he pulls a long pipe from the flame of a small lamp nestled in the sand and brings the stem to his mouth and inhales. He stops and lets the smoke fall slowly from his nostrils as he takes in the full effect. In his right hand, resting on his lap, he holds what looks to be a threatening .45 semiautomatic pistol. He doesn't seem to notice we've returned.

Bradley is lying face down in the sand. I can now see that he's not sleeping. He's dead. What is left of the back of his head is a mess of bloody flesh and hair. A track of bloodied sand runs from the plane's hatch to where Bradley now lies. The blood has blackened the white sand. Flies are attacking the destroyed head. Bradley's concerns over his cargo are over and his trek is complete. He is the lucky one. I guess he doesn't know we have returned either.

"I'm done. Anyone else want some? You want to try?" Preston slowly whispers without opening his eyes. He raises his left arm to hold the pipe extended to the air, offering it to anyone desiring to take a smoke. He shakes the pipe, inviting attention, well, not really shake it; the motion is so relaxed the pipe merely waves back and forth as if a current of air is slowly pushing his hand one way, then another. His language is slurred, not like he is drunk, but as if his words are all linked together, without any space between them. His voice is flat, without inflection or emotion, all while lying beside a dead man.

"I can see so clearly now. We are all going to die, but it's okay. It must be okay, right?" He laughs.

"Shit, Preston, what the fuck have you done?" Toothless asks.

What a stupid question. I'm sure he meant his question rhetorically, assuming Toothless Joe's brain is capable of rhetoric, since it is obvious to all of us what has happened. Preston killed Bradley and found opium somewhere on board.

"Toothless, take the fucking gun before he kills someone else," I shout.

Toothless scowls at me for addressing him as "Toothless." I know he hates his new name. *Well, get used to it.* I would have said it out loud, but I really didn't want to create another fiasco before we dealt with the problems lying in the sand in front of us.

Preston's eyes slide open just enough to make us aware that he is conscious of us. "No way are you taking this." He slowly waves his right hand with the pistol at the sky. He drops the gun and his hand falls to the sand. The pipe remains in his mouth.

Toothless Joe bends down, picking up the gun. He slides it under his pants' belt. "That opium is now mine." He smiles. "But I'll share."

Shockingly, he plops down beside Preston and grabs the pipe. He spies the open cellophane wrapper and the brown, sticky drug and reloads the pipe. After reheating the pipe in the flame, he, too, pulls the pipe to his mouth to take in the smoke of relaxation and escape. He closes his eyes and repeats the action. He is soon lost.

I debate whether I should move in to take advantage of his stupor and grab at least one of the guns he has stuck in his pants. I decide not to try my luck. If he isn't completely under the spell of the opium, I might just awaken him enough to have him kill me. Even slowed by the narcotic, he could overwhelm me with his size and weight.

Simon has already taken a place in the sand to rest. I sit next to him and from my sack shake the leaves and mushrooms we gathered for our food for today onto the ground. We eat, slowly at first, and then as the food wakens the hunger in each of us, we begin to eat as though we are starved. I stuff one handful of raw plants after another into my mouth, barely taking time to chew before swallowing.

Ess doesn't take part in our meal. She is completely mesmerized by Toothless Joe. No, not Toothless Joe, but the pipe that rests in his hand. I am shocked when she kneels beside him to take the pipe from him. I knew Ess had smoked the drug before and that she had been fighting the demon ever since we had been together. I had no appreciation for how strong the drug's grip was, not until now. She takes in the addictive smoke once, twice, three times and then moves into the confines of the DC-3. I hear her sobbing. Eventually, the sobs slow and then cease. The drug has pushed her into a dreamless sleep.

Simon and I are alone.

While Ess sleeps, Simon and I wrap the cargo straps around Bradley and pull his body through the sand to the south part of the island, laying him next to Captain Robert, or at least whatever might be left of the good captain. It's tough work as his body leaves a broad wake, plowing the sand to the sides.

The scavengers of the island have been, and still are, at work feeding on Captain Robert when we deposit Bradley. The captain is no longer recognizable. His body has been moved from where it was first dropped and now appears to have been dragged from the shore to a position half in and half out of the jungle. The bones of his ribs, cheeks and arms are completely exposed from the continuous feeding. We see tracks in the sand that look to be those of pigs. We saw similar tracks at the water spring but had not seen any of these wild beasts. Based on the large chunks of rotting human flesh torn from his skeleton, I'll be happy if we never run across them. The feeding continues as a colony of thousands of yellow ants frenetically cut flesh and carry it back into the jungle. In a couple of days, nothing but bone will remain.

The ants discover Bradley even before we release the strap used to drag him here. Soon, they swarm over his body. It is as if he is covered with a living, moving growth of short hair. I feel an urge to turn away and run, to escape before the ants discover Simon and me and turn us into a swarming bundle as well. I run to the shallow water and beckon Simon to follow me. I doubt the ants can swim, but who knows. We stand next to each other, watching in awe as the ants devour the new flesh. I feel as though I might be sick, but still, I can't avert my eyes from the carnage. Simon gently turns me away and holds my hand as he pulls me back up the shore toward camp.

Preston and Toothless are still sleeping when Ess returns to us from her nap of the dead. Her eyes are red, and I see dark half circles of fatigue marking her face, making her appear decades older than her actual thirty-one years. She refuses to talk, so I don't push conversation upon her.

Ess grabs the pipe again and pulls a pinch of the sticky material from the wrapper to reload the pipe. Placing my hand on hers, I gently pull the pipe away to lay it next to Simon. I blow out the flame.

"Ess, not now, you need to eat. You need to keep your head on straight if we want to have any chance of survival."

"What chance? We're lost and nobody is looking for us. You know that. You see any boats out there?" She pauses and waves vaguely to the sea. "I didn't think so."

She reaches for and grasps the silver lamp but, realizing she has no way to light it, discards it back into the sand. She sticks her hands into Toothless Joe's pocket in hopes of finding his Zippo lighter to reignite the opium-melting flame. Toothless seems to remain sleeping until he grabs her and pulls her down onto himself.

Before I can react, Simon is up out of the sand and kicks Toothless in the head. He pulls Ess free from Toothless Joe's grip. Recovering from the kick, Toothless sits up and pulls one of the pistols from his belt. I am afraid he will shoot Simon.

Ess screams and jumps between the two men, "Stop, just stop."

It hurts me to think that Ess would sacrifice herself for my Simon. I suppose she would do the same for me, but then again, I would never need her help: still, I feel jealous – until I see her fall to the sand to recover the lighter she had pulled from Toothless' pocket. I can't help smiling. She doesn't give a shit about Simon, only the opium.

To be fair, the opium has asserted its control over all of us, whether we have smoked it or not, and it will kill us. It is time to stop.

I see that Preston is now awake and is watching. He's smiling. "Hey, Thompson, or Toothless, whatever your name is, did you get a feel? Was it good? I'll bet it was."

I glare at Preston. He ignores me.

"No, seriously, was it good? 'Cause I'm gonna get me some, too. Her boyfriend there doesn't have what it takes to keep her happy and satisfied, but I do." He stands up and begins rubbing his groin.

I am unsure as to what to do. Before I can act, Simon moves from Toothless and attacks Preston, pushing him back into the side of the plane. Preston responds like a cat and pounces on Simon, knocking him to the sand. Preston begins to punish him with fists to his face, right, left, right, until the thunder of the pistol freezes him.

"Done, get up off him." Toothless points the gun at Preston. Given how stoned he is, I doubt he'll be able to hit him if he fires, even at this close range, but Preston stops. He stands up and brushes the sand from his clothes, looks at Simon.

"Next time, prick," Preston says.

I walk toward Ess, but before I can console her, she moves to help Simon. She grasps him. She kisses him. Simon is beginning to really bother me. Just because he stepped in to get pummeled doesn't make him worthy of her affection. Hell, I'm the one who got us moving to escape Singapore. I'm the only one who genuinely cares for her.

I move off to the side while they pick up what is left of the plants we had gathered earlier today. We are all on edge due to stress and starvation. We are all still so hungry; maybe eating will help. I'll let them cook what is left and prepare it for themselves. For some reason I don't want to be with them now. Perhaps after the mushrooms and ferns are boiled, I'll take my food into the forest to be alone for a while.

CHAPTER 12
It Calls

Tonight, Toothless and Preston are hitting the opium again. In the past, I have used opium several times myself and found it to be insanely seductive and addictive. Simon had been the only one able to get me to stop. I guess I will forever owe him for this gift, but even now I see the smoke drifting into the air and am dying to join Toothless and Preston. I recall my bouts with cramping, nausea, and anxiety when I stopped. That memory is all that keeps me from sitting in the sand next to Toothless and taking a small pinch of the opium for myself. I sniff at the air in hopes that the airborne drug will somehow make it to the membranes in my nostrils, taking me to a land of forgetfulness with no cares. That said, I suspect we will die quickly if I succumb to the urge, leaving only Simon to care for us.

Closing my eyes, I try to visualize every aspect of smoking and how good it would make me feel. It is beyond tempting. In my mind I am observing as a third person, I can see me scraping away the residue in the pipe's bowl from the previous smoking. I see me pinching off a small blob of concentrated opium with my fingers, rubbing the sticky drug into the glossy ceramic bowl, heating the mixture until it begins to turn into that irresistible vapor that will sweep all of my troubles away. I can even taste the smoke as the acidic fume crawls down my throat and up into my nasal passages. Then, I pull the pipe from my mouth and smile.

I feel a soft touch on my arm, shocking me back into the real world, wrenching me out of my fantasy, opening my eyes to find Simon's nose only a few inches from my own.

He whispers so as no one else can hear, "Andy, I know what you are seeing and feeling. It is not good, don't give in. I could have lost you and it would have been the end of me, too. For me, fight." Simon stands up and walks back to the fire next to Ess, where I should be sitting.

I fear that Preston and Toothless are now trapped by the opium dragon and I doubt they possess the strength to defeat him. Maybe they have fallen to the dragon before. In any case, certainly they are now prisoners and always will be, just like me. The difference? I have Simon. They don't have anyone to look out for them, someone who cares if they live or die. They are hopelessly addicted, and they will remain in a clouded stupor for our remaining time on this island.

I thought Preston to be useless from the first time I met him and now he certainly will be nothing more than a drag on our resources. Perhaps we just let him smoke himself to death; it wouldn't be much of a loss. In fact, it would mean our food and water supplies would go farther. No, his death would not be a loss at all. But Toothless is different. We can't afford to have Toothless lost to the drug. Even though I despise the man, it would be bad for us if he becomes a casualty; he has already proven useful for all of us. I doubt we would have survived this long without him. Well, him and Simon.

I hope that Simon and I can pull Ess back from the dragon. It constantly beckons her, and I fear we have little hope of protecting her. As she scans the camp site, her eyes invariably dwell on the pipe. Sleeping next to boxes of the drug may be too much for her. I should throw the drugs into the sea, but I cannot bring myself to dispose of it even though it might be the only way to save us. Its call is so strong.

Fighting the urge to smoke is tiring, and I feel that sleep might be my only savior. I move to the fire, sitting next to my brother for a few moments of peace and support before turning in. Simon looks to me and then to Ess. He stands up, stretches, and moves to the plane, stepping over the outstretched legs of Preston and Toothless to enter what has become our dormitory. Ess and I follow. I don't want to be left outside with the pipe. It takes strength I don't possess to avoid the call of the drug. On my way to the plane, I pause only long enough to make sure Preston and Toothless are still alive, not that I would do anything if they weren't. They appear comatose and their chests rise and fall with each breath. They are still with us. There is comfort knowing they have not left the living, yet. My eyes are captured by the pipe held in Preston's outstretched hand. I successfully fight the urge to join them and turn into our sleepy sanctuary. I win the battle … for tonight.

I must have stared at that pipe for longer than I knew. Entering the plane, I can see by the dim firelight that has managed to intrude into the darkness that Ess and Simon have already fallen asleep. Simon's soft snoring informs me he has descended into a dream world that I should not and cannot interrupt. Surprisingly, Simon has taken my spot, lying across the folded-out chairs. Even though I am moderately miffed by his encroachment on my space, I am relieved to not be spending another night on the hard, steel, fold-out seats. Instead, I will have the relative comfort of the significantly softer padded cushions on the copilot's chair. True, I will not have the advantage of stretching out my entire frame, but I will get some relief from the bruises that have developed from spending the last three nights lying on steel softened only by several folds of canvas.

CHAPTER 13
The Pipe Takes Its Toll

Day four—

The morning light is just beginning to break through the foliage, turning the leaves from black to vibrant green. It is a new day. There are only two people behind me in the cargo bay. Perhaps Toothless and Preston never woke from their fog to come inside. That would be a pity for them after seeing how the bugs and crabs lit into Preston on our first night. Or they woke early and are already out looking for food. I doubt it.

I slept fitfully last night, remaining awake for hours before finally falling into a shallow sleep, a sleep that failed to leave me refreshed or energized. Instead, I feel incredibly lethargic and want to close my eyes again and rest in this seat for the rest of the day. I would too, if not for the hunger pangs and thirst along with the knowledge that in the next several minutes the sun would begin to work its magic and heat the insides of what remained of our plane to the point where it would become uncomfortable; no, uninhabitable. Time to wake up.

I twist my legs into the aisle between the pilot and copilot chairs and stand as upright as the ceiling allows. I am stiff and sore beyond description. The copilot's chair was not as comfortable as I had anticipated. Tonight, I will take back my place in the cargo hold. Sorry, Simon.

I move to Simon's side and shake him. He starts and opens his eyes to focus on me. He nods in recognition, but whispers, "I need to sleep a little more" and closes his eyes. There is no reason to push him. This has to have been a tremendously tumultuous time for him. It also seems to have done him a world of good. I can't recall when he has stepped out of his private world, even with my prodding, and help. It's ironic that he is becoming more of a person just when there is no need or appreciation. Nobody cares or recognizes the change other than me.

I turn to the other side of the fuselage to wake Ess. She smiles and throws her legs off the bench to sit upright and asks, "Where is everyone?"

"They never came in last night, but I have not been out to check. You want to go out first or would you rather I lead the way?"

Hoping that Ess might choose to show me some affection, I am in no hurry to leave the confines of the plane. But she seems to be distant, not acknowledging our relation whatsoever. I ache for her to throw her arms around me and kiss me. She doesn't. She stands, stretches. I should have been the one to initiate some action and give her a hug, but she seems incapable of any emotion other than sorrow. No longer does she love me. Maybe she never did, and I was just a fling. Even if she did love me, she blames me for our predicament. How could she not? Maybe she will never forgive me, and I'm not about to ask her to. She pushes her way past me and exits the hold.

She screams my name, jolting me out of my self-pity. I jump through the door prepared to fight, but no fight is necessary. Instead, I see Ess shaking Preston. He is gray, quite literally, and stiff. The opium pipe I saw him loosely holding last evening is now gripped tightly in his right hand as if he had died while in the throes of seizure. I guess this was possible, given the amount of opium he had smoked; an overdose seemed likely. The extinguished oil lamp appears to have been kicked and now lies several feet from where it lay last night.

Toothless is sitting where we left him last night. His eyes are glazed over. Had he not been swaying slightly, side-to-side, I would have thought him to be dead, too. He talks. At least, I think he's talking, only I can't make out what he is saying. It is just mumbling gibberish. Simon has quietly materialized beside me and is also watching as Toothless attempts to communicate.

Simon whispers, "Take his guns."

He, of course, is right. This is our chance to disarm Toothless Joe. I can't help thinking that it's our last chance. We push on Toothless' shoulder and he topples onto his side in the sand, exposing two pistol grips sticking out above his belt. I grab both guns and then set about foraging through his pockets in search of bullets, Zippos, anything. Fishing through the front pockets of his dungarees, I find bullets of both sizes, .38 and .45, to fit the guns lying in the sand next to me. The second pocket gives up a couple of Zippo lighters and a bone-handled folding pocketknife. The haul is better than I expected. I decide to keep the revolver, a lighter, and the pocketknife and gather up the rest of the items to be hid in the plane. Someplace only I know. I check my revolver to ensure the cylinders are occupied by bullets and push it under my belt the same way Toothless had carried the gun. The first Zippo and the knife, I place in my front pants pocket. The .45 semiautomatic and the other Zippo hide under what had been the captain's seat, stuck up into the padding of the seat pan.

When I step outside again, it is with a new confidence borne from being armed. Toothless is no longer the threat to me, or us, that he has been since our first day here on the island. Smiling at my resourcefulness, I can now protect Simon and Ess. Toothless just snores with his face embedded in the sand, the grains sticking to the insides of his nose and mouth as he breaths. Thankfully, his involuntary reactions caused him to close his eyes before they landed in the pillow of fine silicon.

Ess remains beside Preston in disbelief that he is dead. Why she seems sorrowful, I have no idea. Death is obviously confounding her understanding of the world as she continues shaking his body, lightly now, as if she expects him to wake from a drug stupor. It is hopeless.

Placing my arms around her shoulders, I hold her tight. She doesn't reciprocate, but thankfully she stops shaking Preston and moves her hands into her lap and she doesn't pull away. Rather she continues to sit on her knees and looks at what had been a person just several hours earlier. Granted, not much of a person, but still a person. I attempt to pull Ess up from the sand. She gives no resistance and rises without acknowledging me or Simon. I guide her back to the hatch of the plane and she disappears into the darkness without me.

Simon picks up the pipe and the lamp. I am afraid he will toss them into the sea. "NO!" I yell.

He stops. There is a sadness in his face as he places them back onto the sand. He knows that I have yet to conquer the dragon and can't bring myself to dispose of these damning tools no matter how hard I try. He moves off to sit alone in the sand with his feet just encroaching on the cool water, his eyes facing off into the distance. He has left me with my cross to bear on my own. I drop to the sand.

It is a tumultuous time sitting so close to the opium pipe and Preston. For hours I am tempted by the drug and fortified by seeing what it does to people. It is like a trance as I fight an internal battle to not pick up the pipe and smoke. I move my hand to my shirt pocket at least a dozen times to finger the Zippo residing there. But so far, I have avoided succumbing to temptation. Unconsciously, I have righted the lamp and it is sitting between my outstretched legs. For the first time in years I pray, hoping for something to pull me from this spot before I pinch off a glob of the sticky opium.

Toothless pulls himself up out of the sand to a sitting position and coughs, shocking me out of my daze. He realizes instantaneously that he has been relieved of his weapons. "What the hell? Which of you fucks has my guns?" Then, patting his front pockets, he realizes he is missing more than just the pistols. "You—fuck—got my bullets! And my Zippo? I want my Zippo back. Now!"

He gathers himself up and continues to cough, hacking up the sand his breath had pulled into his mouth and windpipe. His anger pulls me out of my weakness, and I jump to my feet, prepared to run, if necessary, completely forgetting that I had the revolver sticking up from my belt until I see Toothless Joe's gaze freeze on the weapon.

"That there is mine. Give it to me or I'll kill ya."

"I give it to you and you're sure to kill me."

We glare at each other in a standoff. He quickly realizes that I'm not going to relinquish the gun back to him, at least not now. He sits back down and drops his gaze to the sand.

"Why'd you take it? I wasn't going to hurt ya. Or your gal." He turns his eyes to Preston. "He was the only one who'd hurt us. I was gonna protect you. Well, at least we don't need to worry ourselves about him now." He averts his gaze back to the sand.

Without needing to, I volunteer, "I have hidden away the other one. You won't find it, so don't even bother looking."

Toothless shakes his head. "Well, then you better figure out how to start a fire. I ain't doing it no more."

I contemplate the challenge and pull the Zippo from my shirt pocket and flip it to him. "Now you own the fire making and I have the gun. We need each other."

He smiles, shakes his head, and says to no one, "Just lazy and don't have a clue how to get the fire going." He rolls over to push himself up out of the fine sand again to stand tall. I think it is to show off his obvious size advantage over me. He stretches before continuing to speak. "You see if you can find some wood from those whiskey crates that hasn't been soaked and I'll see if I can find some more dead wood that might actually burn." He heads off into the jungle.

As Toothless leaves, I notice I am shaking terribly and my hand has involuntarily migrated to rest on the grip of the revolver. I hope my voice didn't quiver and betray my desire to appear to be in control. Obviously, I am not, even though I have the gun. The gun is the power, not me. Acknowledging my weakness, I do as I am told and begin foraging through the crates to find wood that might still be dry enough to burn. I keep my back to the sea, facing the jungle in fear that Toothless might try to sneak up on me.

Simon continues staring out into the sea. He is oblivious to my small confrontation with Toothless Joe. It would have been nice to have his help and support, but he seems to have descended back into his autistic approach to life. He is disappointed and angered by my inability, my weakness, to dispose of the opium pipe and lamp. His need to approach life's problems logically must be struggling with the paradox I present. He knows that, even though I want more than anything to rid myself of the temptation, I am incapable of removing the very items that tempt me. He must consider me a mess, an incredibly weak individual. And he is right … and I can't believe I am now reliant on him.

As I unstack the crates of liquor, I find a couple that have escaped being soaked by rain. I pull them from the stack and empty them of their scotch bottles. Hoping to bolster my confidence a little, and to stem my desire to try a little of the opium, I unscrew the lid of a bottle and take a quick gulp. The liquor burns my throat, but the peaty taste is so comforting I take another drink. The good scotch tastes wonderful as I swirl it over my tongue. Then it is time to work as I break up a couple crates, the open bottle at my side. I no longer fear Toothless Joe. In fact, after several more mouthfuls of liquor, he is no longer a threat; he is just a foggy memory … as are Simon and Ess. I am intent on breaking away the wooden slats when Toothless lays his large hand on my shoulder.

"You best take better care of that pistol, or I'll take it away from you," he says as he drops the bundle of dead branches that he had been carrying with his other arm. "I don't know that any of these will be dry enough to burn, but if you lay them out in the sun, maybe we will get lucky by the time we need to cook. I'm going to see if I can get another load." And he was off into the woods a second time.

Sitting dumbfounded, I can't understand why he chose not to take the weapon from me. I hadn't been paying any attention. Perhaps he remembers I still have another pistol somewhere so there's no need to pick a fight now. He might not be as stupid as I thought; he needs us, and he knows we need him. We are mutually dependent on each other. We will live together or die. My heart is racing, and I am breathing fast. Toothless Joe's surprise visit has rattled me.

Pulling the bottle back to my lips, I take another swallow, a large one, before sitting it back in the sand. I close my eye to let the alcohol soothe my nerves. Not thinking, I take another mouthful. Soon I will be drunk.

I call to Simon, "Let's get out of here and do something."

Simon doesn't bother averting his gaze from the sea, but answers, "Like what?"

"Explore the island."

Simon looks at me incredulously. "We need to stay here for now. You can't leave Ess with Toothless out there." He waves in the direction of the forest. "Or with the dope in there." His hand swings around to the plane.

He is right, always is, but I need to keep myself busy. The last thing I need now is to be reminded of the pile of free opium that is begging to be smoked. Simon senses my problem and walks over to me and, as a dad helping a little child, he pulls me up by the arm and walks me to a shaded spot in the sand.

"Take a rest. I'll get the fire going," he says.

I'm grateful for his concern, but I hate him for his strength. Who the hell is he to think I need to take a nap? Still, I fall quickly into sleep, hating my brother because he is good.

CHAPTER 14
Can He Be Trusted?

I wake from a peaceful slumber to a sky that has turned from an unvarying light blue to a full pallet of rich colors—spanning from an amazing burning red orange in the west to a deep violet as my eyes moved across the sky to the east. Evening was descending on us, marking the end of another day in paradise. At least, it would be a paradise if I didn't know that tomorrow would always be the same: wake, catch or gather our food, eat, drink, nap, and then go back to bed. The only deviations from the monotony being that of dealing with death. It's not fun. I take it back; this isn't paradise, it is hell and I brought Ess and Simon here with me.

Simon has held true to his promise in getting the fire started. Its light cuts through the darkness only so far. Beyond the light boundary it is black. That is where I sit. Three bodies are silhouetted against the light of the fire, their identities only surrendered by the significant difference in size. Simon is sitting on the far right, with my small, thin Ess right next to him. Then there is a space and Toothless Joe's large, angular body sits alone on one of the whiskey crates. They are talking and laughing, but I can't discern what about, nor do I desire to. What could warrant laughter? I can't remember ever hearing Simon express real joy. I think I'll stay here for a while and not intrude on their fun. Although I am angry at missing out on whatever they found so amusing. So be it.

They are eating and that's good. Simon has noticed that I am awake and watching. I see his eyes glint as he turns his face towards me. He smiles and slides closer to Ess. *ASSHOLE!* Ess smiles and leans into him.

I stand and brush the sand from my clothes. To make it perfectly clear that Ess is mine, I walk over to the fire and sit to Simon's left. He tries to ignore me. I can tell. Although I am glad he has grown since being confined to this island, I am aggravated that he appears to be making his affection for Ess clear … and Ess doesn't seem to mind. Shit.

I tap him discreetly on the shoulder. He continues to ignore me, so I whisper, "Listen up, Simon. Stop the flirting with my girl. She's off limits, completely off limits." Finally, Simon acknowledges me and moves from his perch, allowing me to slide in next to Ess. I check to make sure my gun remains in its place under my belt and then reach down to grab one of the branches on which an unlucky crab has been skewered for cooking.

Toothless doesn't seem to notice or care that I have finally joined the dinner party. He's fallen quiet, as has Ess. He is quietly picking at the white meat from his crab, intent on making sure he gets every morsel. We can't afford to waste any of our food. It is our second most important commodity, right behind fresh water. It is odd that we have begun to act as though the most precious item is the dope that resides in the hold of our permanently grounded plane.

My eyes dart to the plane's hatch door just as Simon disappears into the dark hole. I know he is safe with the drug, so I stay outside with Ess and Toothless Joe.

We quietly eat the rest of the meager catch, hoping to stave off hunger and malnutrition another couple of days. We may not be starving, but I can see and feel that we have all lost weight since God has dropped us here. Eventually, we will need to escape from this prison or die.

Ess taps Toothless and asks, "Can I borrow your Zippo? I think I could use a smoke."

Toothless stands while sticking his hand in his pocket to fish out his lighter. Instead of handing it over to Ess, he walks to the oil lamp and lights it himself.

"You want to go first?" he says, and he hands the pipe to my Ess.

She greedily accepts it by grabbing it in both hands. She doesn't even pause to scrape the residue from Preston's last smoke. She hurriedly pulls a pinch of fresh brown goo and wipes it against the ceramic edge as she holds the bowl over the tiny flame of eventual death; it always seems to end in death. It is then that I know I have lost Ess, not to Simon, or Toothless Joe, but to the opium. Her eyes smile, not in joy but in release, as if she doesn't have a care in the world. The drug's like that, pretending to be the solution for every concern even while it amplifies every problem. The Ess I knew, or that I thought I knew, is gone.

Toothless waits patiently for his turn with the pipe. The allure of the smoke is so strong that he sits next to the dead and swelling Preston without seeming to notice. He needs to be moved tomorrow.

In one way, I am thankful Preston's body is here. Had his smell not become so objectionable to me, I would have succumbed to the smokey temptation along with Ess. As Ess reclines against a wooden crate, I can see that the drug has already worked its magic in clouding her mind. She's oblivious to the crate's sharp, uncomfortable edges and her eyes are half closed while the cloud of drug vapor rises and falls from her nostrils, enveloping her head in a fog so thick it obscures her physical features. She appears close to death, closer than I ever desire to come. Although I am repulsed by her dispassionate countenance, I long for the drug even more. Preston's stink empowers me to shake loose from the opium's grip and forces me to retire to the cargo hold, our sleeping quarters, to join Simon. I have escaped the drug tonight. Ess has escaped the island.

It's a dark night; the moon is barely a sliver in the night sky and clouds mute the stars. The inside of the plane is darker still. Before I can park myself on the bench to sleep, I hear Simon from his perch up front, hidden behind the bulkhead.

"She is not worth it, Anders," he says.

"Fuck you, Simon. How dare you say something bad about anyone. Shit, you don't even know how to act like a normal person."

Silence. Then, "You're right, but just know that I care for you. I think Ess is lost, and she'll take you with her if you don't stop her. Maybe you can save her, but you are going to have to get rid of the dope to even have a chance. What do you love more? Her or the opium?"

It was a question, but I don't know if Simon wanted or expected an answer. He already knew the answer; I want them both and am unable to acknowledge that I need to make a choice. For Simon, the choice really wasn't Ess or the drug; it was really a choice of living or dying. Not ridding my life of the drug meant I would eventually give in. He knows me well.

The darkness became all too quiet until Simon interrupted the solitude again. "Where did you hide the other gun, Anders?"

"Why do you care? Just be happy knowing it's safe."

"I really cannot be happy unless I know. It is how I am wired. Where did you hide it?"

I didn't answer him, knowing that each time I responded he would ask again until eventually I gave in to his incessant questioning and told him. Why I don't tell him doesn't make any sense. He is my brother, and he would never hurt me. But I am concerned that if he had the gun, he wouldn't need me.

"Never mind, Anders. I already know where it is." Then silence again.

Who would have thought Simon capable of playing a game like this? He never plays games. He must know.

"So where is it then?" I prod.

"I will never tell you, but it has a new hiding place."

He must think he's funny. "Simon, where have you hidden it? Simon. Simon?"

There is no response, just the gentle sound of long breathing, Simon has fallen asleep. I don't think him capable of pretending to sleep, so the prick has left me hanging. I will need to check my hiding place in the morning after everyone is outside. I pull the revolver from my pants and wedge it between me and the seat back.

There is no noise outside. Through the half open door, I see Toothless reclined on one elbow smoking the pipe. His eyes are just slits, and I doubt he can see me spying on him from the dark. Ess's prone legs are just visible, the rest of her body hidden by the door frame. I will stay awake to watch and make sure Ess is safe from Toothless Joe. Even drugged, I don't trust him with Ess. Even sober, she would be no match for him if he wanted his way with her. In her current state she wouldn't even know to defend herself.

CHAPTER 15
Where O' Where Has He Gone?

Day five—

I wake to Simon. His face reflects concern—no, not concern, but fear. He says three words, "Toothless is gone," and disappears out the door.

Toothless is gone. The only sign left of him is the depression in the sand from his buttocks where he had been lying last night before I fell to sleep. I am not a very reliable sentry. Ess is perched leaning against the fuselage. Her chest rises and falls as she breathes; it looks as though she has survived a second bout with her dragon. Preston lies in the sand as if he is our camp sentinel. He no longer looks stiff and is noticeably bloated. We need to move him from our site before the ants and pigs find him … and us.

Perhaps Toothless found sleeping in the sand impossible with the fleas and the crabs and moved to another location? In his drugged condition, who knows where he could be. Simon and I will search for him later. I doubt he could go far. We would need to search for him to ensure he, too, has survived. More importantly, I wanted his Zippo back.

I reach for my pistol for comfort and realize I have left it in my makeshift cot and return to the plane for it. It's gone. I fall to my knees to see if it has fallen to the floor, under the seats. No luck. I am frantic as I crawl on the floor, throwing discarded clothes and torn cardboard to the side, hoping to find the revolver that was my only salvation against Toothless Joe. It's not here. My hands pad my pocket for the pocketknife. It, too, is gone. Toothless must have them. A hand falls on my shoulder; it's Simon.

"Lose something?"

"You know I did. Do you know where it is?"

"If you do not have it, I think Toothless must. He came in for a few moments last night, but quickly went back outside. I thought you knew."

"Why would I know? How could I have known?"

"But I thought you were watching," he replied.

I had intended to watch Toothless, and I should have watched him. I wanted to make sure Ess was safe and only now do I realize I don't remember anything after watching Toothless smoke for a few minutes.

"Asshole," I shout at Simon, expressing an anger that should have been focused on myself. I push Simon aside and storm out of the plane.

Ess grabs my arm. "He killed him, didn't he?" She pointed at Preston.

Although more of an assertion than a question, I doubted that Toothless would have taken the effort to kill Preston, but now I notice his head is severely canted to the side as if his neck is broken. I hadn't even noticed this earlier. He must have died in a fog and felt no pain in death, but the drug had certainly not caused it. Opium had some help, that of two strong, large hands at the ends of Toothless Joe's arms.

"He hated him just because he was rich and spoiled, but that wasn't a reason to kill him," I lie. Preston was scum and deserved to die. He was a waste. More importantly, he scared me. I wish I'd had the nerve to finish him off myself. There is no reason to share this with Ess.

"Ess, I don't think Toothless has it in him to kill. If he did, he would have shot him a couple of days ago. Preston earned this. He just smoked himself to death. How stupid." I lie again, ignoring the broken neck.

Ess doesn't buy what I am selling. "Why do you defend Thompson, or Toothless Joe, whatever you call him? He's a jerk, and he will end up killing you and me if we don't stop him. You need to man up and get him now."

She is furious; tears of anger are running down her cheeks. I can't reason with her now. After being next to the body for all yesterday and last night, now she is distraught and frazzled at the sight of it. I think finally seeing the broken neck and dead eyes, really looking into that lifeless face, and seeing the body begin decomposition has deranged her. She never really looked into the dead faces of Captain Robert or Bradley. Seeing a murder this intimate, knowing a person did this with their bare hands has unhinged her. She needs time to collect herself.

"Look, you stay here, and I'll find him. It looks as though he stumbled into the jungle over there. He was so doped up last night, I'm willing to bet he didn't make it too far before going back to sleep. Hell, he might be dead, too." I turn to the trees and begin to walk away from Ess.

"You can't leave me here alone," Ess cries just as I enter the jungle. One can't underestimate the feeling of guilt I feel at this moment. Her plea is an accusation of something, but I'm not sure of what. She wants me to protect her from Toothless and I plan to. I can't take her with me now because she will be useless in her current frame of mind. She'll be safe by the plane with Simon. Although he might not be perfect, I know he cares for her and would defend her if needed. And it won't be needed. Toothless is out there on the island somewhere, not here. I leave her with Simon and Preston.

In reality, Toothless frightens the crap out of me. Even though I am younger than him, I rarely tackle anything more physical than the occasional swinging of a cricket bat in a friendly club game or lugging my reporting bag and typewriter from location to location to cover a story. I'm soft. Toothless is hard. He could beat me soundly without breaking a sweat. That said, I am the smarter man by a long shot. My wits should give me the upper hand. That, plus his just recovering from a night of drugs should make him vulnerable. He'll be exhausted and dehydrated. I am counting on it. Maybe, if I am lucky, he ran into some wild pigs or a poisonous snake or the crazy yellow ants and is already dead. If that ends up being the case, I'll be able to snag back the revolver and his lighter and return to camp a hero.

Somehow, I don't think it is going to be that easy. More likely, Toothless has already recovered from last night and is irritable as hell. That, combined with the fact that he hates me, doesn't bode well for me. I will be lucky just getting him back to camp. I can always light up his pipe for him and watch him kill himself.

There is no way to track Toothless in all this vegetation. He might be watching me, quietly laughing at my attempt to find him. I am "it" in an adult version of hide-n-go-seek. It is so dark and dense here that I doubt I would even be able to find my way out if not for the smallness of the island. I look for broken branches, footprints, anything that will give me a hint as to which way to go. Not seeing anything apparent, I listen for any noise not belonging here in the jungle and am rewarded with nothing but the incessant sound of birds chirping, bugs buzzing, and the breeze blowing. I have no idea which way to proceed so I move straight ahead, forging my own trail through the flora. I walk into a spider web spanning from tree to tree. Although I see no spiders, my imagination instantly kicks in and I am convinced that I am now covered with eight-legged monsters intending to make a feast of me. I beat myself frantically with my hands to either crush or brush them off, running blindly in the jungle without any concern of direction. It is only when I trip over a fallen tree and crash into another that I can stop and attempt to regain my composure. After several minutes my breathing and pulse slow to a more normal rate. I can still feel the spiders crawling on me even though I know they are nothing more than figments of an overly active imagination. The part of my brain that makes up such exciting and engaging news stories for readers is now working overtime to frighten me, and I have no control over it.

My eyes jump to a movement, a black spider about the size of a silver dollar is crawling quickly up my arm. I swat it away just before it can reach my shoulder. Jumping up, I begin beating myself again; it is an uncontrollable reaction. The adrenaline rush wears off and, once I am satisfied that I am rid of the spider, I calm. Time to move on, but this time I hold my arm out cocked upward at the elbow to break any new webs before they can touch my face. I move forward slowly, my eyes darting both side to side and up and down. I hate spiders.

I also hate being hungry and thirsty and right now I am both. When I left camp, I forgot to fill a bottle of water from the stash in our cooler chest. Sitting on the jungle floor to rest a moment, I realize how crazy hunting for Toothless seems. Searching for him was foolhardy. Unlike me, he wouldn't get lost on this small island. Why look for him anyway? So, what if he killed Preston? What am I supposed to do if I do find him? Say I am "concerned?" Attack him? I'm a fool. I will just return to camp.

CHAPTER 16

The Hunt

Thompson stands silently, hidden just inside the cover of the foliage. He has been here for several hours, ever since retrieving his revolver from that prick, Andy. Thompson had been lucky that Ess's boyfriend was such a sound sleeper. He hadn't even stopped snoring when the first mate rolled him on his side to recover the gun. He'd been lucky, and Andy was even luckier. Had he awakened, Thompson would have merely choked him and wrenched his neck as he'd done to Preston. Preston had fought a little, but under his drug induced stupor he was no match. Thompson was surprised at how much he had enjoyed killing that lazy leach on society. Although the crash had been terrible and he had lost his closest and only friend, the captain, he could now see that some good had come from the accident. He hadn't been a particularly religious man. He had seen way too much death and devastation over his life to believe there was a god, unless it was one with a bad sense of humor. When he was a kid, his family's priest suggested to him that God provides free will to the Earth and doesn't impose Himself on us living here. Thompson's dad died from a bout with pneumonia later and he had hated God for allowing his dad to be taken. The hate had faded with the years and was now replaced with a strong dose of doubt, until now. The opium had opened a new understanding. He could see now that God had stranded him on this island for a purpose: to rid some chaff from the earth. It was a shame to have lost Captain Robert, but it was the price that had to be paid to eliminate Bradley and Preston. They were bad people.

Preston was lazy and spoiled, so spoiled you could smell it on him. It was a stench that could not be washed away. Thompson could still smell it on his hands, even after washing them in the sea water and rubbing leaves and dirt over them.

Bradley was different. He had controlled his only friend, Captain Robert, for years. Now that Thompson had seen the opium cargo, he understood. The control was money, and lots of it. Bradley was filthy rich, and he bet that Captain Robert had been, too. Yes, Bradley may have been rich, but he was also a dangerous and ruthless soul. To survive in his business you would have to be. By murdering him, Preston had delivered Bradley to the hell he deserved. Maybe a little earlier than expected, but deserved, just the same. It was funny that Preston had now joined Bradley in the same place, for eternity.

Thompson pulled the branches aside, just enough to improve his view of their camp without giving away his hiding place. He saw that the journalist's girl had been left alone. He had seen her boyfriend traipse off into the woods some time ago, leaving her with a dead Preston. He watched as she attempted to drag Preston's body from the camp, but she had given up after moving him only several feet. It would only be a matter of time before Preston's swelling with the gasses that accompanied decomposition would tear open his body. Maybe it already had. Even surrounded by lush growth, Thompson could smell the sour, sweet, sickening odor as it became stronger and more pervasive.

Thompson enjoyed looking at Ess from the confinement of the trees. From here he could stare without her seeing him, without him scaring her. He could dwell on all the small curves of her body without her knowing. The journalist was a lucky guy. He might just need to get rid of him, too. Thompson unconsciously slid his right hand down to his crotch to rub his manhood. As his penis became hard, he could feel his breath deepen and he imagined how it would feel to be with her, to be in her. As he rubbed, his pelvis began to thrust again and again. He could not help but make noise.

He pulled his hand away. No, that would be saved for her. He moved off into the jungle in search of the journalist.

*

I turn around in a circle, looking into the jungle for any sign as to what direction I should take to return to camp. I am lost. My bout with the spider has left me without any recollection as to how I got here. I look for broken branches, footprints, anything, but see no sign to give me a hint from where I have come, just thick vegetation everywhere. The sun is almost completely hidden by the canopy of trees. I sense that something, someone, is watching me.

In rapid fire, I yell, “Who’s there? Toothless Joe, I came to make sure you’re okay. Is that you?” There is no response. Then as light as a breath of air, I feel the soft touch of a hand on my shoulder. Swinging around aggressively I come face to face with Simon. “Damn it, Simon, I could have killed you.”

“You? Kill me? You are the one that is at risk the way you have been frantically running about. You must be lost, so I came to help.” He looked over my shoulder into the trees behind me. “Have you seen any sign of Toothless?”

“Nothing. He seems to have disappeared.”

Simon taps me on the arm lightly, points into the trees and beckons me with his other hand to follow him. I do. Why I trust him now, I don’t know, but I do. He has never really let me down. I tell him of the spiders and he just stares at me. My spider induced hysteria is lost on him. Truly I don’t know how he found me, but he is a godsend.

I feel sorrow for Simon. Until being stranded here, he had lacked the ability to feel, to hurt, to enjoy life. At least that’s how I saw it. As terrible as our predicament, the island has been so good for him. I see life in his eyes that I had not known existed before. If I didn't know better, I would think he is enjoying his time here. Personally, I hate it; I am so out of my element. I am threatened. I am afraid. I am lost. I continue following Simon without question.

Simon leads us through the growth, taking care to not disturb any more of the vegetation than necessary. While he is concerned with the plants and the path, my eyes are flashing around continuously, not in search of Toothless Joe, but in anticipation of spiders. Although not logical, I am now expecting to bungle into massive, sticky webs at every turn. Simon doesn't appear to be bothered and moves on without pause through the jungle. There is no way to tell what direction we are walking; the sun appears to be straight-up in the sky, so it provides no guide of direction.

My pangs of hunger and thirst are returning. The shock of the spiders and Simon's appearance made me forget my body's need for a time, but now that the shock has worn off, I am only too aware that I must drink water soon if I am to go on. I can't even sweat. Simon senses my anguish. He stops and drops to the ground.

"Here, let's chew some of this. It will help." He has pulled leaves from a low bush. "This is good for us. Chew it slowly and it will quench our thirst a little."

I grab a bunch of the leaves and begin loading them into my mouth, chewing slowly. Simon is watching me intently. I swallow.

"At least I think they are good for us." He smiles.

I laugh; Simon has made a joke. This is a first for him. Greedily, I load another mouthful of leaves; their coolness and freshness work a miracle in placating my thirst and hunger. Simon appears to be satisfied in watching me eat. Of course, he probably had plenty of water to drink before leaving camp. It would be very unlike him to have left spontaneously in search of me; he would have been prepared before taking one step out of the relative safety of the camp.

I lay back on the soft vegetation to rest before we return to our quest. Truthfully, I don't know whether Simon has us looking for Toothless or is guiding me to camp. I close my eyes while Simon remains sitting stoically watching for signs of danger or Toothless Joe. He realizes that they are likely one in the same.

I don't know why, but for some reason I wake with alarm. Although I see nothing new and Simon remains in his same position, by the change in light I must have fallen asleep for some time. The little sky I can see through the canopy of trees has darkened, taking on the slight violet hue that marks the sun's decline to the sea. We have no more than a couple hours of daylight before we mark the end of another day on the island. Unfortunately, this time we will spend the evening knowing we have new danger on the island, one that is armed, and who thinks I might be unarmed.

Simon shakes his head and stretches as if to pull himself out of a self-induced trance. "We need to return home. Ess is alone," he says.

Return home? With Simon I must consider whether he is referring to Singapore or our camp. Although he never seems to get lost in logical inconsistencies or memory lapses, I can't imagine how he could view the makeshift camp centered around a wrecked DC-3 with opium and whiskey as "home." Then again, he is factual and pragmatic. Referring to the camp as home might just be his acknowledgement that our camp is now the place where we will permanently live from now on. This is his way of telling me that we are stuck here.

I reach up, grabbing a tree branch and in one motion pull myself up to standing. "Which way?"

Simon looks upwards to see that the brightest part of the sky appears to his left; he points in that direction and without speaking begins his trek through the forest. I shake my head and follow, taking only brief moments to snatch some more leaves from bushes or ferns that Simon has pointed out as safe to eat.

CHAPTER 17
Who Watches Who?

Darkness is falling quickly as we finally exit the forest to the beach just south of camp. The camp looks to be empty and completely quiet. The fire is no longer burning, and instantly I am concerned that Toothless has returned and hurt my Ess. I flush with anger. I will kill him. Oddly, I feel no guilt for having left her here alone, just anger at Toothless Joe.

"Ess!" I yell. I yell again. "Ess, I'm here. Where are you?"

The DC-3 hatch pushes open and Ess spots me first and runs toward us. "Andy, where have you been? I have been so scared. I feel as though someone has been watching me all day. I hid inside of the plane because I thought it might be a little safer. It was so hot in there."

"Ess, thank God you're safe. I would never have left you alone if I thought you were in danger." I lie, knowing that I had not been concerned, not even when Simon showed up in the jungle, leaving Ess alone.

"But, what about Thompson?"

"You mean, Toothless?" I smile. "He is still out there somewhere, probably dead, so don't worry yourself."

"But we must worry. I mean, what about our fire?" She looks to the still smoldering ashes. "I'm sorry; I let it die out. And Toothless has the only lighters."

I lift my hand to pull the second lighter from my breast pocket. It's gone. Nothing. Toothless has escaped with our fire.

I look to Preston's body, still lying in the sand close to the plane. It looks as though Ess has tried to drag his body, but with little success. "Did you check Preston? I'll bet he has another Zippo in one of his pockets. Hell, he's an addict. He must have a couple."

"None. I looked." Ess responded. "I hated having to turn him over, but I checked all of his pockets and even the sand where he died. Toothless Joe must have taken it with him."

With no fire, we are in trouble. We can't cook and we can't heat up our water to make sure it is safe to drink. Thank goodness for the scotch.

I dip an empty bottle into our rapidly declining water supply allowing the water to flow into its opening. I add a couple ounces of the whiskey in hopes this would eradicate any micro-organisms that might sicken us. I hand the bottle to Ess and ask her to drink a little. Simon and I lay down the leaves we had managed to gather, and we take our time eating before turning in. No reason to capture crabs. Simon says that it would not be prudent to eat them raw.

I pick up Preston's feet and drag him out of our camp, laboring to pull his body as far as the water south of our home. I will move it farther down the beach in the morning.

Tonight, we will take turns watching for Toothless. Why? I'm not sure. He has a pistol; I have none. He can create fire; we can't. He has the advantage of surprise and cover of the jungle; again, we have none. Our only weapon is a bag of tools and a too-large fire ax. Whoever stands watch will carry the axe. I will take the first watch and Simon will spell me.

Both fortunately and unfortunately, it looks as though we will see some more rain tonight. Fortunate in that it gives us the opportunity to replenish our water supply. Unfortunate in that the night will be almost pitch black. The stars and moon will hide behind clouds, leaving us to live in almost complete darkness, with only a small discernable distinction between the blackness of the jungle and the gray beach. In addition, the rain will mask any noise of someone approaching. I have chosen to take up a position at the very nose of the plane. I suspect Simon has retaken his position to sleep in the co-pilot's seat just on the other side of the aluminum against which I lean. The dense trees provide complete cover from which I can observe the camp site. I feel invisible. I hope the crabs are satisfied lunching on Preston and don't venture as far inland as my makeshift hunting blind.

A light breeze begins to blow in from the north, cooling the evening and making a slight whistling noise as it rushes around the skin of the plane, only to get lost in the branches of the trees before reaching me. I am refreshed by the drop of temperature that has accompanied the storm. The rain was next. First as drops diving into the sea, sounding like waves crashing on a beach, wave upon wave, as the storm approached land. Then it was here. Although the sting of the droplets is diffused by branches before hitting me, I am drenched within moments by a torrent of water pouring off the leaves. I peer out between the branches to our camp, keeping watch, seeing nothing except in those brief moments when lightning flashes in the sky, instantly filling my world with blinding light. Then instantly leaving me in a relatively darker world between flashes. The thunder is deafening, alternating between the rumble coming from distant lightning and the frightening crash and crack when the strikes are close; so close that I can smell the ozone. I want so much to go inside.

The gods must be engaged in war tonight and show no signs of retiring soon. I listen as the water rushes down the metal skin of the plane, off the wing, to flood our cooler to full and overflowing. We will have fresh water tomorrow. I hold my hands as a cup to catch water draining from the leaves above me and channel the cool water to my mouth, swallowing greedily as I take it all in. It is invigorating as the water rehydrates me. I debate waking Ess and Simon so that they, too, might drink down some of this refreshing rain, but decide it is better to let them sleep. It is a good feeling when I realize I need to piss. I move off further into the forest to urinate. Why I feel the need to seek the privacy of the forest makes absolutely no sense, but I feel more comfortable knowing I am completely alone. In moments I return to my post relieved.

The rain has slowed to a quiet and calm shower that is gently relaxing me into a trance. I fight the urge, but I feel a need to close my eyes, even if for a moment. Rubbing my eyes with my fists helps only for a second and then the urge to sleep returns. I lose the battle as I kneel, resting my elbows on the leading edge of the wing, supporting my chin in my hands. I lose track of the world for a moment. Okay, perhaps more than a moment, but not long.

It is no longer raining, and the clouds have thinned just enough to let the moon cast its reflective light on our beach. Sand on the beach appears as a gray strip bordered on both sides by black, on one side a black wall of forest and on the other a black shining surface of sea. All is quiet save for the dripping of water from leaf to leaf then to jungle floor. We have peace.

I have no idea of the time, but I will wrest Simon from his sleep for his turn in watching for Toothless Joe. There is only fifteen or so feet of forest I have to move through to reenter our camp, but the vegetation is dense and sogging wet, so I take my time reaching out in front with my arms to shake the water loose from the branches. Why, I don't know. I am already soaked; the effort is habit only. I enter the black belly of the plane and quietly move from the hatch to the cockpit where Simon will be sawing logs. He is not. Simon's eyes are already open; I must not have been as stealthy as I hoped entering the plane. He nods to the back of the plane. I ignore his gesture.

I whisper, "No, Simon, I'm not going back out. It's time for you to take a turn at the watch."

He nods once again toward the rear of the plane, shakes his head, and rolls to his side pulling his legs up onto the pan of his seat and resting his head against the wall of the cockpit. I want to physically jerk him out of his seat, but that will make a commotion and wake Ess, so I give up and turn to leave. Facing the rear of the plane, the dim moonlight streaming through the windows provides just enough illumination for me to make out a bulge in Toothless Joe's hammock. It is occupied. I look to my side and see Ess sleeping across the fold down chairs. Apparently, Toothless has come home. I sneak to the rear of the cargo hold to peak into the hammock and see Toothless glaring back at me. He is smiling.

"Go to bed, son. We'll have plenty of time to talk in the morning." He holds his hands across his chest as he lies on his back. Below his two hands I can see a pistol gleaming in the reflective light.

I return to the front of the hold and take up my position across from Ess and lie down, too afraid to sleep. As soon as I close my eyes, I hear Toothless rolling out of his perch and I sit up. His hammock is still, it doesn't move at all. I can hear his breathing, slowly in and out, in and out, but other than that, he isn't moving. I lay back down on the seats, closing my eyes and listening, waiting for him to come after me. It will be violent. As soon as I fall to sleep, he will put his vice hands around my neck to strangle me. It will be the same way he must have killed Preston. My eyes pop open only to realize Toothless remains in his cot. There is no movement in the hold, the only activity is my overactive imagination. I will not sleep any more tonight.

CHAPTER 18

Who Will Be King?

Day six—

Simon shakes me violently. His face is a confused combination of accusation and consternation. It is his habit to bring his face close to mine whenever he is intent on making a point, but he never has pulled mine to his as he is now. He has my shirt balled in his fists and has my face pulled so close our noses touch. "How did you let him in here? Are you crazy?"

It is ironic hearing Simon call me crazy, but then again, he is angry with me. He has every reason to be. I let him and Ess down. It is shocking to see emotion from Simon. This is unique and reflects another change in him. I sense that the crash has shocked his psyche to the core and has been more effective in making a man of him than years of counseling. I will lay here quietly rather than push back on him. I have no idea how he will react if I choose to defend myself.

He releases my shirt, letting my head fall back to the seat. He turns to Ess, who appears oblivious to what has just taken place. He grabs her by the shoulder and pulls her up to sit. "Ess, we need to get out of this plane into the open." She stands while he pushes open the door and they exit together into the early morning light.

I hear Toothless from the back of the plane, "Shit, the man is a nutcase." Then I hear him roll over. He is instantly sleeping again.

Toothless sticks his head out the hatch door to find us already preparing for the day. "God, it is a great day. It felt wonderful to twist that little prick's neck until he croaked." Toothless stops to see if he gets any response from us. He doesn't.

"I mean, he was a prick and deserved to die. I just did what you wanted to do. Don't you think? You were just too chicken to do it yourself." He looked to the water where Preston's body still lay, half in the sea and half on dry sand. "Shit, we need to drag that SOB down the beach. He stunk up the area alive and now he is stinking it up dead."

I look to Simon while trying to ignore Toothless' babble.

Toothless pushes by me, grabs the cargo belt he had used originally to drag the good captain to his final resting place and walks over to Preston. He lays out the belt and rolls the body over it so that he can slip the belt under the arms to pull him into the water. The gases that accompany decomposition serve well to float Preston like a boat. Toothless takes off south, knee high in water towing Preston's body behind him.

Once Toothless is out of ear shot, Ess asks me, "What are we going to do?"

I am already stepping into the plane to see if Toothless has left anything of use behind, namely a pistol or lighter. His hammock is empty, and his duffle contains nothing except for spare clothes and a spare belt. I return to the light of the outside, looking to Ess. "Not much we can do, except to live with him until we get a chance to snag his gun."

I sit beside my brother and whisper, "Simon, where did you put the other gun?"

Simon looks to the sand and shakes his head, not commenting.

He then looks up, continuing to ignore my question, and sets about gathering food for the day. "We need to eat in any case.

Toothless is going to make a mistake and we can take him then. You know he is going to need to smoke the opium again. It is only a matter of time. We just can't get ourselves killed first. We'll have an opportunity to take the pistol back when he is doped up."

He pulls up one of the wooden crates that had been emptied of scotch bottles and examines it, turning it around in the air as if it were the most interesting thing in the world for him. He smiles, drops the crate in the sand, pulls up another crate and steps against its side, splitting a couple thin planks from the box. He picks up the first crate, its lid, and the wood scraps he has just broken loose. Then he is off into the plane in search of more parts to complete whatever it was he has already built in his mind. Within moments, he exits again with a couple strips of brightly colored fabric tied to the slats wood and draped inside the crate. He takes what I assume is his newly manufactured trap and heads to the water. As he quietly goes about his business, and it is like a business, he is smiling broadly. Simon appears to be getting great pleasure out of competition, man verses fish or man verses crab, whatever he is intent on catching.

Simon slowly walks away from the camp, toward the northeast, in search of the right place to deploy his new tools. He seems to find it several hundred feet up the beach in a section of shallow water shielded from the sun by where the jungle squeezed the beach to only a few feet in width. Here, perpetual shade from a couple of palms cooled the water, making a shallow that is not only populated by crabs, but small fish and sea urchins. I watch as he kneels, pushing the lid under the water, holding it in place with a rock. He then leans the crate at an angle supported on one side by a scrap of wood. He rests his hand on top of the crate … and waits … and waits … and waits. Suddenly, in a surprise of motion he pushes down on the crate, breaking the thin scrap that had held the box askew. Reaching down into the water it looks as though he is pushing his hand under the lid while pulling the entire box first to its side, then turning it again to bring the open portion of the box above the surface of the water. He pulls the lid away and smiles.

Simon rises from his knees, picks up the crate and walks towards us as water drains out the narrow slits between slats of wood. He sits the box down in the sand and pulls out two small, colorful fish, each about eight inches in length. He drops the fish back into the crate and reaches into his pocket, pulling out a small pocketknife and reaches back into the box to retrieve one of his prizes.

Quietly he sets about slitting the fish up its gut with his little knife. If the fish had been any larger, I doubt the little folding knife would have been sufficient. After slitting the abdomen, he pulls out the small amount of entrails and drops them back into the crate. He looks to me and says, "We've got to save those for more crab bait." He then places the fish against the wood and saws off its head, dropping it, too, back into the crate. He does likewise with the second fish.

Sitting next to Ess, he holds one of the fish out to her saying, "Just scrape the meat off the skin with your teeth. It will be good for you." He takes the second and scrapes the meat with his lower front teeth to show how to remove the white meat from the tough skin. After eating, he gets back up and returns with his box to the same section of water for another round of fishing. I follow him to his spot this time, hoping for another round of success. I am so hungry.

*

Dragging Preston's body to the burial ground was easier than Thompson expected; it was swollen with gases to the point it floated on top of the water as a balloon. His only concern was that the water pressure might cause his skin to rupture, releasing the gas and as a result, killing his buoyancy. He quickened his pace in recognition that it was only a matter of time before the skin would burst open. He had no desire to be nearby when that occurred.

As he approached what was to have been the final resting place of Captain Robert and Bradley, he could see that it had not been the "final" place at all. The captain's torso was no longer laying where he had left it a couple of days earlier; it had been dragged partially into the jungle. Thompson retched when he realized the good captain's legs had been wrenched from the hips and stolen away. Likewise, one of his arms had been pulled from its socket.

The thieves? A couple wild pigs. He didn't need to see the cloven hoof marks surrounding the body or the flattened vegetation. Two were now working on Robert's separated arm. Thompson had seen these types of pigs before; they were prevalent throughout the islands in the Javan Sea. They were odd-looking beasts, so different from those domesticated ones you expected to see on a farm. These would be like large fat dogs with huge heads and snouts. Yet they were undoubtedly pigs: with their large ears and flat noses. And they were vicious in their voracious eating, fighting over every torn piece of flesh and bone. Currently, they were so consumed with fighting for the captain's arm that they failed to notice Toothless standing in the water not more than fifty feet away. So far, Bradley had escaped attack from the pigs. Instead, his body was still being consumed by the ants. Most of the colony appears to have moved on, but the steady feeding continued, albeit at a less fevered pace. Bradley would be the next meal for the pigs as the natural circle of life proceeded without pause. Thompson's only objective was to avoid becoming part of that circle.

Although he thought the water would protect him from the ants, Thompson had no idea if the water would deter the hairy pigs. He prayed that if the beasts had food to consume and did not perceive him as a threat, he would be safe. But he didn't feel safe.

He slowly moved his hand to remove the pistol from his belt and brought it up to point at one of the beasts. He had no idea where to aim. He had never shot an animal like this before. He had no idea if the bullet from a revolver even packed enough power to punch through the hair and bone shielding the massive head. A shot to where he thought the heart ought to be was best. If he shot one of the beasts, he wanted to be sure to drop it before its partner could attack.

He pointed the gun to the sky and fired, hoping the sound alone would be sufficient to scare the gorging beasts back into the jungle. *Bang!* the shot rang out, sending sound waves across the island. Just as when Preston murdered Bradley, the percussion of the gun shot shocked the jungle into silence; birds stopped chirping, bugs stopped clicking and clacking. But the pigs didn't take notice. The two kept eating, but they were certainly aware of him. He would either need to leave Preston here in the water or kill the pigs. The pigs were not going to relinquish their food. He was afraid to go closer.

Oddly, his limited humanity kicked in. He felt it wrong to abandon Preston's body in the water regardless of whether he had been an ass or not. Granted, the sand was not a true burial ground. It had become the closest thing to a cemetery that they had, and anyone's body deserved at least some dignity. He pointed the gun back to the nearest pig that was now lying on its chest aggressively crunching the wrist it had wrested away from the second pig. The second was now intent on pulling the second arm from the captain's body.

Thompson took aim at a spot on the side of the pig's head, between the ear and the eye. He had no idea if he could hit it from this distance. He dropped the cargo strap, stepping on it to ensure the body could not float off and brought his second hand to the gun, creating a fulcrum to steady the pistol. Arms straightened, legs spread out, one slightly to the front to maximize balance, he breathed out and pulled the trigger. Nothing happened.

"Stupid, Thompson," he chastised himself for forgetting to pull back the hammer, cocking the gun. With the gun cocked, he breathed out again, calming his nerves and fired.

The pig stopped eating. Thompson didn't know he had hit the target until the pig began to shake, rolled onto its side, and slowly died. His challenger for the captain's arm, sensing the death and danger, squealed, and disappeared into the brush.

Surprised and relieved, Thompson stood still in the water and took several deep gulps of air through his mouth until he was calm. He could feel his heart slow as the additional oxygen took effect. He kept his eyes focused on the spot in the jungle where the second pig had disappeared: first to make sure the beast did not return and secondly to avert his eyes from the dead, bloated body that now had come to rest against his legs. He knelt in the water to retrieve the straps, blindly fishing around the sand until he had one, then both straps that buoyed the dead ship of flesh. He pulled himself from the water and headed to the beach.

Dragging Preston to the opposite side of Bradley, away from the captain, he figured that the ants would soon move en masse to begin their demolition, hopefully deterring the other pig from adding him to its feasting for a while. After depositing Preston on the beach, he pulled the strap free and proceeded to roll the pig onto the belt to be dragged back to the camp. No reason to let this food go to waste, although the idea of eating an animal that had, until just a few minutes ago, been dining on human flesh repulsed him.

Thompson began dragging the pig back up the sandy beach. Although the pig was not as large as domesticated hogs, probably weighing no more than Preston, the weight was concentrated, making the pulling even more arduous. He stopped, realizing he no longer had the strength to pull the animal the entire way to the camp without some type of assistance. In addition, he did not want to leave the captain as lunch for more pigs. He dropped the strap to the ground and returned to where he had seen the captain being devoured by the carnivorous beasts.

Struggling with the gore and smell, he gathered parts of the captain's body and piled them in the sand. He would spend the next hour digging a grave in the sand to provide the captain and his severed body parts a more appropriate burial. He felt he owed him that. Hopefully, his grave would prove deep enough to keep the pigs from rooting him back up. Thompson did nothing more for Bradley and Preston; the pigs and ants could have them.

After completing his burial, Thompson entered the jungle in search of branches that might serve as a sled to get the pig carcass home.

*

I am alone in the camp. I have no idea where Simon is off to and Ess has walked up the beach alone in search of a little privacy and to bathe in the shallow sea water. I offered to go with her, but to my disappointment she was reluctant to have me join her. I don't think she is up for any extra-curricular activities, not the type I desire. I'll wait for her to return and then take my own shot at bathing. Not only does my body stink of sweat and filth; I look like hell. My hair is greasy, and I haven't shaved in more than a week. Simon's pocketknife should be sharp enough to scrape away the whisker growth, but I will still smell bad. If I were Ess, I wouldn't be interested in getting physically close to me either.

We need to figure out a way to get Toothless to wash and shave, too. His gray stubble combined with his sour breath reminds me of the ancient beggars that used to hound me when I got my first job in New York City. That seems forever ago. His body stench is beginning to permeate the plane. I don't know how long I'll be able to stomach being cooped up with him when we sleep.

Here I am pondering how to get our toothless wonder to bathe when I notice him walking up the beach, returning to camp. He is dragging something behind him, although I have no idea what it is. From this distance, it looks to be a dark log with short branches sticking out of one side. Personally, I am surprised he has come back. He drops the branches and whatever he's been dragging in the sand and continues toward us.

As I look more intently, I see he has not been dragging a log; it's a large dog. No, not a dog, but a pig with a huge head and knotty snout. The head is almost as large as the rest of the body, one ugly creature. Toothless is standing tall and smiling as he walks into our camp. He comes as a conquering king, having brought bounty for our benefit. I guess I should be thankful; however, I can't bring myself to trust the man.

He steps to me directly and drops the two ends of the strap he had been using to pull the carcass into my lap. "You need to hang that wild hog from a tree with this and clean it so we can eat." He reaches into his pocket and pulls out his jack knife. Tossing it to me, he says, "Better get to it before it starts to rot.

"Hang it head down, slice its neck to drain the blood and gut it from here to here." Pointing to his low abdomen and pulling his finger all the way up to his neck. "Make sure you get all them guts out of him, but don't puncture 'em. That'll foul the meat. And find a place away from here to gut him. We don't need to bring his friends or the ants here to eat what comes out of him."

I have no idea how to gut the beast, nor do I have any desire to take orders from someone like Toothless Joe. I brush the straps from my lap, pushing them off into the sand, and defiantly stare back at Toothless. "Gut him yourself." I continue staring until Toothless pulls the pistol from behind his back and points it in my face.

"Don't give me an excuse. Trust me, there is only one thing I would enjoy more than putting a bullet between your eyes." He then averts his gaze for just a moment in the direction of Ess and then returns his eyes to me.

I get the message and pick up the straps and leave, walking south from our camp back to where Toothless left the carcass lying. As I go, I scan the forest for a tree, any tree, that might have a low branch strong enough from which I might hang this thing. I have no idea how to go about gutting and cleaning an animal other than Toothless Joe's few words of direction, but with the encouragement provided by having the gun waved in my face, I can figure it out.

I continue down the beach beyond the animal in search of something from which to hang the pig, before finally settling on a low tree with thick horizontal branches leaning out over the sand. Dragging the pig is arduous. Its weight pushes it deeply into the sand. Even though it sits on top of broad-leafed branches that serve a sled, I am sweating profusely by the time I toss the straps over the branch and set about figuring out how to pull the pig high enough to be hanging. The cloven hoof feet provide no purchase point for the traps. I tie the straps around her legs, but they slip free as soon as I attempt to pull the pig into the air. Eventually, I settle on poking holes through the pig's hide just in front of its hind legs and stick the cargo strap's hooks directly into the holes. I pull down on the straps, yanking the pig's hind legs into the air. I tug a second and third time, pulling most of the body off the ground. I cannot get the head completely off the ground; it is too heavy. Holding the straps tight, I loop them around the tree trunk and tie them off.

Simon startles me by laughing. He has been watching me struggle to hoist the beast from the ground. I think he has become an ass since we have become castaways. He sits silently behind me as I do the hard lifting. He doesn't even bother to help.

"You want some help in cleaning the pig?" he asks.

"So now you want to help? You going to help cut or just supervise?"

I am shocked with his directness when he answers, "Just supervise. Having two people cutting at the same carcass is asking for trouble."

He sits down on the sand with his legs crossed and watches, alternating his gaze between me and the strung-up hog. After returning his gaze, I quickly give up any hope of getting Simon to help with the job and set about cutting. Just as Toothless has suggested, I first cut the pig's neck. Nothing happens until I cut deeper and then deeper again until a rush of dark blood flows over the knife and my hands into sand staining it black. I want to vomit.

Simon says, "Good."

Thank you, Simon. Now shut the hell up, I think to myself.

Pulling the knife free from the neck, I pause to pull myself together and garner the strength to cut down the center of the animal to open its belly, starting from the hind legs all the way down to the front legs. I push in the blade at an angle and begin sawing through the skin.

Simon contributes, "Just saw a little until you get through the tough hide. Then you should slowly separate the skin with one hand while moving the knife blade downward towards the pig's head."

"Simon, have you ever gutted a pig before?" I ask.

"No, but I read an article in a hunting journal that outlined-"

"Read an article, oh, wonderful."

I begin sawing as Simon suggested, until I get through the outer layer of hair and skin. Inserting my fingers to pull the hide outward, I repeat the exercise, digging deeper into the flesh, cutting from top to bottom until I have a two-and-a-half-foot long cut which I pull open to gain access to the pig's entrails. Not knowing any better way to pull the guts from the animal, I try to slide my fingers under the folded tubes that I assume are intestines, freeing them from the meat with the assistance of the knife blade.

Simon interrupts my efforts by saying, "Whoa; be careful with that knife, Anders. You do not want to nick the intestines, or the feces inside will come oozing out. It will be a smelly mess."

"Simon, you know so much about cleaning a carcass, you ought to take a crack with the knife yourself."

Either not getting the sarcasm, or just not caring, Simon responds, "No thanks, Anders, I think you are doing just fine." Then he returns to his staring. He is enjoying this immensely.

As I cut, scrape, and pull, I feel the brown intestines eventually give way and fall from the pig's belly to the ground, making a sucking sound as they fall, leaving a huge cavity in the body. I continue the same process with its other organs, attacking anything that doesn't look like good meat, eventually cutting through the esophagus to remove the stomach and lungs.

Proud of my accomplishment, I look down at my feet that are now covered with blood and innards. I get sick and throw up what little I have in my stomach. I stumble across the sand, entering the sea water, and sit down to rinse the staining blood from my skin and clothes. I sit in the coolness to calm and prepare myself for the return trip to the carcass. I still need to release the straps from the tree, lowering the carcass to the sand.

Toothless is smiling when finally, I drag the pig back to camp, pulling it through the water so the carcass' cavity doesn't fill with sand. The pig is substantially lighter now that it has been gutted. I can't believe Simon left Toothless alone with Ess to pretend to help me with the pig. That said, I am glad to have had his guidance so that I didn't screw up. Cooked pork will be a welcome change in menu for tonight.

Toothless hops up from the sand and walks quickly to meet me before I reach the camp. In one hand he holds the plane's fire ax. In his other is a short log.

"Pull that fucker up here and lay its neck across this," he says, dropping the log into the sand.

I jerk the head up onto the log and stand back as Toothless begins chopping away with the ax. It takes several chops to sever the head from the body, shrinking the length of body that we will cook by more than half. He picks up the head by the ears with both hands, then twists at his torso, swinging his arms backward and forward, releasing the head into the air and out into the sea.

"Let the fish have that."

He reaches down, grasping the remaining portion of the pig and throws it over his shoulder before returning to camp.

"No 'thank you?'" I ask.

Toothless doesn't even turn around to face me, but I hear, "If you think you need it, then thanks." He walks off to our almost empty camp.

He forgets to ask for his knife, and I don't offer it.

CHAPTER 19

The King No More

Camp has been quiet since Toothless' return. Ess whispered in my ear that she was both surprised and scared by finding Toothless at work digging a pit just beyond our camp when she returned from her bath. Although she felt his eyes dwell on her a little too long, drifting down from her face to the wet blouse that clung to her breasts, he had barely acknowledged her. So, she hadn't run. He never even got up from his knees; rather he just resumed digging away sand with his hands, widening and deepening the hole. She had withdrawn into the plane and had been there the rest of the afternoon, waiting for me to return. She didn't want to be alone with him.

By the time Simon and I returned, Toothless had not only dug a cooking pit for the pig, but he had also filled the pit with wood, started a fire and lined the hole with a large piece of scrap metal from the plane and a bunch of large green leaves. This was to be the oven for our pig.

He dumped the pig onto the green leaves and then threw more green leaves on top of the carcass before covering it all with sand, smothering the flame, but capturing the heat to cook. More speaking to himself than any of us, he says, "Dinner ought to be ready by nightfall."

I must give Toothless credit for his food contribution today. As penance for killing, he brought us meat and cooked it for us.

And it is delicious. It is our first food other than leaves, crab, and raw fish in six days.

With our appetites satiated and the sun dipping into the ocean, Toothless disappears back into the plane only to return a moment later with the long wooden pipe, the lamp, and another packet of opium. Today started badly, but appears to be ending well, until Toothless offers me the opium pipe. I close my eyes to blind the image from sight and hold my hands up, palms toward him while shaking my head violently to suggest I'll pass. I know the side-to-side movement is barely discernable. I can't think of anything I want more than the feeling of nothingness to sweep through me. I'm ready to give in until Simon says "No."

Toothless nods as if saying okay and offers it to Ess. She greedily grabs the pipe and takes a shallow draw, then follows it with a slow, deep draw, allowing the smoke to fill her lungs completely before escaping in twin tendrils threading upwards from her nostrils. She inhales again, moving from consciousness to semi-consciousness; it hurts me to watch.

Toothless pulls the pipe from her hands to take his turn at the death alter. He pinches another small glob of the drug and scrapes it against the edge of the ceramic bowl of the pipe before starting his descent into oblivion. He will be lost to us soon.

I look to Simon, and he senses my 'thank you' for him saving me from falling.

"Andy…" He never calls me Andy. "…we need to escape this island soon or we will die." He pauses for me to respond. I don't. "Do you want to escape with Toothless and Ess, or just us?"

I'm shocked he is suggesting we might leave without Ess, but realize that he is not suggesting, but merely acknowledging that if we do not leave soon, Ess will never be able to leave. She will eventually smoke herself to death, as will Toothless.

"Simon, we have to take Ess."

"Okay, we still need a plan to leave. Certainly, no one is searching for us. We have not seen a boat since we have been here. We need to build a boat to float away, without the opium."

I nod in agreement knowing that leaving the drug will be almost impossible for Ess and Toothless. We can make Ess leave, but Toothless? I doubt it.

I rise to go to bed. There is no reason to remain out here watching Ess and Toothless smoke their minds away. Not only is it offensive, but it's also too tempting. Simon follows me silently into the hull of the darkened DC-3.

I pretend to sleep while lying across the hard seats. Simon falls into a deep sleep instantly. His measured breath gives way to soft snoring. In the relative privacy, I can now search the plane to find the .45 pistol I know he has hidden in here somewhere. We will need it before tomorrow is over if we really intend to leave. Dropping to my knees, I begin searching the floor mainly by touch, aided only by the minimal indirect campfire light that manages to invade the cargo hold through the windows and the half open hatch door.

Crawling slowly and silently towards the tail of the plane so as not to wake Simon, my hands reach into the crevices wherever steel and wood are bolted or riveted to the fuselage shell. Simon is smart, he has probably moved the gun several times since first hiding it. I can't be sure if it is still inside the plane, but for some reason I suspect Simon would never conceal it in a place he couldn't get to quickly, and hiding it outside meant exposing it to the rain. He would never do that. The gun was here, somewhere.

I pull open our suitcase and run my hand under the clothes in search of the gun or the lighter. It would be just like Simon to try to outsmart me by hiding the gun in such an obvious place. Nothing. I dump the clothes onto the floor and run my hand around the interior of the case, feeling for anything that might be hidden inside the liner. Again, nothing.

Moving on to Ess's bag, I dump its contents to the floor in search of the pistol. Failing to find anything other than clothing, along with a couple pens and pads of writing paper, I gather up her clothes and stuff them back in the case. I move to the rear of the plane and likewise search Toothless' and the captain's duffle bags. No luck here either; however, I am thrilled to find a carton of cigarettes squirreled away under the captain's clothes. I place the carton onto the seats and return to my search.

Bradley's suitcase, a very high-end piece of luggage, is in the very rear of the cargo hold. The man must have been loaded. The latches are broken, so I assume someone else has already been interested in getting into this case. Not a good place to hide the gun, Simon, especially if you had to break the locks just to get inside. I lift the case from the floor and lay it on the seats. Upon opening the case, I find only a bunch of balled up clothes. Given how fastidious Bradley had appeared, someone else had obviously rifled through the case. It wasn't Simon either. There is no way Simon could return clothes into the case without first folding them. It was a Simon thing. Hell, he even folds his dirty clothes. No, this was either Toothless or Preston, and given that Preston found the pipe and oil lamp, he must have been the culprit. This and the opium explain why he killed Bradley. It was also probably where Preston had gotten the very .45 I am looking for. Unfortunately, the pistol isn't here now. Bradley had a second case, the briefcase that he had held in his lap during our entire flight. It is missing. *Okay, Andy, find the briefcase, find the gun.*

I return the seat where I placed the cigarettes and sit while still looking for the missing case. My attention is drawn to the pile of corrugated cardboard boxes that still occupy the center of the cargo hold. Screw the noise; nobody is going to hear me anyway. I begin moving cartons, looking for any opened boxes. Although some of the boxes have torn or damaged sides, I feel nothing other than cool cellophane packages when I insert my hand to explore. Thank God I don't rub up against spiders or other creepy crawly things. As I get to the bottom layer, I see it. Hidden between two boxes is Bradley's leather briefcase, its locked leather flap torn away. Unfortunately, it feels empty when I pick it up. I run my hand through the interior; empty. I shake it and hear a muffled thump. Good try, Simon. I win. I sit the case on the floor and run my fingers around the interior base until I find a hold to pull the fake bottom free. There is no gun, but there are bundles of paper money, lots of them.

I pull two of the bundles from the case and hold them up in the faint light. They are British notes, and someone has squirreled them away. It is hard to imagine that someone other than Preston was that person. If it had been Toothless, he would have hidden the money in his duffel; maybe he doesn't know about it. I replace the bundles in the briefcase and place the case back in its hiding place, piling the opium-laden cardboard boxes back in their places. No gun, but a wonderful find, that is, if we ever escape this place. Maybe I will be able to afford quality scotch even without selling my stories to the newspaper.

A yawn escapes me. I will resume my search for the .45 tomorrow. It must be in here; Simon wouldn't have hidden the gun outside of the plane for fear that Toothless would once again get his hands on it. I'll check under the controls in the cockpit and the toolbox tomorrow. Right now, I want to go to sleep and dream about how I will use the money once I get home.

I am tired and I need to sleep, but the excitement of my find has me wide awake and I consider going back outside when I hear Ess's voice. It's frantic but muffled. I am surprised since I thought both Ess and Toothless were both well on their way to oblivion when I left them. I rise from my bed and peek out a window to spy on the druggies. Toothless has not succumbed to the effects of the drug completely. Not in the least. He has pulled down his pants and is lying on top of Ess, my Ess.

"Simon, help me," I yell as I run out of the plane and launch myself at the prone First Mate. I hit him hard with my shoulder and knock him off Ess. He is too doped up to defend himself as I roll back on top of him and begin to pummel him with my fists. Right, left, right again, pounding his face without concern for my hands or him. I just want to kill. I pull my fist back to strike again, but Simon stops me before I can unload.

"He is out cold, Anders, time to stop. We need to check on Ess," he says.

He is right of course, but I want so much to continue pounding Toothless, but that can wait. I stand up and, as a final attack, strike out with my foot hard, kicking his exposed testicles. I feel and hear them crush. Even unconscious, he rolls on to his side pulling his legs up in an involuntary reaction to the debilitating blow. I hope he dies.

Ess, still under the drug's effects is quiet, but tears are running down her face. She is fumbling with her hands to close her torn blouse and cover her exposed breasts. She hasn't been raped, but had I fallen asleep, she would have been. Toothless can't be trusted.

I pull the gun from Toothless Joe's waistband, point it at his head and debate pulling the trigger. I want to, I need to, but I cannot bring myself to kill him. I stick the pistol under my belt and consider what to do with the man. We can kill him or jail him, but we cannot release him; he is too dangerous.

Simon and I pick Ess up from the sand and walk her into the plane to give her privacy and relative safety from this monster. Simon gives her his seat in the cockpit and picks up her valise to find her another blouse. This is a side of Simon I have rarely seen. Sensitivity is not one of his strong traits. Compassion is completely alien. Even now, I'm not sure if this action is one of care for her or one of his prudence and his embarrassment at her nakedness.

"We need to tie him up. Let me get the netting from the cargo hold." Simon disappears once again to the rear of the plane. I follow.

He gathers the rope netting in his arms. "We can figure out what to do with him tomorrow, but for now this will have to work."

I grab the netting and exit the plane with Simon prepared for another fight, but there would be no more fighting tonight because Toothless is gone.

*

Thompson rolled to his knees as soon as he was alone. His mind was no longer fogged by drugs. Not even the opiate had been strong enough to numb his nerves against the effect of Andy's kick to his groin. Although afraid to look, he could tell his genitals had been badly bruised and were swelling. The pain would not allow him to straighten up, but he knew he had to run before Andy returned with the gun and killed him for what he had tried to do to his girl. If the roles were reversed, he would do the same.

He pulled himself up to one knee, using a crate to steady himself, then pushed through the pain to stand. Even though he could not pull his pants all the way up over his testes, he held them high enough to allow him to shuffle his feet without tripping.

"Kick me in the nuts? You asshole. I'll kill you," he whispered through clenched teeth as he stumbled into the jungle.

After only several paces, tripping through the vegetation, the pain caused him to fall to the ground. He looked down to assess his damage, but in the dark could not tell how serious an injury had been inflicted by Andy. He reached down to touch, but even the light pressure of his fingers resulted in excruciating pain. He became nauseous. He had never hurt like this. His touch told him his testicles were huge, already swollen to more than twice their normal size. He couldn't help but wonder if he would die from the hemorrhaging. If so, he hoped it would be quick to make the pain leave.

Knowing he couldn't go any further with the trauma, he pulled leaves over the top of him to hide when Andy came hunting. It was only a matter of time, and he did not want to die meekly, unable to walk or defend himself. He passed out.

*

He's out there right now, staring at me from the protection of the trees. To my eyes they serve as an impenetrable wall of black on this night, hiding that bastard—Toothless—from what he deserves. I pull the pistol from my belt.

"Toothless, you're a dead man. Get out here now and I will at least make it quick," I yell.

Nothing. I see a movement at the edge of the trees not more than twenty feet from where I stand. I pull back the hammer on the revolver and fire into the dark not caring what I hit. Creatures that had fallen quiet for the night are awakened and begin to stir. There are noises I had not noticed before as the hidden animals of our island begin to move. I cock the gun again and fire blindly into the trees, hoping I hear a scream, a shout out in pain, begging for mercy; anything to tell me I hit the SOB.

Nothing.

Simon lays his hand on my trembling hands. My whole body is shaking. He is steady and calm; he always is. "Anders, let us just put it away and save this for tomorrow. We will begin the hunt early. Okay?"

The firelight shows the concerned look on his face. He is right, of course; he always is. I break open the gun, exposing the cylinders, and pull out the spent cartridges. After replacing them with new bullets, I close the gun again and reach behind me to stick it back under my belt.

Simon stops me and takes the gun from me. "My turn to watch tonight. You get some sleep and I'll stay in there somewhere —" He points to the trees that show the nose of our plane. "—and wait for Toothless to return." He pauses, then moves his face close to me, looking me directly in my eyes., "I do not think he will come back tonight, but I am going to make sure we are safe."

He turns from me and seems to almost float through the darkness, disappearing into the trees before I can object. I hate not having the gun. I can't move from where I stand. Perhaps I am in shock, so I sit down onto the sand.

CHAPTER 20
Hide and Seek

Day seven—

Morning was breaking for the seventh day on this prison of nothing but sand and trees. The sun with a brilliant red hue was just beginning to peek through the foliage high up in the trees but had yet to make its way to Thompson as he lay mostly covered in leaves and ferns on the floor of the jungle. He had not slept at all last night; not because of any remorse related to his actions, but because of the severe pain he was experiencing. He'd hoped the pain and swelling would subside by morning. It was not the case. If anything, the pain had spread from his groin to his abdomen, leaving him nauseous. The hours lying still had not helped at all.

He reached under the leaves to examine his testes. Fortunately, one was unaffected; however, the second was huge, stretching the scrotum taut. It was painful to the lightest of touch. He could not even roll over without reliving the pain of Andy's initial kick. Pushing back the leaves he took his first look at his damaged testicle. Pink skin had been replaced by a deep purple extending up into his lower abdomen. Blood appeared to be seeping from his penis and he felt a huge urge to urinate even though he'd had nothing to drink for hours.

He tried to roll over in hopes of pushing himself to a standing position. It was too painful to move. He gasped in agony, hoping it had not made him inadvertently cry out in pain since he must still be close to the camp. He would not have made it far into the jungle before collapsing. Eventually they would find him. The pain was so awful, perhaps discovery wouldn't be so bad if Andy would kill him quickly, but that didn't seem like something he would do. No, Andy would kick him again and again, leaving him to cry out, begging to die, but Andy was cruel and wouldn't waste the bullet.

He rolled to his other side, supporting his damaged organ with his hand. Although feeling as though he would vomit, he could at least move to his knees, leaving his parts dangling free. There was no way he could pull his pants over the swelling. Perhaps his loose underpants, but his dungarees needed to be discarded. He moved his leg opposite the damaged testicle up to place his foot flat on the ground, providing him a point to push himself up to standing. Reaching to grab a tree branch with his free hand, he pulled himself upright. Well, partially standing; he remained hunched over at the waist, the ache preventing him from standing straight. Using his toes, he slowly pulled his pants down, alternating from side to side. He couldn't reach down to pull them with his hands without compressing his gonads, sending him into spasms. Once relieved of the long pants, he could start walking.

He was miserable and intent on redemption by returning the favor to Andy; however, he would need the gun to exact his revenge. Ess was safe for a little bit. He couldn't imagine when he would be healed sufficiently enough for him to have his way with her. That bitch. If she would have just kept her mouth shut none of this would have happened. It's all her fault. She would pay, too, eventually.

He stared through the trees in hopes that he would be able to see the camp and get a sense of what Andy was up to. The trees hid the view but he could make out voices. He couldn't tell what was being said, but it was clear that they were still in camp.

Thompson debated what to do. What could he do? Soon he had to move away from camp, but realistically, he could not walk far. Standing was painful, sitting was worse and not an option. It would be too painful to try to stand again. So, he stood, leaning against a small tree for support, hoping that if his fellow castaways entered the jungle in search of him, they would enter far away from where he was perched. At least if they went in search of him, it would leave the camp vacant. He could return to camp in search of the .45 and the knife. He needed those to get restitution for the damage inflicted on him, and he would make Andy beg before killing him.

*

Simon struts out of the trees and sits next to me. “Brother, why did you not go in to sleep? I had it covered,” he says. “You wasted the opportunity to get some rest and maybe even to comfort Ess. That is what you should have done. How do you think she is doing?”

“You know, I don’t know, and I’m not sure I care. Hell, what was she doing staying out here smoking dope with that ass, anyway? Shit, she was just asking for it!”

“She might have been stupid and foolish, but even you cannot think she was asking for it.”

Even me? Since when does Simon think he has a right to lecture me?

Simon continues, “But you are right that the opium has to stop before she can be any good for us. I know you love her, but you will never get her to leave the mountain of drug sitting in the plane. At some point, I think she will sacrifice escaping from the island for escaping from life in general.”

I am not sure I love her at all, but feeling obligated, I answer as if I do. “Damn it, Simon, if she stays, I stay. Just get used to it.” I can’t believe Simon is getting under my skin. I know he’s correct. Ess is nothing but a liability. Hell, she wasn’t pulling her weight when she was sober, and the time she is sober is getting less and less. I’ve seen it before. So has Simon. It doesn’t take much to become addicted to the drug. It makes you dependent on its ability to numb all your feelings. Although it sounds repulsive, once you fall into the arms of the drug, it loves you. The feeling becomes irresistible. It's a beautiful smokey whore waiting to take away all your inhibitions, who you hate but can never leave.

Simon flips the pistol to me. "Shall we go find the fucker?"

I have never heard Simon swear before. This has been a week of firsts. I stick the pistol under my belt and hesitate before answering. "What about Ess? Should we leave her?" I'm more concerned she will start smoking the opiate again than I am that Toothless will return to camp while we are hunting him. I pat my pocket to ensure our lighter remains safely in my control.

Simon shocks me by flippantly responding, "How can we care, Andy? She is caught up in a web of drug addiction. We lost her when she took her first drag on the pipe. You should have known. You should have stopped her."

I am mistaken in thinking the response as flippant. Simon is just pragmatic. I don't know what to say. I didn't control her. I never did. Hell, she's a big girl. It's not my fault she got hooked. "Enough!" I yell at myself as much as at Simon. "Let's just go," and I head into the jungle without a plan or direction. I trust Simon will follow me.

I keep to the north part of the island, paralleling the beach with the intent of slowly crisscrossing the island until we run across Toothless or some trace of him. It is a stupid tactic, and my brother knows it. To him, my search is as if I am purposely trying to avoid contact with the man. On some level, I suspect I am. I wouldn't know what to do with the guy if I ran into him anyway.

Simon seems to read my mind and asks from behind, "So, what do you want to do when we find Toothless? Capture him, beat him, shoot him, or what?"

I can sense him smiling at me, knowing full well I haven't a clue. "Simon, what do you think we should do?"

"I think we should shoot him and leave him in the jungle."

"And why is that?"

"Two reasons: first, if we capture him, we must take care of him; and second, we didn't bring the straps to tie him up. He will be able to run away, leaving us no choice but to shoot him. So, we should acknowledge that likelihood and act accordingly; we shoot him on sight." It is tough to argue Simon's logic. I am about to agree when he cuts me off, "But, it doesn't seem quite right, does it? You have a tough call to make, brother."

I stop and turn to face Simon. "What would you do?" I ask pointedly.

He smiles at me and says in his superior way, "I think we return to camp and figure out how we intend to hold him if, and when, we capture him. Otherwise, why pretend we are hunting for any other purpose but to kill?"

I wait to see if he has anything further to contribute. He falls silent, obviously done. He stares back at me to see if I have taken in what he said. Then he turns around and heads back to camp. This time it is my turn to trail behind. Sometimes I hate Simon.

*

Thompson leaned against a tree, mere feet from the edge of the jungle, hoping the low foliage and shadows were sufficient to hide him. His genitals throbbed and his legs hurt from standing but he couldn't sit for fear that he would never be able to stand again, especially if he needed to get up quickly. So, he stood bent over at the waist, legs splayed open so as not to touch his ruined gonad. He no longer thought it damaged, but destroyed. It continued to swell and the bruising had darkened to black.

The camp appeared deserted, but he doubted that. More likely they were not yet awake. He hoped to take this opportunity to at least grab a bottle of water. He was parched. Just as he was gaining the nerve to steal into camp, he heard voices from the far side of the plane. They were still hidden by the fuselage but headed his way. He closed the branches and limped away from the beach; he could not risk a confrontation now. He couldn't run; he could barely move, and the pain was not getting any better. He pushed through the growth, the branches scraping and cutting into his bare skin as he moved. *Shit, what asshole doesn't wear pants in this stuff,* he cursed himself.

Each step reminded him of his injury. He only wanted to get to a place where he might sit without jostling his gonads. Looking down, he noticed fresh blood had once again begun to seep, staining his shorts a deep, dark red, almost black. He felt a terrible urge to urinate. He paused his halting and slow progress to relieve himself. Gingerly pulling his shorts down so as not to place pressure on his crushed testes, he could see the discoloration had spread and the swelling had migrated to his abdomen. His scrotum was beginning to resemble a water balloon. He tried to urinate, but rather than the clear stream he'd expected, he could only accomplish a trickle of bloody fluid that ran down his leg. The anemic urination came with an unbearable cramping. It felt as if his insides were being pulled out along with the crimson urine. He doubled over in anguish. Despite the extreme agony, it was being quickly displaced by fear, a fear he might die from his injury.

Thompson closed his eyes, waiting for the pain to subside and return to the constant ache he had experienced ever since Andy kicked him. His soft tissue was no contest for Andy's bony foot. Although he was never a religious man (sometimes he even questioned the existence of God, any god), he found himself slipping into prayer. He doubted it would help, but what could it hurt? Of course, why would God care for him anyway?

Just pulling up his shorts turned into a massive ordeal. Any movement of his testicles was almost unbearable. One small step at a time, always leading with his right foot, then gingerly dragging his left leg up next to his right, he moved further into the jungle. He was unconcerned with breaking branches and leaving a trail; he doubted his hunter had any ability to track him through the growth. If Andy found him in this stuff it would be by dumb luck, not his tracking skill. He wasn't concerned he would find him as long as he could stay on the move, no matter how slow.

He stopped to listen. He didn't want to go too far into the jungle because he needed water badly. He was already beginning to feel the headache and fatigue that accompanied dehydration. The camp provided water to quench his thirst and opium to hopefully numb his pain. Both were becoming critical.

Thompson reached to pull up a handful of loose ferns. He thought they looked to be the same as the ones they had picked for food in the past few days. Unfortunately, he couldn't be sure, but he had nothing to lose. He placed the torn growth into his mouth and began chewing. The taste was bitter, but also refreshing. Hopefully, the leaves would not kill him; he needed the modest moisture they provided. He pulled some more leaves and stuffed them into his mouth, relishing their coolness and the taste of chlorophyll. His mouth full, he continued crushing the leaves with his teeth, sucking the meager liberated liquid down his throat. If these plants were poisonous, he would get sick soon. He'd probably die. He didn't care. If he didn't get water soon, he was dead anyway.

He closed his eyes in anticipation of pain as he leaned into a bush for cushion as he lowered himself to the ground. He would worry about getting back up later. For now, Thompson would be satisfied staying below the view of searching eyes while he continued munching the ferns.

*

When Simon and I return to camp, we're surprised to find that Ess has remained cooped up inside the DC-3. She's managed to lock the door to prevent Toothless from getting at her. Although I am happy to see she is protecting herself, her fear confirms our need to capture or kill Toothless. He can't be allowed to roam freely on our island. None of us will be safe if he is on the loose.

I knock on the door and receive no response. I knock again, this time louder. From the broken windshield she whispers, "Andy? Andy?"

"Ess, come on, open the door. You're safe now."

In moments we hear the latch mechanism scream and the door opens. The bright sunlight makes seeing anything inside the relative darkness of the plane almost impossible. Ess doesn't come out.

Her voice materializes out of the gloom, "Did you get him? Did you kill him? You need to kill him."

"Come out, Ess. He isn't dead, but he's not here. You're safe now and you need to eat and stay strong."

She doesn't respond and she doesn't come out of the plane. She is being irrational. Screw her. I do not know why, but I know she can't be allowed to fall under the control of her fear; none of us can. I enter the plane and grab one of her arms and yank her outside.

"Get over it, Ess. It's time we stick together to get out of this. Pull yourself together, dammit."

I must have been too rough. She falls to the sand and is crying. She lies there glaring up at me. She looks as if she wants me dead. But I'm not the problem, and I turn away to escape her anger.

I nod at Simon to get his attention. Regardless of Ess, we need to figure out what we will do with Toothless once we capture him. Hell, we need to figure out how to capture him. Right now, our only option is to shoot him. Toothless is certainly tougher than me and could take me in a fight. Simon, well, I don't think he could even hold his own with me, let alone with a bruiser like Toothless. I walk to the far edge of camp and turn my back to the sea, keeping the plane and the edge of the jungle in my sight. Simon follows me.

"Anders, as I see it, our options are pretty limited," Simon says, laying out the various alternatives he sees that could enable us to capture and control Toothless. None of them seem to be particularly good. Realistically, we don't have any way to incarcerate him. One of us would have to guard him every minute of every day. Our resources to provide food and water would be severely stretched, until, eventually, we would all starve.

After I point out my concerns with each of his options, Simon pauses and asks me pointedly, "So what do you want to do?"

I know what Simon wants me to say; he has laid out our options in a way that makes our required action self-evident. His question is rhetorical; he knows what we need to do. He just wants to force me to say it. I don't want to admit it.

He asks again, "What do we need to do?"

I give in to him. "We need to kill him, don't we?"

"Yes, if we want to live, he needs to die. It is as simple as that." He looks at me and he senses my agony in agreeing with him. "Anders, I am not suggesting that this is a good alternative or that we will enjoy carrying it out. It is the only alternative."

Simon hurries over to the DC-3 and disappears inside, only to return a few moments later brandishing the .45 that I was searching for yesterday. I hope he knows how to use it. The way he is waving it about, he'll probably end up shooting himself, or worse, me. It's a lot more complicated than the revolver, yet he treats it as a toy.

"Where was that?" I ask.

Simon smiles at me, "Under the Captain's chair, right where you left it."

"You never even moved it?"

"No need to. You were already convinced I had moved it, so it was best just to leave it there."

I must hand it to Simon; he is intelligent, and he managed to outsmart me again. Now we each have a pistol. Simon looks toward Ess and then back to me as if to ask, *Do we leave her*? I shake my head and mouth to him that I will stay here at camp while he takes the first crack looking for Toothless. I'm not concerned for Simon now that he has the pistol. I leave my revolver tucked in my pants and watch Simon duck into the trees, pushing away branches with one hand while holding the .45 in his other. He vanishes into the shadows of the foliage. I hear him call to me, "I will be back in an hour, and then it is your turn hunting." Though I have no idea how he will know when an hour is up, I expect he will be back in camp right on time.

CHAPTER 21

Gotcha

Simon pushed through the dense growth. Although the island is small, the growth provided an almost infinite number of places to hide the hunted from a single hunter. His ability to systematically search the island would be impossible. Toothless had a significant advantage, being able to move from hiding place to hiding place under the cover of dense growth and a continuous cacophony of bug and bird noises. Simon's advantages centered on the gun in his right hand, an uncanny commitment to process, and his ability to remain stealthy. Moving quietly was critical, and so far he had been anything but quiet. He was almost rampaging through the trees and brush without any regard to the noise he was making. The excitement of the chase had surprisingly overwhelmed his logic. He stopped, finally realizing how his enthusiasm would ultimately doom his pursuit. He slowed his progress to a crawl, taking the time to continuously scan his surroundings in search of a sign, any sign, of the first mate.

Hoping not to miss any fresh signatures of Toothless as he progressed, Simon restructured his haphazard search into an organized pattern, moving directly east away from the sun that had already begun its descent in the sky. Once reaching the beach on the other side of the island, he would move southward several yards, then return to the west, keeping the sun to his face. Although tedious, he believed this provided him the best opportunity to succeed in his quest. He would move slowly enough to ensure that no trace of Toothless or his movements would escape him.

The island was not large, but at this pace he would need significantly more time than the hour he had mentioned to Anders. He hoped Anders would stay at the camp and not confuse the search by bringing Ess into the jungle. He also thought it very possible that Toothless would eventually need to return to camp for water. Of course, the draw of the opium would be even stronger. Toothless was hooked on the drug, and the attraction would be impossible to ignore. Simon took comfort in knowing that if his search failed to yield Toothless, they could still set up a trap at camp. Either Toothless Joe would eventually show up in camp or he would die in the jungle. The question would be when. Until they were sure he was dead, they would be in danger. No, it was best to ferret him out before he had a chance to hurt them.

On the second pass of his search, Simon found that he was on the track of Toothless, but he had no idea what to make of it. There on the ground, not more than several yards ahead of him among some crushed bushes, were a pair of tan dungarees. This didn't make any sense unless Toothless was smarter than they thought and was using these as bait. That meant Simon had turned into the hunted. He dropped to kneel, hoping to conceal himself in case Toothless was waiting for him to enter the trap.

He tried to slow his breathing, but he could feel his heart racing. He could almost feel that Toothless was close by. He needed to listen and wait, turning his head slowly from side to side in hope of catching a movement, a color, anything that did not belong in the sea of green and brown. The dungarees should have provided some camouflage; it was not logical for Toothless to discard them even if he was trying to set a trap. Something was wrong with this picture.

It was quiet for a prolonged period and, after convincing himself that roles had not reversed, Simon stood and slowly approached the pants. As he approached, he rotated left, then right, swinging the pistol in front of him, scanning the forest. His nerves were beginning to fray, and his gun hand was shaking. He had no doubt that if he saw movement, he would shoot without concern for who or what he shot. He hoped his brother and Ess had remained in camp. Simon brought his second hand up to the gun in a vain attempt to stabilize his hold.

He knelt to pick up the pair of pants. They were stiff and stained with dried blood. He was certain they belonged to the first mate. He was now stalking an injured or already dead man. Next to the discarded pants, he noticed a low bush that had been almost completely crushed. The low-lying plants next to the bush were flattened as if someone had laid upon them. Simon searched the ground for signs of animals that might have killed Toothless. In particular, he looked for the cloven hoof prints of a pig. Without a gun, Toothless would be no match for wild, hungry hogs.

But there were no animal tracks. He did see footprints, human footprints, and they led back to camp. There appeared to be no attempt to hide the path; in actuality, the tracks were obvious, too obvious. Either Toothless didn't care if he was being followed or he wanted to be followed. Simon moved off the path, deciding to parallel the tracks through the jungle. He stopped every few yards to listen and observe. Nothing seemed out of the ordinary, other than the damaged plants indicating the recent passage of a person.

Long before getting to camp, his stealth and persistence were rewarded; he heard a halting breathing accompanied by faint groans. He moved silently towards the sound. He practically tripped over a prone Toothless. The man had covered himself in leaves, making him almost impossible to see. Had he not heard the groan he would have thought the man dead.

Toothless' eyes remained closed, but Simon could make out the small movement of the man's lips as he struggled to talk. Simon pushed away the leaves exposing a gaunt, gray face covered with peppered beard stubble. He pushed away the rest of the plants to expose the rest of the man. Simon was shocked. From head to foot, the man was filthy and covered with scratches. He still wore his long-sleeved work shirt, but his thin legs were bare and enveloped with small cuts from the branches he had pushed through. They were streaked with dried and cracked blood. The front of his undershorts was soaked in wet blood and urine. Simon leaned down to hear the struggling voice.

"Huh-uh," Toothless chuckled. "Looks like you caught me. I guess I ain't too threatenin' now. You ain't going to let me die, are you?" Toothless never opened his eyes to recognize who he was talking to, but he trusted it wasn't someone intending to hurt him again. His lips turned up slightly to show he realized that instead of being captured, he'd been rescued.

Simon stood up, debating what to do. He fondled the grip of the pistol safely tucked under his belt, knowing that he could end this all by pulling the weapon, placing it against the first mate's head, and pulling the trigger. That would be the best way for this to end. He and Toothless would be the only people to know what had happened. For Toothless, that knowledge would only be a moment, but for Simon it would be forever, and that was too long. Logically, he knew Toothless represented no risk to them now. He still might be useful to their being able to escape the island alive. He pulled his hand away from the gun and knelt to Toothless' side.

"Let's get up, you old pisser. Time to face the music back at camp."

Toothless whispered, "I don't think I can stand."

Simon's response was direct and honest. "If you cannot get up with my help, I will leave you here to die. You choose."

Toothless opened his eyes as he gripped Simon's arm. "I ain't gonna die lying here in my piss and blood, so let's go, but you gotta take it slow." He kept his right leg stretched out straight and pulled his left up to a bent position. "Pull me up, but don't jostle my nuts. They're hurt bad, really bad."

Simon pulled on Toothless' arm slowly, wresting his body from the ground as gently as possible. Despite his effort to lever him up to standing with a slow, continuous pull, avoiding any sudden movement, the first mate cried out in anguish. It was obvious any motion was excruciating. Certainly, Toothless was not going to be an escape risk. Something was seriously wrong with the man. The effects of Ander's kick should have been long gone by now, but it looked as though they had gotten progressively worse.

Simon inserted his left arm under the first mate's right shoulder and around his back to support him as they limped through the brush to the beach. He kept his right hand on the butt of the pistol in the unlikely event that Toothless might grab for it. Simon laughed. Here they had been so afraid of what Toothless might do to hurt them and now it was apparent the mean bastard would not be able to hurt anyone for a long time, if ever.

*

It's been hours since Simon went on his hunt, and I'm concerned that he is late. He's never late … unless he's lost. To my relief, Simon and Toothless break out of the darkness onto the beach not more than ten yards from me. I never heard them. At first, Toothless Joe's appearance is shocking. He looks ancient, years older than the man who escaped yesterday. His face is gaunt and gray, accentuated by the gray stubble of more than a week without a shave. He looks as though he is paralyzed on his right side, dragging the foot through the sand. Simon is as much dragging the man, as the man is walking. Simon continues directly into the center of our camp and drops Toothless to the sand. He falls with a whimper. Simon then moves behind Toothless Joe and pulls him to the fallen tree, propping him up in a sitting position. Toothless' legs are splayed out wide in the sand and his head falls back to rest against the wood. Toothless grimaces noticeably and closes his eyes tightly. His face is damp with either sweat or tears, or both.

Simon sits next to me and quietly whispers into my ear, "Anders, you hurt him bad when you kicked him. I think you probably ruptured one of his testicles."

"Good for me then; he deserved it."

"No, I don't think you understand. He might die from this."

"So, what if he does; it's not my fault."

Simon changes the subject. "Where is Ess?"

"She got up just after you left on the hunt and shut herself away in there." I nod toward the hatch door. "She's still in there. She's never come out."

"Aren't you concerned?"

"Shit, Simon, she's my girl; of course I'm concerned. Just drop it. I'll check on her when I get around to it. She'll be fine. Especially now that we have Toothless. Shouldn't we tie him up or something?"

Simon let his eyes drift over to where Toothless lay against the tree. "We can, but I don't think it is necessary. I doubt he can stand up without our help. He is hardly dangerous."

"It's great that you feel safe; it wasn't your girl that he raped."

"He did not rape her."

"Okay, okay, tried to rape. Fuck him, Simon. I'm getting the cargo straps to tie the fucker up so he can't try anything like that again." Simon stares at me and shakes his head like I am the one screwed up. Sometimes I hate Simon.

I hop up anyway and grab one of the cargo straps that lay in the sand next to our whiskey crates. I am not sure how to tie the old bugger up. I don't want to give him any warning about what I am going to do for fear that this might all be an act and he might fight me. I tie a noose in the strap and sneak up to Toothless' side and flip the noose around his head. In the same motion my knee pushes him onto his left side. He cries out in pain but doesn't fight. I grab his right hand and pull it behind his back and loop the strap up around his elbow and tie it off with a knot. Then I pull him back up into a sitting position and push him over onto his right side and repeat the process with his left arm, pulling the two arms together at the elbows. I pull him back up to sitting again and loop the remaining portion of the strap once again around his neck and secure it with a loose knot. "There, I don't think you're going anywhere now."

I walk around to face Toothless. He doesn't open his eyes, but I see the spittle bubbling from his lips. Simon motions for me to come back and sit next to him.

"Anders, he is helpless. Why treat him like that? Did you notice his shorts? He hemorrhaged badly. Bet he still is." He pauses. "We might need to perform some kind of surgery."

"You've got to be kidding, Simon. We can't cut into that guy. We don't have a clue as to what we would be doing. Plus, we don't have any surgical tools. What are you thinking, that one of us tear into the guy with the same knife we used to gut the pig? God, we'd kill him for sure. By the way, when did you become a doctor?" I say sarcastically.

"I am not a doctor, and you are right that I really do not know what I am doing, but we cannot just let him bleed to death. Can we? Look at him," Simon says.

I get up and approach the helpless Toothless. "Hey, Toothless, mind if I take a look?"

Taking no response as acquiescence, I kneel and pull back the top of his shorts to look at the damage. It is worse than I could have imagined, and I can't help but be proud that it was I who inflicted so much damage on the prick. I laugh silently at my pun. His scrotum was a deep purple, almost black, and swollen to more than twice the size it should be. The skin is pulled taut. Discoloration has spread up into his abdomen and covers the inside of his right leg and his penis. Blood and pus are oozing from the urethra. Hell, I almost killed this guy. He's a wreck. Even though he is seriously injured, I can't comprehend how Simon expects to save the guy by cutting into him. What is he thinking? How would he even know where to start.

I pull the shorts out further to get a better look. Toothless groans in agony. Simon is right; this guy is going nowhere. Tying him up was a joke. The man is in obvious pain, so I release the straps.

We have choices to make with Toothless: let time heal the injury, play God and perform surgery, or shoot him, putting him out of his misery. I can't help but think the latter is the best choice, but I vote for the first. Even then I realize that we will have to do something to care for him while we try to relieve his agony. The obvious answer to the pain was something we had in abundance and was sitting only feet from us in the cargo hold. We have enough opium to kill his pain a thousand times over, maybe ten thousand times. I stand up to fetch a bag of the brown, gooey stuff.

"Not yet." Simon stopped me by placing his hand gently on my arm. "He needs water and food first or we may as well kill him now."

He's right, so I grab a bottle of our precious water and take it to the first mate. He never opens his eyes, but he opens his lips for me to pour in the cool, life-giving fluid. He closes his mouth, and I can see the cheeks move in and out as he pushes the water around with his tongue. He swallows and opens his mouth for more. This time he opens his eyes and tears begin to flow. I tip the bottle again to his lips and pour. He greedily takes a gulp, swallows, coughs, and opens for more. I know he has not had anything to drink for the past day.

CHAPTER 22
Killing the Pain

We sit around the fire silently. No one bothers to speak. The food has been sparce today and what we do have, some ferns and mushrooms, is getting tiresome. Tomorrow, Simon and I will catch more crab to feed us. We need the protein.

Our energy is waning and, even more so, our morale is at a low point. I fear we are finally resigned to the fact that we will never leave this place.

The allure of the opium is calling me. It calls us all— except for Simon—but tonight, only Toothless has given in to the temptation. He has taken to the drug ever since we released him from the straps. As soon as his hands are free he asks for the pipe and the oil lamp. He's monopolized their use since then. The thick smoke numbed his pain, but it is doing nothing to help him heal. Blood continues to ooze slowly, leaving the sand sticky and stained brown in a spot between his legs. He doesn't seem to notice as he inhales the opium vapors. I pull the pipe from him occasionally to ensure he doesn't overdose on the drug. Each time I grab the pipe, I long to take a draw for myself, just one. Simon's gaze is the only thing giving me strength to not succumb to the temptation.

Ess sits on the opposite side of the fire. She hasn't spoken since leaving the confines and safety of the plane. I can't tell whether it's anger or fear that motivates her silence. Perhaps it's jealousy that we let Toothless smoke the dope to numb his pain and yet offer her none of it to numb her anxiety caused by having to share space with this man she considers an animal. I can't blame her.

Simon is silent, too. He seems satisfied and happy just sitting and watching. He appears intent on observing our actions, as if we are an experiment and he is the scientist. His eyes flip from one of us to another, but each time he looks at Ess, his gaze dwells just a bit longer than with the rest of us. Perhaps he expects Ess to eventually explode in anger and strike out against Toothless. So far, he must be disappointed with the experiment results. There hasn't been any blow-up, no yelling, no screaming. But maybe that's the point, we don't know how to communicate any longer. We really don't have anything to say.

We have been unable to establish any feeling of normalcy or trust with one another. Taking Toothless alive torpedoed whatever trust Ess had in me or Simon. I am sure she looked to me to be her protector, her knight in shining armor, and slay the dragon (that being Toothless). And she had a right to expect that, but it would have been wrong. Simon was right to not take Toothless' life just because he could. The old man was no threat to us now. Killing him would not have rolled back to a time before he assaulted my Ess. It might have made Ess feel a little better, but I doubt it.

No, we had fallen into a world of distrusting and detesting each other. Only Simon and I maintain our bond. I think that if we are saved, Ess and I will part ways quickly. She hates me now; not like she hates Toothless, but she still hates me. I earned her hate when I made her board this damned flight more than a week ago. I am in the same predicament as Toothless; I can't turn back the clock. I understand why she can't forgive me, but its tiring and I am beginning to hate her, too … for punishing me by locking me out of her life.

Although the edge of Toothless' pain has been temporarily dulled, Simon is right about the surgery. After feeling the first mate's forehead, it's obvious he has developed a fever. He is burning up. Simon tells me this is related to an infection or perhaps something he calls necrosis. He says that the man's testicle might be dying, and if it is, we need to remove it. I can't bring myself to purposely cut into another human being. I don't know if I could do it even if it meant saving a life. Maybe Simon will take care of it, but he is typically one to supervise. I can't imagine him stepping up to do the cutting. I would ask Ess to complete the task, but I think she would prefer sticking the knife into Toothless' throat. I can't ask her to consider doing anything to help him.

We all know that the opium is, at best, a band-aid; it addresses one of the symptoms of the injury but fails to provide any type of real solution … unless we are happy knowing that the solution is nothing more than keeping Toothless effectively sedated until he dies. I am okay with this, but I think Simon hasn't gotten to the same conclusion. He approaches everything logically. If we are committed to watching the man die slowly, it would only make sense to conserve our resources and put him out of his misery quickly. In his mind, to enable him to continue living obligates us as his community to strive to provide a cure for his malady. I am sure his "cure" implies some type of surgery. I struggle with the idea and even more with who might be called upon to complete the procedure. Given that I am unwilling to let Simon shoot the man, I expect the onus falls on me to cut into him and I am sick with anxiety.

I move to sit close to Toothless. Although I am not sure he will understand anything I say to him in his current state of fog, I want to prepare him for what I think we will soon be doing to him. I struggle with how I will begin.

"First Mate Thompson, I want you to listen closely." Toothless is staring blankly into space as if I don't exist. I am confident he hears me, but I am also sure he is not capable of internalizing anything that I have to say. I will try to communicate with him again once the drug effect starts to wear off. I lift the pipe from his limp hands.

CHAPTER 23

Bet'cha Didn't Know I Was Gonna Do That

Day eight—

This morning has been extremely productive for our small tribe of survivors. Simon and I got up early this morning just as the sky was moving from black to gray so we could take advantage of the wealth of crawling crab meat that attacked our beach each night. We have been lucky enough to capture enough of the critters for a feast. The crabs are being held captive in a couple wooden scotch crates that sit in shallow water only several feet from our camp. We hear them scratching and scraping against the wood in hopes of escape. I am confident they are incapable of knowing their only escape will come through a visit to our campfire. They will be breakfast, lunch, and dinner today.

Although we have now addressed one need, we will need to address another by the end of the day; we are running dangerously short of fresh water. Unfortunately, we have had no rain for the past three days. We will need to refill our water bottles from the muddy spring in the middle of our island. The water will taste terrible, but after a generous addition of alcohol, Simon and I are comfortable it will be safe. None of us want to experience the intestinal problems Preston invited by drinking the untreated water. I can't afford to become ill. Our camp can't afford me becoming ill. Today I think we should add a double dose of scotch to ensure the drink is safe.

Simon has gathered empty bottles for our trek inland. I am prepared to acknowledge this will become our daily routine until we escape this island. I look forward to the exercise and welcome anything that diverts my thoughts from our predicament; however, I have trepidation of running into one of the pigs with whom we share this land. I check my pistol to ensure it's loaded. I look at our remaining crates of scotch. Once we run out of the scotch, we will need to either leave the island or we will die from dysentery. Given our current condition, I have no doubt the scotch will outlast us.

Before leaving, I sit down beside Toothless to share with him our concerns regarding his injury. It's important to have this discussion before he launches once again into his opium smoking.

"First Mate Thompson, we need to talk about your injury. I don't think there is much chance that it is going to heal on its own. Would you agree?"

Toothless nods almost imperceptibly in agreement, but I do not think he has any idea as to what I am alluding to. Realizing that I need to be more direct with the man, I say, "We need to remove you damaged testicle and I don't know how to do it without killing you."

Toothless' face changes almost instantly, from one of question to one of anger and fear. "Andy, no fucking way you're chopping off my balls. You better hope I die because once these —" He points to his crotch. "—stop swelling, I am going to kill you, you pecker."

He continues, "You kicked me like a chicken-shit and now you're going to neuter me? You stay away from me or, or…"

As he struggles to come up with another threat, all I can think of is a new name for the toothless wonder. Since he will soon be ball-less, I can call him "Nutless Nelly," or something equally demeaning. The new name will fit well, plus I like the sound. I start to laugh. I am not laughing at Toothless, but it sends him into a tirade of invectives, none of which are having the effect he intends. I can't help myself; the louder he yells, the louder I laugh.

Toothless swings a fist at me, and although the punch is feeble at best, the force pulls him over onto his side. I laugh even louder when he cries out in pain, and I know now that I can cut into this prick. I gather myself from the sand and toss Toothless his precious pipe. I leave with Simon to get our water. I don't bother helping Toothless right himself in the sand. Let him take care of himself. For all I care, he can just lie there until we get back.

We have been successful in our effort to replenish our water supply and we have returned with bottles filled with a murky, foul-smelling liquid we will need to drink to survive. I am still angry with Toothless for the swing he took at me. I am tempted to serve him water before we treat it with the alcohol. Toothless should be thankful for Simon. He has become his only defender.

Upon entering camp, I see that Ess has taken up her spot in the sand, on the opposite side of the campfire from Toothless. I am proud of her. She's replenished the wood supply and has a nice fire going. She has already roasted and eaten a couple of our crabs. Their shells litter the sand next to her. I'm glad she hasn't waited for us to begin eating. The lack of food has been particularly hard on her. If she was thin before we were stranded, she is now emaciated. She looks like the very prisoners of war we had hoped to avoid becoming. I suspect she has enjoyed withholding food from Toothless.

Toothless remains lying on his side exactly as I left him. Well, not "exactly." He has started to bleed more profusely. The dark stain of blood is spreading in the sand below him. In addition, he has soiled himself, and the stink is unbearable. I can once again smell the smell of death. The feeling of déjà vu overwhelms me. We will soon be saying goodbye to another of our shrinking band of survivors.

Simon ignores the smell and sits down next to our injured compatriot. I deposit my armful of bottles into the sand and begin adding a little scotch from our remaining liquor supply to each bottle. Simon has been really nothing more than company. He didn't offer to help carry a single bottle. Thank you, Simon.

Although Simon appears sympathetic to Toothless' plight, I can see that he has no intent of helping the poor man sit up. After completing my treatment of the water, I crawl over to where Toothless lay and motion to Simon to move aside so that I might pull the old man away from the soiled sand. Despite my intense disdain for the man, I can't stand watching him lie in his own feces. After sitting Toothless upright, I move around behind him and grasp him under his arms to pull him to the water's edge. I will wash him, not selflessly, but selfishly; I can't stand the odor.

I pull him through the sand and ignore his cries of pain. It is shocking how light he has become. In the week plus that we have been stranded, his body has deteriorated more than the rest of us combined. I don't know how he has not bled out.

Toothless relaxes once his body reaches the water. I am not sure if it is the coolness or the buoyancy that has provided the relief, but I am thankful the crying has stopped. I consider leaving him in the water, but quickly realize I can't. His bleeding and seeping will attract hungry crabs and fish. No matter how sorry the individual is, I don't think he deserves to be fed upon while he is still living.

I pull Toothless' jackknife from my pocket and cut the shorts from his body. I can see no reason to keep them. Every time the first mate moves, the shorts squeeze his testicles and make him convulse in agony. Every time he craps, they get soiled. Every time he leaks blood or urinates, they hold the moisture next to his skin, resulting in rash. They really serve no purpose. Plus, we have no prudes here; his exposure isn't going to shock anyone. Lastly, I have no concern for his dignity. He lost any right to that when he attempted to rape Ess. After cutting away the shorts, I toss the knife back onto the sand. I can't bring myself to push it back into my pocket until the smell of shit and piss is cleaned from it.

The thought of rubbing the man's butt and privates with my hands to cleanse away his excrement is repulsive, so I resort to merely splashing water against his skin. That is as close to a cleansing as I will provide. As I splash and splash to wash away the dried filth and blood, the water in which I stand becomes stained a reddish-brown. I want to vomit.

I drag him around in the shallow water hoping the sand sliding against his backside might scrub the remaining dried feces from his legs and butt before dragging him back onto the beach and his previous spot, propped up against the fallen tree trunk. After leaving him sitting, I return to the water to rinse any traces of his pollution from me, but I will enter the water further up the beach to avoid contact with the sewage infected sea. Upon entering, I walk briskly, kicking the water wildly as I go, hoping the agitation rinses me clean. Then I kneel in the water and rub my hands and legs with sand to scour away the contamination. I only return to land after satisfying myself that I no longer have any vestiges of Toothless' foulness on me.

Reaching into the crate that holds our crabs, I toss one onto a small scrap of aluminum sitting in the embers of our fire. This piece of metal—a bent piece of scrap torn from our plane when we crashed—is the most expensive cookware I have ever used. At first, the crab attempts to escape the heat and flames. I push it back to the center of the aluminum sheet with a twig until it finally succumbs to the heat, collapsing with its legs curled underneath it. Simon tells me it's ready to eat once its color has changed. The full process takes less than a minute. I use the same twig I use to kill it to now pull it from the fire and leave it on the sand to cool. I repeat the process with a second crab, one for me and one for Simon. Toothless can wait until we have finished our meal.

Toothless is as alert as he has been since taking a swing at me. He is not staring at me as much as he is at what I am holding. His eyes follow my hands as they pull morsels of meat from the crab shell. He sucks at his lips each time I push the delicious meat into my mouth. It is enjoyable watching him covet each bite I take. He's starving and needs nourishment and water to replenish the blood that has been constantly leaking from his body. I'll feed him eventually, but I want him to know who the boss is. He doesn't have his gun to hide behind any longer. I am the king in his world.

Simon intervenes and throws a crab into the fire. He tired of watching me taunt my helpless captive much like a cat might toy with a mouse before killing it.

I give in to Simon and finish cooking the crab for Toothless. Perhaps I have been wrong in tempting the old man. Certainly, I've enjoyed it far too much. After letting the crab cool, I toss the dead ten-legged creature to a dying two-legged creature. It lands in the sand only to be grabbed greedily by the toothless wonder. He first pulls the legs from the body and proceeds to suck the white meat from the shell. It's gross watching him eat. Fluid streams from the corners of his mouth as he sucks one leg after another, discarding the emptied shells onto the sand. He struggles with the pincers until he crushes them between his molars. He then starts to tear at the body. After failing to break the shell, he looks to me as if pleading for help. I reach into my pocket to pull out his knife and realize I left it lying in the sand after cutting away his shorts. I stroll back to the water in search of this most precious tool, and smile at seeing it glisten in the sun. Although I had intended to wash this before returning it to my pocket, screw it. I fold up the knife and toss it to Toothless. *Knock yourself out,* I say to myself.

Toothless tries to catch the knife and fails. He is incapable of any quick, coordinated movement. There is no reason to be concerned that he might use the knife as a weapon against the rest of us. He picks up the knife, unfolds it and begins to stab at the underside of the crab, trying to break through the armor and release the remaining portion of sustenance. I watch him work the crab until I get bored and throw another crab into the fire for myself. I throw a second in the fire for Ess. She needs the food more than me.

After eating, Ess silently disappears into the plane again. She no longer speaks. She has no desire to be with us, preferring the solitude and darkness of the cargo hold. I want to follow her, but

Simon stops me, saying that she might just need time for herself. He assures me she will eventually snap out of this. I don't think so. The stress, the loss, and the malnutrition are having a devastating and potentially permanent effect on her, both emotionally and physically. I feel helpless.

Simon leaves my side to load the long wooden pipe with the sticky opium and hands it to Toothless. He could tell the pain had returned to our captive, but I'm still shocked to see him offering the drug for relief. Simon has always despised the drug and its effect on people. He is my rock who I cling to in my effort not to delve into drug use again, but he knows that Toothless needs the sedative. It is no longer recreational, but medicinal. Simon is the closest thing we have to a doctor. I am glad we have him, even if his bedside manner lacks something to be desired.

He has refilled the oil lamp and lights it for Toothless. "You will need to take a few large draws before the pain subsides. Do it now."

Toothless willingly takes Simon's direction and inhales the vapor deep into his lungs. I am not sure why Simon feels the need to provide the instruction. Toothless is always glad to smoke the dope. Now he has an excuse.

The effect, although not instantaneous, is obvious. His pupils dilate; his eyes glaze over; his mouth relaxes. He takes the smoke in again and again. I am concerned that he might overdose until Simon pulls the pipe from Toothless' loose grip. Simon reloads the pipe and leaves it next to the first mate in case the pain makes its way through the fog.

He returns to my side and lays his head against mine and falls asleep. I am touched by his show of affection. I can't recall when Simon has initiated touch with anyone. It took years to get him to the point that he was comfortable being touched. This is another breakthrough. It's too bad the progress will start and end here on our little beach. I lean into Simon and fall into a deep, deep sleep.

There is a scream. My eyes flip open just in time to see Ess leap from the plane. Simon is nowhere. The scream comes again, not from Ess but from across the embers of what had been our cooking fire. It's Toothless.

I see his eyes wide and wild and looking to the ground in front of him. His hands are held in the air. They are blood soaked. In one hand, he holds his knife, in his other, he holds what had been his scrotum. He has castrated himself.

I have no idea what to do. The blood, so much blood.

Ess rushes to the still smoldering campfire. She tears away her blouse and wraps in around her hand before reaching into the embers to retrieve the red-hot aluminum we had been using to cook our meal and shoves it against Toothless' lacerated skin, cauterizing the wound and squelching the flow of blood. She drops the aluminum as the heat burns through her blouse, blistering her hand. She has saved the life of the person she most wanted dead. Toothless passes out.

I am frozen and can only stare in shock, amazed that a man could do such a thing to himself. It's even more shocking and amazing to me that Ess would act so quickly and courageously to save the man who had tried to damage her. Had she just stood by, she would have watched her nemesis bleed out. Had she thought about what she was doing, I have no doubt she would have left him to die.

CHAPTER 24
Did I Sign Up For This?

"What type of person takes a knife to himself like that?" I ask more to myself than to Simon.

"Someone who is absolutely committed to living," he answers. "Anders, you and Ess better be careful of that man. He will do anything, and I mean anything, to get even with you. Did you get the knife back?"

I nod and pull the jackknife from my pocket to show him that it's safely in my control and out of the hands of that crazy man.

"You know, maybe he is not as crazy as you think," Simon says, as if reading my thoughts. "None of us were too excited about pretending to be a surgeon. He did us a favor. I am willing to bet he knew we would never be up to it and his death was going to be the result."

Toothless remains unconscious and will remain so until we know how to care for him. Simon has been placing a small amount of the opium directly into the first mate's mouth whenever he begins to stir. He admits that each time he administers the drug this way there is huge danger Toothless could just slip away from an overdose. Lucky him.

I douse his gaping wound with the scotch in hopes of stopping infection. He cut into himself with a contaminated knife, while he himself was still filthy. He may have traded one type of death for another. I pour the scotch onto cloth I have torn from a shirt in the captain's duffle (I don't think he would mind) and gently dab the area surrounding the cut.

The gash is huge and there is no chance for it to heal unless we can close it. The plane's meager first aid kit provides no help, failing to include any sutures. In fact, the kit is of little use for any of the challenges we have faced on the island. It includes only a few small cotton bandages, a little bottle of ethanol as an antiseptic, a small pair of scissors, a roll of adhesive tape, and a bottle of aspirin, the cure for everything. I have already used up all the bandages and the antiseptic.

I am at a loss as to how we can close the wound without sutures and look to Simon for a solution. He doesn't disappoint. After scouring the plane and luggage looking for a needle and thread and striking out, he has come up with another option. Armed with a pair of dikes from the toolbox, he has cut some of the aluminum wiring from the now useless controls in the cockpit. After stripping away the insulation, he has cut and shaped the wire into numerous small hooks he hopes he can use to tie the wound together. I have no idea if the wire ties will work, but we really have no other choice.

We roll Toothless onto his back to best expose the cut and Simon and Ess set to work on closing the cut. Simon is armed with the pair of needle-nosed pliers and the hooks, Ess with a pair of normal pliers and her fingers. The wire is stiff and the end cuts are blunt, so they tear more than pierce through the skin. After Simon pushes one of his hooks through both sides of the wound, Ess pulls the skin together by crimping the wire with her pliers. Simon then moves on to push through the next aluminum stitch, slowly closing the gaping hole. After completing the process, Simon sits back to look at his and Ess's handywork. It will leave a large scar, but he hopes it is good enough to give the old guy a chance of living.

I think Ess would be more than happy if the old bugger dies, but she relishes the opportunity to see First Mate Thompson as a newly created eunuch.

Using scotch as an antiseptic, I douse the freshly stitched tissue. It seems like such a waste of good booze. It would certainly be more acceptable if Toothless were conscious and I could at least see him writhe in pain as the alcohol contacts raw flesh and torn skin. In any case, the man better be glad we have an abundant supply of the scotch because if it came down to me being able to enjoy a good stiff drink or him getting an infection, the drink wins out. I pull the bottle to my lips and take a large swallow, allowing the liquor to burn my throat. It reminds me I am alive.

We have been busy addressing Toothless' injury and have forgotten to eat our stock of crab. They now appear to have died in the crate. Simon tells me we should not eat the crab now that they have died for fear of intestinal disease. I don't agree with the risk; however, I am not prepared to debate him. I dump the dead crabs out into the sea. Ess watches me dispose of the creatures. I am sure she would take the chance eating them if I gave her the opportunity. Tonight, we will go to sleep hungry.

From the cigarette carton I liberated from Captain Robert's duffle, I had grabbed several smokes and place them in my breast pocket. I offer one to Ess to curb her hunger. She declines. Instead, she grabs the discarded opium pipe and prepares her own solution to kill the hunger pangs. Although she sits only a few feet from me, she is a world away. Her universe is one of cloudy escape. I am choosing escape, too; albeit mine is one brought on by drinking scotch and chain-smoking my way to a nicotine-induced sleep.

Toothless mercifully remains unconscious and now lies by the firepit on the hard canvas cushions we pulled from the folding seats in the plane. When he wakes, I wonder if he will even be aware of his self-mutilation. I'm not sure what to do with his severed scrotum. I've picked it up from the sand and dropped it into one of the emptied scotch crates. If they'd have been mine, I don't know whether I would want to see them before we buried them or threw them far out into the sea. Toothless is either the bravest or craziest person I know. Simon would say that he was neither, just pragmatic. He must have known his dying testicles needed to be removed or they would kill him, and he realized I was incapable of doing what needed to be done. Well, maybe I was incapable, but Simon would have eventually given in and performed the surgery. He probably would have even been able to save one of the testicles for the time being. I guess Ess would also have been glad to cut on Toothless. In her case she likely would have preferred using the fire ax, chopping off his penis along with the scrotum.

Simon sits almost stoically in the sand by the water, just beyond the light thrown by our small campfire. He is only a faint silhouette against the water illuminated by moonlight. Although I can't see his face, I can feel his eyes boring into me as if he is accusing me that I would have been too weak to do what needed to be done with Toothless. I can sense his shame in me as I drink myself into a stupor. I can even feel his pity as my girl descends further into her tunnel of despair and departure from sanity. Tonight, I realize that Simon will outlast us all. I am worldly, but he knows what makes the world tick, more so than I will ever know. I thought I was the one of action, but he has proven me wrong again. He is a man of results. I am a pretender.

Today, life on this island has become more tenuous for us. It is an island full of my fears. I fear that when Toothless awakens he will be unable to deal with the pain. The physical pain will be huge, but living with his self-castration may prove even more terrible. Toothless will pray to die. I fear Simon may have saved this man only to have the unpleasant opportunity to watch him die slowly. I fear Ess will not be able to pull herself from the drug in time for us to escape the island. I fear I will fall to the temptation. I fear Simon will leave without us.

Tonight, I will sleep outside with Toothless and Ess. Neither of them will be moving inside; the drug has defeated Ess's ability to move, and I worry that moving Toothless would tear away his sutures. My solitary Simon moves from his perch on the sand to disappear through the cabin door. I imagine he will enjoy his typical, refreshing, sound sleep in his co-pilot's nest. Although

Ess and Toothless have fallen into a deep sleep with the help of the opium, I am not sure it will be refreshing.

The three of us will be visited by crabs soon, so I gather what little wood we still have in camp to feed the fire to deter the little beasts.

CHAPTER 25
Reckoning Time

Day nine—

Surmising from the closed hatch door, my brother Simon has yet to wake up from his peaceful slumber while I've been awake for hours, though I've resisted the need to open my eyes and start the day. Last night's combination of booze and cigarettes has my head throbbing. The bottle that remains nestled in the crook of my arm is almost empty and from the look of the butts scattered about in the sand, I must have gone through a couple dozen smokes. I feel like shit and, apparently, I earned the feeling.

I roll onto my side only to find Simon sitting beside me. He is staring intently at me, no, through me, as if I am a figment of his imagination. I assume he is disappointed in me. Well, why shouldn't he be? I am disappointed in me, too. I need to step up to my responsibilities. Instead, when I should have been gathering food and water, I was imbibing scotch.

He says to me, "I will catch some crab for breakfast, but you stay here until you pull yourself together. You are worthless in your current state."

What? My brother is chastising me. If I did not feel so punk, I would smack him on the side of his head to remind him who is the boss. Who am I kidding? Simon has become the mature and responsible brother. I deserved his reprimand.

Simon pulls the bottle from my arm and pours what little amber liquid remains into the sand, then kicks the dead cigarette stubs into the now dormant fire pit. I curl up in the warming sand and close my eyes, drifting back into a fitful sleep.

*

Simon waded into the shallow, cool water to gather the crates he laid out as traps. In one, he has captured small fish that had been calmly treading water before they were tempted by his lure. In another, he managed to trap several crabs as they clambered over each other to get a portion of the bait; Simon found a use for Toothless' dismembered body part. He knew it was disgusting to use the rotting flesh, but he had few other options. They needed the food, and the scrotum was convenient and too useful to disregard. The crabs went crazy over their treat. There would be no burial for the first mate's body part.

Simon realizes he would not be able to tell his tribe what really happened to Toothless Joe's gonads. It would make eating the crabs seem like cannibalism. He did not think it prudent to open that possibility, and for Toothless, the outcome could be dangerous and gruesome. Even if they died here on this island, he did not want them to lose their humanity. No, he would just say he threw them out into the sea if the first mate or Anders inquired about the severed scrotum.

He gathered up his sea bounty and set off towards camp, comfortable in knowing his effort should stave off starvation for another couple of days. They were all losing weight, but in general, their caloric intake was sufficient to keep them alive. Although the food might be adequate and tolerable, it was hardly preferable. They would eventually need a change if life here was to remain bearable.

The challenges to their survival had grown substantially over the two days. With Toothless' injury, he could no longer contribute to the success of their small community. He was a liability. Ess had been capable of helping, but she had fallen into addiction. She, too, would now be nothing more than a liability. Simon could not understand what Anders saw in that woman. Even her success as a journalist had been more a result of her looks than her talent. Anders could and would help them survive, but realistically, Simon remained concerned that it was only a matter of time before Anders, too, fell victim to the opium or the booze. Simon was their only lifeline, and the weight of the responsibility was beginning to tell on him.

Upon entering the camp, he was surprised to see that Toothless was wide awake. He had pulled away the cloth that covered his injury and was touching the wire sutures as if testing them.

He raised his eyes to meet Simon. "Why'd you save me?"

Simon could not tell from the tone if the comment was intended as a true question or an accusation. He chose to consider it a real inquiry. "Because you would have done it for me if I had needed your help."

"But I didn't need your help, I took care of it, and I would have either lived or died as a result. Who cares now? We're gonna die here anyway," Toothless says. He stared at Simon with a questioning look, "What did'ja do with 'em? I wanna see them."

"I am sorry, Toothless. I do not have them anymore. I threw them into the sea. I could not imagine you wanting to see them."

Toothless grimaced. To Simon, it was unclear whether the expression was pure annoyance to the unwelcome name Anders had given him, anger at having his body parts disposed of, or just pain.

"Trust me, you would not want to have seen them," Simon says.

"How could you know?" replied Toothless. "They were mine and mine alone. I had a right to see 'em before you just tossed them to the fish. I wouldn't have done that to you. How could you?"

Simon knew he was right. Now he was glad he had not shared how he'd disposed of his testicles. He changed the topic. "How is the pain? Are you hungry?"

"Fucking terrible, and yes. What you got there in your wooden boxes?" Toothless' interest had redirected to the crates. Obviously, hunger was overwhelming his pain.

"Breakfast for all of us. You are going to owe me once you get well enough to walk. Do you understand?"

"Sure, sure. I get it. You all kick the shit out of me and then it is somehow my fault, and I should feel grateful to you. No farting way, thank you. You will take care of me until I am good and healthy. And you should be glad to do it. If it weren't for me, you wouldn't have survived your first couple days here."

Simon rolled his eyes and then focused directly on Toothless. "It doesn't matter what you did for us in the past. If you cannot pull your weight soon, and I mean real soon, you are dead. I will let you starve. Oh, and by the way, I didn't throw your nuts into the sea. I used them as bait for the crabs. You can choose to eat them or not for all I care. In fact, I hope you decide to pass. It leaves more for us."

It was rare for Simon to get angry. In fact, prior to being stranded on the island, he rarely expressed any emotion.

Simon continued to address Toothless, "…and we have a lady here." He nods toward Ess who is still sleeping in the sand on the other side of what had been the campfire. "So you better get yourself prepared to put on shorts. I know it is going to hurt like hell, but you will be putting them on anyway. I am not going to have you sitting around exposed."

Simon dropped the crates where he stood and moved off into the jungle in search of firewood. From the cover of the growth, he yelled back to Toothless, "Don't even think of messing with the crabs or I will make sure you don't eat again."

*

Simon is making me proud, jealous, and ashamed, too: proud my brother has stepped up as a provider; jealous that he seems to have gained strength and has become our de-facto leader; and ashamed that I have become needy. While I have been moping around with a hangover, he has been doing what a responsible individual should do. He has made sure each of us has what we need to survive. It's odd, even though I know that I'm becoming dehydrated, my thirst has left. Instead, I only feel the hunger pains. Simon makes sure I drink before eating. He says that I need the water more than the food. I'm not sure I agree with him, but I admit my headache is finally beginning to subside. I hope I can take a few bites of food without getting sick.

He's cooking the fish and crab together on the sheet of aluminum. Our faces watch in anticipation as the little sea creatures fry, we are all hungry. We find it impossible to pull our gazes from the sizzling food. The smell is wonderful. Even in my parched state, my mouth is watering.

I don't want to share any of the food with Toothless. I can't understand why Simon insists that we are responsible to care for him just because he can't care for himself. Fuck him. He's the cause of his own problem. I should kill him just because … well, just because. I hate the guy. My hand hovers over the pistol grip sticking out from my belt for just a moment.

Ess is quiet and has made a point to sit far away from me. It appears she is purposely avoiding me and becoming fond of Simon. I hate it and I'm beginning to hate her. Maybe she's friendly to Simon just because he has become the purveyor of our food. I understand that. Losing to food is better than losing to the opium to which she has become addicted.

She raises the opium pipe from her lap and inserts the ceramic bowl into the little oil-lamp flame and leans down to suck the smoke deep into her lungs. I know she is lost to me now. She lives only for Bradley's pipe, the oil flame, the Zippo, the little brown sticky opium, and the scarce food and water supplied by Simon. She only gets up from the sand when she needs to relieve herself. Even that act has fallen prey to the opium. As if she is afraid to leave the proximity of the drug, she has taken to defecating in plain view just beyond the tail of the DC-3, always keeping us and the drug in her view. Prudence has all but disappeared. She's broken and I doubt she can be fixed. At least, I know I can't fix her. Since she likes Simon now, he can have her.

Simon tosses a crab onto the sand next to Toothless. The first mate greedily grabs the hot beast without concern of burning himself and pulls a pincher from the little body. He stuffs the morsel, shell and all, into his mouth and begins to crunch. His eyes roll upwards to the point that only the whites are visible. He is in ecstasy.

Simon pulls a second crab, along with a couple of small fish, from the fire. He lays them on a large leaf that serves as a plate and carries them over to where Ess sits. Unlike Toothless, she barely acknowledges the food. The opium has already deadened her appetite. Simon waits for a moment for her to take the offer. When she fails to respond, he places the leaf on the sand beside her.

I patiently wait for my turn as Simon returns to his cooking. He tosses a second crab to Toothless before loading a second leaf with crab and fish. He brings the meal over to where I sit and plops beside me to share our breakfast.

Whispering to himself, I hear him say, "We cannot go on this way for long. This is not enough food for us to survive."

I answer, "You're right. We'll get more when we go inland to replenish the water."

"That's the point, Anders. Since we both need to go to carry back the water and the food. We will need to leave him with her." He points towards Toothless. "Is she safe? Is he safe?"

"Of course, he is safe. What do you think she is going to do? Slit his throat?"

Simon looked at me as if to answer *yes*. He says nothing.

"Simon, she couldn't hurt him if she wanted. Hell, she is so loopy I'd wager she can't even walk."

"So, if Toothless wants to hurt her, she will not be able to defend herself."

"Toothless isn't going to be hurting anyone for a while." I chuckle before continuing, "He's a eunuch, probably not going to hurt anyone ever again." I pull the gun from my belt. "And if he does, I'll use this on him."

Simon shakes his head and grabs a crab that has cooled enough to handle. Unlike Toothless, he cracks the shell and pulls the white flesh with his fingers. After placing the meat into his mouth, he says to Toothless, "You are going to be sorry for chewing up the shell and eating it. It is going to hurt like hell when you need to crap. You might even tear yourself up inside."

Toothless stops just as he was about to pop another leg into his mouth. "I can't possibly hurt any more than I do now, but maybe you're right. I don't want to shit blood, too." He pauses from stuffing the leg into his mouth and instead he copies Simon, pulling away the shell from the meat with his fingers.

Looking across the flame, I notice Ess has started to pick at the fish. If she wasn't going to eat it soon, I was planning on taking it for myself. We cannot afford to waste anything.

CHAPTER 26

I Am a Savior?

I feel compelled to rescue Ess from the opium. Is it because I am burdened with the guilt of knowing I'm the reason she is here in the first place or maybe it's because I, too, feel the pull of the drug? But I don't want to be faced with taking care of her because she is unwilling to care for herself. It sounds selfish, but I can't let her negatively impact me.

After eating, I take the pipe from Ess and hand it over to Toothless. He would be needing it to deaden his pain soon. I will enable his addiction, while rescuing Ess from hers. I will be her savior. Simon says I'm foolhardy and acting rashly. What he wants to say is that I'm being stupid. He thinks cutting her off from the drug might hurt her more than the drug itself. I can't agree. I pull Ess up from the sand, forcing her to stand. Holding her around the waist to steady her, I walk with her to the jungle in search of food, and escape from the temptation waiting for her in our camp. Simon trails behind. It is about time I retake my position as leader.

We leave Toothless behind with his precious pipe. It's empty, so he will need to get up from his bedding if he wants to load the bowl. Crawling to retrieve the opium and the oil lamp will be hard, but we all know the promise of the numbing relief of the drug will win out. As the anesthetic effectiveness of his most recent dose wears off, the pain from his wound will become excruciating. I doubt anything will be able to stop him from getting to the drug. He will be lost in the oily smoke from the pipe when we return. I only wonder how long he will wait before he makes his move. The longer he waits, the more painful it will be. It would be fun to wait and watch, but I won't.

We have also left him with a pair of underwear that Simon pulled from my luggage. Consider it a gift, Toothless. Hopefully, he will take the opportunity to put these on and cover himself while we are off on our quest. Nobody wants to see the ugly gash and his penis. I am sure Toothless would rather not have to look at them, either. If Toothless doesn't have the shorts on by the time we return, he had better be comatose because I will pull them on over his legs and injury and I don't intend to be gentle. If the gash tears and begins bleeding again, tough.

Ess' intoxicated state makes our trek inland even more difficult and slower than I expected. She moves from tree to tree, grasping at branches to provide her stability. It's embarrassing watching her stumble and wobble from hand-hold to hand-hold. Quite frankly, I'm surprised she doesn't fall. It's aggravating though; she is slowing our progress. At this rate, we will not finish our food gathering before dark. I resist the urge to reach out to help her with her balance, and even stop Simon when it looks as though she's going to tumble and he reaches to grab her. If Ess can't keep up, I'll leave her behind. We can retrieve her on the way back. It is impossible to drum up any sympathy for her. Hell, I didn't stick the opium pipe in her mouth. I'm not the one who has become addicted. Surprisingly, even though she struggles, Ess still manages to stay with us. She knows if she doesn't, she'll be left in the dark jungle by herself. Fear is a great motivator.

Simon and I have quietly come to the same conclusion: everyone contributes to the tribe's success or we don't survive. Even Ess, in her drugged stupor, must be getting it. She needs to begin pulling her weight or we'll let her die. We can't take care of her and Toothless. They need to be held accountable for their own predicaments. Ess must wean herself from the opium. Toothless … well, he's a challenge. He needs to heal fast, or he's going to starve. I should not understate the positive; as long as he can't walk, we don't have to worry about him hurting us. I don't know what to do with him once he is able to walk again. I wish Ess would have let him bleed to death. It would have made things so much easier for us.

Our first goal today is water. Although the meager spring at the center of our island provides a questionable source, it is our lifeblood. We have not seen rain for days and the sky remains cloudless. This muddy pond is our only fresh water source. We can tell we're getting close to the spring as the ground begins to give below our feet leaving faint depressions in the soft earth that fill with seeping water as we walk. Several steps before I see the pool of murky water, I feel the suction of the muddy soil gripping my feet. A peaty odor accompanies the glistening black soil, a witness to the ages of perpetual dampness spreading out under the trees.

On the far edge of the water, I see that we are not alone. Several wild pigs have laid claim of the life-giving water and are noiselessly staring at us in defiance. I am concerned that approaching closer to fill our bottles will invite a confrontation. Although I can't suggest that I am capable of divining the pigs' intentions, as if they even have the ability to act on intent, these beasts view us as both a threat to their water and as a likely meal.

Sensing my concern, Simon whispers to me, "We better back off until they leave."

"And if they don't leave?" I say to myself as I silently back-pedal through the swampy dirt and muck, praying the hogs don't consider us a threat. Afraid to turn my face away from the beasts, I can only hope that Simon and Ess are moving backwards, too.

It was a mistake bringing a drugged Ess into the jungle. It was a terrible error in judgement and one that becomes more profound when I hear a grunt and the slap of mud when Ess falls backwards into the slop. I am not sure if it was the noise or the sudden movement that agitates the pigs, but they have lost all interest in the water. They fling up mud and water with their cloven hooves as they pace aggressively on their side of the muddy pool. I have no idea how long it will take them to attack us, but they will attack. We can't wait for them to circle the pool and trap us. I pull the revolver from my belt and fire wildly at the pack of beasts. The first round splatters the mud in front of the hairy animals while the second round sailed high over their heads. I am wild and shaking. I can't calm myself.

The pigs are frozen initially by the gun's explosion, but only for an instant. They are agitated even more and charge at us directly from the other side of the pond, heading directly into the mud and water. I shoot again crazily and have no idea where this round goes as I turn to run. Behind me they splash, grunt, and squeal. I will be killed unless I can outrun them.

*

Simon drew the .45 semi-automatic with his right hand and knelt to steady his aim as the pigs frantically clamored over each other in their desire to kill. He was shaking, so he brought his left hand up to steady his aim. He fired; once, twice, three times into the lead pig, a huge male boar, before the beast crashed into the mud headfirst, dead. A second continued directly at Simon while a third veered off to the side, focused on Ess. Simon pulled the trigger as the second monster was almost upon him. The bullet crashed into the animal's eye and exploded out the back of its head, knocking it instantaneously to the ground. Simon trembled as he pulled the trigger again, shooting the already dead creature. He stared in shock at the bloodied pig that had come so close to killing him. He felt numb and incapable of movement until Ess's cry jerked him back to life.

The third charging pig had grasped Ess's arm in its jaws and was flinging her thin body back and forth. True, Ess had lost weight since our arrival to this island, but the pig was throwing her about as if she weighed almost nothing. Simon was in awe at the beast's strength as he pulled the gun up again to fire. Afraid that an errant shot would hit Ess, he approached the murderous pig to gain a better aim and fired, hitting the pig in the rear haunches. Even though he could see the red dot where the bullet stuck home in the animal's side, the pig's aggressive tossing and tearing was uninterrupted. Simon stepped closer and pulled the trigger again and again, this time taking aim at the pig's cobby body, each bullet tearing hunks of flesh from the pig as they tore through the body and exited.

The pig stopped its tugging and throwing and fell to the ground; yet even as blood poured from its wounds, the pig refused to release its jaws from Ess's arm. The crazed animal continued to bite deeply into Ess, crunching through muscle, tendon, and bone. Simon placed the muzzle of the gun against the pig's head, just below the ear and fired and continued firing until the gun was emptied. The pig's jaws finally stopped moving. Ess was quiet. Simon hoped she was unconscious, not dead. He bent his knees and fell back into the mud, falling into the slimy muck with a muted thud. There was no other noise; the other pigs had fled.

After several minutes (or even hours, Simon could not be sure) the noises of the jungle returned, jogging him back to life. Ess remained unconscious and her arm was still enclosed in the dead pig's jaws. The blood from her arm was streaming down and over the pig's coarse hair into the mud. Removing his leather belt, he wrapped it twice around her arm just above the elbow before looping it through the buckle to cinch it tight around her thin arm; nine days of meager rations had ravaged her body. Her body was now going to be devastated further. Instead of merely being thin, he was sure she was going to lose the arm or bleed to death where she lay.

He shoved his gun's barrel into the mouth of the pig in a futile attempt to pry open the huge, locked jaws. Failing to even budge the jaws, he looked for a branch to stuff between the teeth to apply more leverage to his effort. Although he failed to find a strong, loose branch in the muck, he did find the revolver Anders had dropped as he ran away. He cracked open the cylinder to find the gun still had three bullets. He hoped these would be sufficient to free Ess's arm from the toothy vice.

Placing the revolver's muzzle against the pig's lower left mandible, he fired, shattering the bone. He tried to pry the teeth apart, again failing to budge them. Moving to the other side of the massive pig head, he fired into the right side of the bony jaw.

Finally, he could pry away the teeth, freeing the damaged arm. While no doctor, he was sure the arm was lost. Through the torn flesh he could see the crushed bone and torn tendons within. The only thing that had prevented the arm from being torn away completely was that on one side of the bite the pig's teeth had dug deeply into the elbow joint and had not been able to break completely through. Had the animal lived to throw its head one more time from side to side, Simon believed the joint would have broken and the pig would have had its trophy along with a free meal.

Simon got up from his knees and stuck the pistols into his front pockets. He pulled Ess's limp body up in one continuous motion, throwing her frail body over his shoulder, and began his trek back to camp. He could only pray she would survive long enough so that she might die in the light of the sun, not in this dark, dank jungle. The forest had lost its innocence and had now shown itself to be a center of malice. He would need to be more careful when he comes here in the future for water.

Water? That would need to wait until tomorrow. He could return later today to gather one of the pigs as food, but he doubted that he could bring himself to return to the spring today. Certainly, he would not return until he reloaded the pistols.

CHAPTER 27
Bad Decisions

Shots ring out behind me and then there is quiet. I fear the calm is nothing more than a sign that those hairy monsters have overtaken my brother and Ess. I am alone and must continue running, hopefully back to camp, but in all honesty, I don't know where I'm going. My direction of movement is purely a function of tree avoidance and a vague idea of where the danger remains behind me.

One might expect I would go back to save my brother and girlfriend, but that requires rational thinking and bravery, neither of which I have now. Terror has a grip on my actions and has left me no choice but to run. My legs pump without thought or effort. It's as if they don't even belong to me, as if I am floating through the trees. I should be tired, but the adrenaline rush has masked any fatigue. When I break out from the jungle into the sunlight blanketing the beach, I fall to my knees, thankful to be alive, even if that means being alone. I fall into a deep sleep on the warm sand.

*

Simon cradled Ess in his arms as he followed the same trail that led to the spring back to camp, his progress slow and monotonous. Ess' blood soaked his shirt as it dribbled from her wounded arm. Had he not applied his tourniquet he had no doubt Ess' life would have already drained from her body. She would be dead. He marched on despite physical exhaustion, knowing that

Ess' only chance for survival depended on his speed in getting her to camp. His mind drifted from his physical duress to thinking about what he would need to do once he got Ess back to the plane. He dreaded the responsibility that awaited him. He hoped he had the bravery and the skill to do what needed to be done, and he hoped Anders would already be in the camp to assist him.

As Simon saw light breaking through the cloak of vegetation, he summoned additional strength and broke into a trot. He exited the jungle just as his legs gave way, tumbling both him and Ess to the sand. Ess grunted, but thankfully, remained unconscious.

Leaving her where she fell, Simon rose to his hands and knees to crawl into what was now a deserted campsite. It was not completely empty, just quiet. Toothless had managed to find the motivation to pull on a pair of Anders' undershorts and was now propped up, sitting in the sand directly in front of the cargo door. He was present in body only. He didn't even notice when Simon pulled him away from impeding the only access to the cargo hull. Obviously, the opium anesthetic was working. Simon didn't pause to consider how his tugging on Toothless might pull at the sutures. He didn't have the luxury of time to worry about the first mate's problems.

He disappeared into the plane, returning an instant later with the fire axe and several tools from the plane's toolbox, ready to perform what he thought a necessary, but gruesome, bout of surgery. He intended to amputate the damaged arm before Ess could reawaken.

His first task was rekindling the campfire. The flame would be necessary to sterilize the tools and cauterize veins and arteries. He had no idea how to complete the surgery, but he knew that once started, he would not be able to turn back. Being able to staunch the blood loss would be critical to saving the young woman's life. Realizing he would need more wood to fuel the fire, he ran into the woods to gather as much dead wood as possible.

The area closest to the camp had already been scoured of dry wood, so the gathering took significantly longer than he expected and hoped. It was fully an hour before he returned to camp with an armload of branches that would have to suffice to keep the fire going through the surgery and into the evening. He pried loose a couple planks from a whiskey crate and using the fire axe, he chopped the kindling into strips to get the fire started.

Thankfully, Ess remained unconscious. Simon brought his face close to hers to feel her breath. Turning his head, he moved downward to place his ear tightly against her chest, listening for a heartbeat. Although faint, it was steady. She was still alive.

Toothless had recovered from his drugged stupor and was now intently watching Simon's actions. "What you gonna do there?" he asks, knowing perfectly well what was going to happen. To Simon, Toothless seemed to be enthralled at the promised gore.

"I am going to save her life, I think," Simon responded without looking at the first mate.

"You think?" Toothless laughed. "Looks to me like you're planning to kill her. You're really fucked up. So, when did ya become a doctor?"

"I am not a doctor and I never want to be a doctor. You guys just keep getting hurt. Just so you know, I saved your life, too. Maybe you should just say 'thank you' and then shut up. You are not helping."

Toothless frowned, obviously angered at Simon's comment. "Look, you little piss ant, I saved you all when we crashed. If it weren't for me, you'd have been pig food a week ago. And just so we don't forget, you didn't even have the guts to save me. If I didn't have the guts to cut myself, you would have just let me die. I saved my own life."

Simon didn't have the time or energy to argue. "Sure, sure, Toothless." He dismissed the first mate as he set upon getting the flames to catch.

Not to be deterred, Toothless continued. "You cut into her, you might as well just kill her. Why not dig into the captain's duffle for a couple more bullets and shoot her right here—" He pointed to the spot between his two eyes. "—and be done with it. It would be a hell of a lot more humane and a lot less painful. Whatch'oo gonna do if she does live through the amputation anyway. Shit, she'll die in agony. You need to stop and think."

"Look, old man, I do not have time to think anymore. I must save her now. What I do later, who knows? I guess Ess and I will deal with the consequences. You know all about consequences, right? They are the reason you no longer have balls, so shut up or I will take away your opium."

The threat hit home and Toothless bit back his retort and fell silent as he watched Simon prepare.

Once the fire started, Simon pulled the canvas cushion that Toothless had used as a bed the previous evening closer to the flame. It was stained with sweat and blood, but it would need to serve as a hospital bed once again. In final preparation, Simon headed into the plane to assemble the remaining items he thought would be needed to successfully perform the amputation: clothes to serve as bandages, wire to serve as sutures, and a short length of the cargo straps to tie around the remaining stump of an arm to stem the flow of blood and ultimately help hold the wound together. He grabbed another hard, canvas cushion from a chair; he needed something to keep his tools from lying in the sand. Lastly, he grabbed a packet of the raw opium. He would rub it into a cloth and stick it into Ess' mouth between her lips and gums. He hoped it could keep her from feeling the excruciating pain that he was about to inflict upon her.

As he exited the plane and looked at Ess' diminutive body, he questioned, just for a moment, his commitment to doing what needed to be done. Shaking off the feeling of temporary doubt, he prepared for the operation. He laid out the pad on the sand and doused it in scotch. Then he methodically began the process of sterilizing the tools by first pouring scotch over each item and then inserting them briefly into the fire, burning off the alcohol. He laid each item out on the pad: a pair of cutting dikes, a pair of pliers, a large wood-handled screwdriver, and several pieces of aluminum wire cut to various lengths to be used as sutures. Next to the tools, he laid strips of linen he had torn from his brother's shirts. The cut straps lay next to the linen strips. The last item was gruesome, the fire axe with its flame blackened blade.

Simon stood and took the bottle of scotch and poured a big gulp into his mouth, hoping the liquor might provide him with some magical fortitude for what he was about to do. He then drenched his hands with the alcohol. He rubbed the alcohol between his fingers and up his arms, hoping to kill bacteria and lowering the chance of infection.

He patted his pockets and found the jack knife. He smiled as he opened the knife and poured the liquor over it before tossing it onto the pad along with his other tools. It would have been a huge mistake to start the surgery without a blade more delicate than an axe.

Now to begin. Simon knelt to loop his hands under Ess's shoulders, pulling her up to a sitting position against the fallen tree that had defined the edge of their camp site. He gently pulled her damaged arm up to lay over the trunk. He then wet his hands once again with the scotch and took a second large swig before setting the bottle upright in the sand.

He grabbed the axe handle and positioned himself on the opposite side of the tree trunk. He lowered the blade just above the elbow and below the belt tourniquet. He raised the blade and lowered it slowly again to where he wanted to strike. His hands shook as he brought the blade up a second time over his head to strike. He paused and lowered the blade again to the target. He did not know if he could do what needed to be done. Toothless stared quietly, seemingly unable to pull his eyes away.

Simon breathed in and out before raising the axe a third time and then pulled down hard, striking to sever the damaged arm. In his anxiety of striking too high on the arm, he failed, and the blade hit the forearm, cleaving through muscle, tendon, and bone before embedding itself in the wood well below the damage inflicted by the pig.

The anxiety was gone now, replaced by a sense of duty and urgency. Simon wrenched the axe head free from the log and he raised the handle high over his head and chopped down again, this time cutting cleanly through the arm exactly where he intended. A second portion of arm fell to the sand by the previously severed forearm and hand. He vomited. Toothless cried. Ess screamed.

CHAPTER 28
What Have I Done?

It's odd when you fall into that world halfway between sleep and awake and you can still dream. I Know this is a dream. Simon is gone and I am alone with Toothless. I am killing him with an axe. I see myself striking down again and again, plunging the head of the axe into his body. Blood droplets spatter against my face. I am coated with blood. He is the cause of all my troubles and must die. There is no sorry for what I am doing, but I am now truly alone. Then I wake up.

My eyes look up the beach to our camp just as Simon pulls down with all his might with the fire axe. I hear a scream as I jump up from my slumber to run to my brother.

He has fallen to his knees, bile streams from his mouth, tears from his eyes. He is mumbling, "Pull yourself together, dammit," and he gets to his feet and moves to the other side of the fallen tree.

I follow him and see my Ess lying on her side in the sand with no right arm. My God! What has Simon done? "Simon. Simon, you've killed her."

"Stop, Anders. Just get out of my way. I am saving her."

He kneels and picks her frail body from the ground and quickly but gently lays her on a canvas bed. Without talking, he starts to work with tools from our toolbox. Hell, he is using tools from a fucking hardware store to perform surgery. My brother has gone crazy. I have always known him to be off; I just never was willing to admit it. Now I have no choice. He has gone nuts right in front of my eyes.

Even with what seems to be insane behavior, I can't stop him now as he works feverishly to stem the flow of blood from Ess' arm. Her poor, beautiful arm. I choke back a sob and walk to the other side of the fallen tree and sit down beside the severed pieces of arm. He hit her twice. My God. My God. I will kill him … once he saves my Ess.

I get up to my knees and turn around, leaning against the bloodstained wood. I doubt the stain will ever wash away. I watch as Simon pulls a screwdriver from the fire, its tip glowing red with heat. I can barely see what he is doing as he crouches over Ess, one hand wielding the burning screwdriver, the other a pair of pliers. He touches the heat to one part of the arm staunching the seeping of blood then he moves on to another part. I am in awe of my brother even while my hate boils.

Simon is working into the evening using the glow of the fire as his only light. He breaks from his work only to stretch his back. He takes a moment to dip a cloth into a packet of sticky opium and he places the end of the cloth in Ess' mouth. He then crouches over and begins working again. My back is hurting sympathetically, just watching him. I have no idea how he can continue.

The moon is high in the sky when he is finally finished.

Toothless has been sitting quietly the whole time, watching. Once Simon stands, Toothless mutters more to himself than anyone else, "Damn good job," in admiration. He then pulls up the opium pipe, lights the oil lamp and starts sedating himself.

I am speechless when Simon lies down on the sand next to Ess and falls into a deep sleep. He almost kills my girl and now he rests beside her. That is where I should be lying. I will take this up with him in the morning. He will pay for today. I can't believe he almost got Ess killed in the jungle. He's going to pay.

CHAPTER 29
Who Will Watch His Back?

Day ten—

Everyone sleeps late this morning. Yesterday left us more tired than we realized. And now I am hungry and thirsty, angry and confused. When I sit up, I see my brother is already up the beach with his little traps, trying to catch us some more food. Ess is sleeping soundly. I can see her breast rise and fall in a steady rhythm. Toothless is awake, but not alert. His eyes are open, but not seeing anything. The only thing that tells me he is alive is the smoke trickling from his nostrils. He must have just taken another draw from his pipe.

I rise and walk to Simon. I don't know what I will say or do to him. All I know is that he needs to stop trying to take Ess from me. He needs to stop making me seem unimportant and insignificant. I am important. Hell, in the newspaper business, some might think me exceptionally important.

Standing behind Simon as he watches his traps, I remain silent, waiting to see how long it takes for him to acknowledge me. I wait … and wait.

Finally, I break the silence. "What did you do to Ess, you prick?"

He doesn't even turn to me as he answers. "I saved her." He pauses and then continues, "You almost killed her."

He turns around to face me. "What in the world happened to you out there, Anders? We could have been killed and you just ran. I thought you were brave. I was always smart, but never as confident as you. You were never afraid of anything and I, hell, I was not even capable of speaking to others unless it was about something technical, or you were with me. Now you have shown yourself to be more of a coward than I ever was.

"It hurts me even to talk to you now. I am ashamed that I ever looked up to you, that I ever considered you my savior, my guardian. Did you even come back to check to see if we were okay?"

"Of course," I lie, "but, I couldn't find you." I could tell from Simon's eyes he knew I was lying. I never could hide anything from him.

"Look, Simon, there was no way I was going to be of any help out there. I fired the gun but missed. It happens. I'm not a good enough shot to take down a wild pig. I couldn't help, and you should know that. You just needed to run. Why didn't you?"

"I wanted to, but I could not," he says.

"Why not?"

"The pigs caught us. One grabbed Ess and was going to kill her. He had her arm in his jaws and was ready to rip it clean off. It was terrible. I was so scared, but I could not run away and leave her to die that way. You should not have, either."

He's right, but I can't give him the satisfaction by agreeing with him. He already believes he's right all the time. "If I would've stayed and tried to kill the pig, I could have missed again, maybe even ending up shooting Ess. Hell, I could've shot you, too. I was wild with my aim. How'd you stop the pig?"

"I shot him with my pistol. Your gun, you know, the one you dropped when you panicked, I had to dig it out of the mud after you ran away. I had to use it to pry the dead pig's jaws from Ess' arm. She would have died, and probably should have, out there in the woods." Simon turned away from me.

I know this is his way of stopping the conversation, but I'm not done, yet.

"Simon, you might be smart, but you don't know anything. Yes, I panicked; anyone capable of experiencing fear probably would have. You just don't feel. You never have. How can I even explain panic to you?"

He turns back to face me, and for the first time I can ever recall, I see nothing but anger in his eyes. I can see it bubbling up in him, making him want to burst, but he manages to control it. He says in a measured and quiet voice, so quiet I need to strain to hear, "Anders, I have fears. I feel pain just like you. I may not be able to express it, to show it, but I feel it. I was afraid out there. Really afraid. But I did not let it take control over me. I did not let it make a boy of a man. You did." He turns back to his fishing.

I sit down on the beach and watch. I've nothing more to say, at least nothing he would listen to. What can I say now, anyway? It's best to let him calm down. I need him to take care of Ess.

It's then that I notice both of his front pockets bulge with pistols. I doubt he will voluntarily relinquish control of these in the future, but I will need to get these back. Given how angry he is with me, he can't be trusted.

Simon reaches into the water and rights one of his crates. He relishes being better than me at gathering food. He is our famous fisherman and his crates have proven to be extremely effective traps for fishes or crabs, or whatever. I shouldn't be jealous; He is our only source of food, and for that I am thankful, genuinely so. I need his ingenuity to help keep us alive until we can be saved.

Be saved? That will never happen. Looking out to the sea beyond Simon, there is nothing but blue interrupted only by occasional flat green islands that don't look much different than our own shitty atoll. It is hard to believe we haven't seen one boat, one plane, not anything, and yet here we are in the middle of a brewing war. I would have thought we might see or hear signs of battles, but nothing. Since the second storm a week ago, we haven't even seen clouds. We are perfectly alone.

When Simon starts back to camp with his bounty, I follow. I feel like a tag-along child trying to catch up with his older brother. To the casual onlooker, it would seem as though I might be a vassal showing fealty to my lord. I jog to catch up and walk by my brother's side; I will allow myself to be subordinated to him.

Back in the little sandy enclave that has become our home, and probably always will be, little has changed. Why should it? Ess lies still on her hard canvas pad. Simon makes sure she stays that way when he pulls the rag from her mouth to apply a dab more of the opium onto it before reinserting it under her lip. Toothless still looks lost in his hazy world. I look closer and notice he has changed. His face has taken on a sickly pallor and sweat is beading from his brow. He looks ill. Simon moves from Ess to place his hand on the old man's forehead.

"He is burning up," is all Simon says as he pulls up the man's shirt to expose minute red lines snaking up from his groin. He pulls the shorts out to see the repaired injury and is repulsed by the odor. Toothless had rid himself of a dying or dead testicle; now he faces an equally dangerous infection. The skin surrounding the injury is bright red and pus is leaking from the cut held together by the wire stitches.

Simon grabs the half empty bottle of scotch he had used to disinfect his surgical tools and splashes the amber liquid directly on the wound. Even under the influence of the drug, Toothless winces in pain. Without penicillin, the infection would either advance until it killed the first mate, or his fever would kill the infection. Either way, the next couple of days will define whether he lives or dies. The old man's infection provides me a foreshadowing of what to expect with Ess. After Simon is done dousing Toothless, I take the bottle and dump the alcohol over my poor Ess' stump. I don't know if it will help stem infection, but I can see no other options.

There is little else for us to do other than cook our food. Over the next couple of days, we will be faced with challenges. The first is just to make sure Toothless and Ess eat and take in water.

Keeping their wounds clean of infection will be a second test, one that may prove insurmountable.

We set about cooking in complete silence and find the effort a welcome diversion from our troubles.

Simon finally breaks the quiet. "Anders, I know you were terrorized by the wild swine. I was, too, so I forgive you."

I am moderately surprised at Simon's attempt to make peace with me, but I shouldn't be. I understand this man like no one else. He needs me and, quite frankly, I need him. Making peace will be critical to our survival, especially now that we are on our own. Granted, we still have Ess and Toothless with us, but they can't be counted on as an asset now or possibly ever. Personally, I would relish putting a bullet between Toothless' eyes. I'll never forgive him for what has happened to Ess. Simon might blame me, but I know where the blame truly lies: the first mate. Had he not attacked Ess, this devastation would never have been set in motion. Eventually, I will kill Toothless.

"Thanks, Simon, but I don't need, nor do I want, your forgiveness. Really, all I want from you is to continue catching us food and take care of Ess until she heals. By the way, when are you planning to give me back the guns?"

"Anders, that is not going to happen. Quite frankly, unless you know where there are some more bullets, the guns are useless. Why do you want them, anyway? It is not like we need to be afraid of the first mate and I suspect you are not excited to go with me into the jungle to replenish our water."

"Simon, I'll go with you to get water and I know where the bullets are. I have them hidden away," I lie, knowing full well they are still sitting in Bradley's and Captain Robert's luggage. "I'll swap you bullets for one of the pistols."

Simon smiles. "Anders, I lied. I already have the bullets." He pulls out the .45 first and shows me that the magazine has been reloaded. "I got these from Bradley's valise. I found the bullets for the revolver in the captain's duffle. I do not need your help finding them. We can talk about arming you when we go back to the spring."

Is he kidding? My God, he's playing games with me, treating me like a little kid. *We can talk about it*? I could pound him into the sand and take the guns if I wanted to. I could and I probably should, but I won't, yet. I smile and respond, deceptively, "Sounds good." I can tell from the look on his face, Simon doesn't trust me.

"Look, Simon, if you think I am going to run again, I won't."

"No, Anders, I do not think you will run, but I do think you would kill the first mate."

"And what if I do? Even you must agree he is of no use to us, and he's an individual who can't be trusted. Hell, once he gets to the point he can walk without pain, he'll be looking to kill me, and you, too."

"Anders, don't you get it? It does not matter. For now, he is not a danger to any of us, so how would shooting him be anything but murder? You cannot lower yourself to his level. We have time to think about what we will do when he gets better. You know, I don't even think he will be very interested in hurting us if he gets through this. Why would anyone want to live alone on this island; it would drive one crazy! No, I think he needs us more than we need him, so we are safe."

He is smiling at me in a smug, 'know-it-all' way that serves to piss me off more. Simon is trying to push my buttons, and he is succeeding.

I pull a couple crabs from the fire and crush their shells with the pair of pliers Simon had used to fashion sutures. Hopefully, we'll never need these to perform surgery again. "Simon, why didn't we use these before to crack the shells? They work great. You want me to crack some for you?" Even though he's angered me, I am calculating that a conciliatory approach will be more effective in reestablishing some trust between us. I need him to give up at least one of the pistols, then, murder or not, Toothless is a goner.

He responds without looking at me as he prods at a couple crabs with a thin, green branch, pulling them from the flame. "Sure, and while you are at it, go ahead and pull the meat out of these to feed the first mate and Ess. They need the food more than us."

I do as he asks and pile what looks to be a meager amount of meat on a piece of torn, flat aluminum. It used to be part of our plane's tail. Simon grabs the makeshift platter and first makes his way to Toothless. He attempts to feed him a bit of the delicate white meat by pushing it between his lips and through the gap in his teeth that was now occupied by nothing but gums. Toothless' eyes open as the savory taste sets in. He whispers a silent "thank you" and opens his mouth for more. Simon feeds him another pinch of food and waits for Toothless to chew and swallow. This exercise goes on until the meat is gone and he returns to me and the fire in search of another crab for Ess.

I comment, "You know, we only have a couple crabs left. If you feed them to Ess, you're going to have to go hungry."

"I got it. Let's first see if she will eat at all. If I go hungry for now, I can feed myself first from our next catch."

I strip the meat from our last two crabs, laying it on the piece of metal, and give it back to Simon to see if he can get Ess to eat. I doubt she will wake up to eat anything, but I watch hopefully as he gently pulls her up from the mat to a sitting position, leaning her against the fallen tree still stained with her blood.

Simon grabs the food and brings it up to below her nose for the smell. She opens her eyes and glances down at the meat he offers her before raising her stump to eat. I don't think she knew her arm was missing. I can't bear to watch. I close my eyes.

Nothing happens, at least not the crying or scream of agony I expected to hear once she saw the ugly folded skin where her elbow and the rest of her arm (her long, lovely, beautiful arm) should have been. I open my eyes to catch her staring into the face of Simon as he feeds her the crab. She chews, swallows, and opens for another bite, and another, until the meat is all gone. She refuses to look at her arm or at me, instead choosing to gaze either at Simon or directly into the fire. Her face belies the emotional and physical anguish I know she must be experiencing.

Simon returns to sit next to me for a moment, then stands up to retrieve one of our few remaining bottles of murky water. He takes it to Ess. At first, she turns her head to the side, avoiding the drink, but, finally, she relinquishes and opens her mouth to allow Simon to pour in a few drops for her to swallow. She coughs as Simons pours in a second swallow, so he waits. She coughs again and vomits up, not only the couple swallows of water, but the crab Simon had just fed her. She looks down at her lap to see a glob of undigested food and bile. Although the amount was pitifully little, it had fueled huge hopes that she might be able to recover. Simon brings the bottle to her lips a third time, tilting it just enough to dribble the water into her mouth. She accepts the drink without gagging.

This process continues until Simon has given Ess most of the murky, scotch-laden fluid. Hopefully, she won't die from dehydration this evening. I should be thankful that Simon is caring for her, but I am jealous. He has displaced me in my role as leader, caregiver, and boyfriend, and it isn't fair.

Fair? I laugh to myself as I stare into the fire; nothing is fair on this island. Well, I take it back. I'm losing a damaged girl to my damaged brother. In a way it makes perfect sense. They deserve each other.

My attention is pulled away from the flame as Simon returns to Toothless, sharing what little water that remains from his bottle. Toothless' cheeks are sunken, and his lips are so parched the skin cracks as he opens his mouth. Small droplets of blood ooze from his lips and disappear into the stubble of his unshaven face. He needs the water more than Simon or me, but I can only see his drinking as a waste. Our precious water should be reserved for me, Simon, and Ess. If Toothless dies, who cares?

If Toothless lives, who cares? I do, and Simon should. I can't see how we can let him roam free if he gets better. But then again, how can we jail him? Even if we could figure out a way to imprison him, who is going to feed him? I'm not.

CHAPTER 30
The Routine

Simon kneels in the mud, filling a scotch bottle with the brown water from what now has become our personal water supply. I am not sure where the pigs have gone, but I see no signs of their return to the spring since our encounter yesterday. I do see that Simon managed to kill three of the beasts before the rest ran off. The brown piles of flesh are now attracting flies. Having heard some terrible stories of pigs' cannibalistic viciousness, I am surprised the animals that survived from yesterday hadn't returned to feed off their friends.

We should take one of the boars back to camp as food. As if reading my mind, Simon looks away from his bottle at me and shakes his head. "These pigs are really starting to stink from decomposition already," he says. "We need to pull them away from the water before they foul our only supply."

He is right. He is always right. Certainly, these hulks of wasting flesh are no longer fit for us to eat. In fact, just their rotting represents a hazard to our water source and our existence.

After filling the remaining bottles, Simon and I set about dragging the pigs away from the pond and back into the jungle. Even though I want to stop because it is hard work, Simon insists we drag the beasts away from camp, meaning we would eventually end up dragging each animal hundreds of feet to rest on the other side of the swampy ground. By the time we're done, the sun has already begun its daily slide into the sea. He gathers up the bottles and loads them into our netting, rolling them tightly to keep them from bouncing against each other and breaking. He transfers the makeshift sack onto his back and motions for me to follow.

"This water should take care of us for another couple of days, don't you think?" I ask Simon rhetorically. As our numbers on the island have dwindled, I find myself asking questions that really don't need answers. It's as if I need to talk to myself for no other purpose than hearing a person's voice. It makes it less lonely for me. Simon doesn't seem to have this problem. He is perfectly happy keeping his thoughts to himself and speaks only when he is providing direction. That's the way he has always been. He's lived in relative solitude his entire adult life; this is not such a change for him.

He surprises me by responding, not so much to my question, but to our circumstance, "You know, Anders, I think we will be making this march each day for as long as we're trapped on this island. Perhaps you and I need to spend our time on these treks thinking about how we can get rescued or how we might escape."

I give Simon an incredulous glance, "Rescue? Now? If you could have put some thought into this a week ago, maybe my Ess wouldn't be broken." I don't know why I use the term "broken," but it seems so appropriate. Her spirit, her hope, had been dashed long before her arm was crushed. Emotionally and physically, she is certainly broken and would never be fixed. She is beyond repair. I wonder if Simon has included Ess in his thought of rescue or if he's already written her off, too. And what about Toothless? I can't bring myself to rescue him. If he had been upfront with us from the beginning, we never would have been here in the first place. No, Toothless will not be saved.

As we march back to camp, we do it in complete silence. Simon's thinking process for our rescue doesn't include me. Why should I care? If his plans succeed, I don't need to bother myself with contributing to the solution. I am perfectly happy just following along … Until we get home, then I will be boss again.

I follow Simon as he breaks clear of the jungle to enter our campsite. Ess is still sitting against the fallen tree trunk. It is pleasing to see that her eyes are open, and she doesn't appear to be in any pain. Although she doesn't acknowledge us by talking, I see her eyes thirstily follow Simon as he deposits his load into the sand.

Amazingly, Toothless is missing. When we left, he looked to be at death's doorstep, delirious and sweating with fever. Either the infection has been pushed back by the fever and the scotch, or perhaps he has moved into the forest to die. I can only hope.

Looking up the beach, I see that my hopes for his death will be delayed for some time. It looks as though Toothless is truly on the mend. While I thought he had been unconscious most of the time since his surgery, apparently, he managed to pay attention to Simon's fishing and trapping efforts. I see him ankle deep in the water with Simon's crates. I doubt he will have any success with his efforts, but I guess I am glad to finally see him making the effort to help us. At least he's not waiting for us with the axe as we exited the forest. I see the axe head is buried in the wood just behind Ess's head. I fear Toothless is well enough to bury it in me.

All is quiet, so I sit and watch as Simon pulls out a bottle of water and mixes in a generous amount of scotch before offering it to Ess. She opens her mouth to let him pour in a swallow. This time she doesn't choke or cough, and she opens her mouth for a second gulp. This play repeats itself (she opens her mouth, he pours in murky water, she swallows) several times until she has imbibed almost a quarter of the bottle. Even though there is little liquor in the water, she is drunk by the time she is done. She leans her head back against the log and nods off to sleep. I hope it is a painless sleep.

I, too, feel a need to sleep and recline back into the warm sand and close my eyes.

*

Simon takes the water bottle to Toothless. The first mate makes no notice of his approach until Simon takes a seat in the sand.

Toothless pretends to check his traps, occasionally pushing his hands into the water to prod a crab into his trap. He finally breaks the silence. "Fever broke this morning after you left. I hope you don't mind me taking a crack with your traps."

"Not at all. Are you having any luck?" Simon paused. "What are you using for bait?"

"Oh, nothing much, just some stuff I found lying in the sand. It looks like the crabs like it though. I've been lucky so far." Toothless nodded towards another crate that sat half submerged in the water. This crate still had its top affixed and was serving as a jailhouse for its captive crabs.

Simon stood and brushed the sand from his pants before walking over to the crate to look at this day's catch. "Wow, you really have been successful. Looks like we will not need to starve tonight. You are planning on sharing, right?"

Toothless turned to face Simon. "Look, I done wrong when I went after the girl. I was the dope; I was the one that done it. I can't blame you for what happened to me. I got to be truthful, I wanted to kill you all, but now I know it ain't your fault that I got hurt so bad. It was my doing and it ain't going to happen again. All I want is to get off this island alive and we need to do it together."

Simon looked into the man's eyes. What he saw was a man who had aged twelve years in twelve days. A man who no longer looked as though he could hurt them even if he wanted to. He was a man who had lost his muscle, his anger, his very confidence. To call him spent would be wrong; he was merely resigned, resigned that he needed help to live, resigned that he had done wrong and he had no friends on this island, resigned that he was no longer the man he had been twelve days ago. Nothing would ever be able to change that, to give him back his manhood.

Toothless continued, "You know, I tried to throw it away after you left."

"Throw what away?" Simon asks.

"The pipe, that fucking pipe. I never should have tried it. That opium Bradley brought on the plane is bad stuff. I thought I could resist it, but I couldn't. Never could. I can never forgive the Good Captain. He got addicted to the money; I got addicted to the sticky brown shit. He paid for his smuggling. I guess we both did. I am sorry it looks like you paid for it, too." He smiled and continued, "Hey, but look at it this way, at least the Japs didn't get you."

"At least not yet," Simon countered. "Hey, before I forget, here is water. You are going to need to drink a lot of this if you want to keep the infection at bay. Plus, you are going to need to keep yourself clean with the alcohol."

Toothless smiled again. "I'll take the water, and I already took the opportunity to keep myself doused with the scotch. Damn waste of good whiskey though, splashing it where my nuts should be. I splashed a good amount in my mouth, too, just to fight infection from the inside. I sure as hell hope we get off this place before we run out of booze."

Simon smiled at Toothless' attempt at humor. He was righter than he knew about getting off the island before they ran out of the scotch. No scotch, no antiseptic, no drinkable water.

Simon turned away from Toothless and called over his shoulder as he walked back to camp. "Don't take too long in catching dinner, we are all hungry."

*

I wake to the smell of roasting crab. The sun has set, and the only light comes from our campfire and starlight—silvery threads of light reflected off the mirror-smooth sea. Although most folks would kill to live in a paradise like this, seventy-five degrees both night and day, no wind, no rainstorms for the past several days, I find myself longing for change. It won't come tonight. I stare at the cloudless sky and its infinite spread of stars and realize Simon is right; we will be returning to the spring tomorrow for water. There will be no rain tonight.

I roll to my side and watch Simon playing chef again, cooking us crab. My stomach aches with hunger. I hope he and Toothless have been successful with today's harvest. Simon sits beside Toothless, separated from him only by a wooden crate that, I assume, contains the creepy-crawly crabs waiting their turns to be thrown into the red-hot cinders to cook. I want to move closer to the fire and grab some food, but I choose instead to lie here quietly in the shadows, attempting not to draw the attention of our toothless wonder. Although I know Toothless isn't a danger to me, I have no desire to tempt him to anger; better to leave him alone. I will deal with him later.

The aluminum platter is piled with crab. It has been an abundant catch. I will wait to eat since it looks as though there is more than enough for all of us to fill our bellies tonight.

Simon breaks into one of the crabs and holds the little beast up to his nose. He shocks me when he passes on stuffing the meat into his mouth. He must be hungry. Instead, he pulls the white meat from the shell and takes it to Ess. He begins to feed her. HE IS FEEDING my girl again. I can't believe it. He's taking advantage of another opportunity to steal her from me … and he is doing it right in front of me. I don't show my anger because I'm sure he is purposely attempting to rile me. He has succeeded, but I'm not going to show it. I will not give him the pleasure of knowing he has angered me.

As he feeds Ess, he pretends to not notice I am watching his every movement. He ignores me as he gently presses the meat between her lips with his fingers. I guess I should be happy she is getting much-needed sustenance, but I can't be happy that Simon is pretending to care for my girl. I know he is doing this just to piss me off. He will pay for this.

She smiles as she opens her mouth to accept the delicate meat from Simon's hand. She chews, swallows, and opens her mouth for more. It is like watching a baby bird being fed by its mother. *Give me a break. Can't she feed herself? Did she lose both hands? I don't think so. Stop feeding her, Simon, and let her feed herself; she isn't helpless.* But then I catch myself. I guess she is helpless, at least for the time being. I should be happy Simon is taking care of her as I asked him to. Why can't I just be happy about it? At least she isn't wasting our food this time by vomiting it up into the sand.

I turn away from them. I'm disgusted at watching Simon trying to impress this woman. I am more disgusted that Ess appears to enjoy eating up the attention as much as she enjoys eating the crab. My stomach growls with hunger. Sarcastically, I wonder if Simon will feed me, too. Probably not. He doesn't want to screw me. Well, maybe not physically.

As I stew, I hear Toothless breaking into his crab. His eating is as disgusting to hear as it is to watch. He groans with pleasure as he sucks the meat into his mouth. I hear the cracking of shell as he breaks off another piece of the crab. I turn back to watch the beast as liquid drools from the corners of his mouth. I find the sound he utters as he chews less gruesome if I watch.

The man eats as if he hasn't seen food for days. In truth, I guess that is the case. The little he ate yesterday was not enough to sate a mouse, let alone an adult man. He pushes the meat from the shell with his fingers and tongue. He tears at the shell with his teeth. He is ravenous. I wonder if there will be anything left for Simon and me once he's through. Although he is looking at me, I don't think he really sees me. He is completely lost in the ecstasy of tasting and relishing his meal. He is so one-dimensional, capable of doing nothing other than devouring his meal.

A silhouette passes in front of me as Simon walks between me and the fire to return to his seat next to Toothless to eat. He looks at me and smiles as he pulls another couple of crabs from the flame. He quietly sets about breaking and stripping the shell from the meat, his method a striking contrast to that of Toothless.

Efficiency and neatness were apparent in how Simon prepared his dinner. These were two adjectives that could be applied to everything he did. I longed to see him, even if for just a moment, succumb to hunger pangs and just stuff a leg into his mouth, crunching it up and spitting out the shards of shell to the sands, but that was not Simon. I think he is not capable of acting in a rash fashion.

He tempts me as he takes his time pulling meat from the shell … taking his time to make sure I see the food he is preparing for himself. He realizes he is upsetting me by not inviting me to sit by the fire with him and by not sharing his food. I'm not going to let him get to me. I'll wait until they are done, then I'll eat whatever is left. I'll piss in their water. That will teach them to ignore me.

Simon continues staring at me as he eats. Slowly, he takes morsel by morsel to his mouth, pausing only to close his eyes to savor the taste. I know he's hungry, having gone without food yesterday. That was his fault, not mine. There was no reason to waste food on Ess. She couldn't keep her food down; he should have known.

I lay still in the shadows, watching jealously while Simon eats. Simon wins. I feel stupid when I rise to move next to Simon's side opposite Toothless. Sitting down I begin to share in Simon's pile of food. He doesn't seem to care that I am taking part of the food he liberated from the crab shell for his own benefit. Brothers must share.

CHAPTER 31
Not Paradise

Our campfire wanes as we sit in the sand after our first decent sized meal that any of us have had in days. I can't remember when my stomach was last full; it is now. It's a good feeling.

Simon falls to his knees, looking up at the star-filled sky. Quietly, he says, "You know, if we are going to get out of here, we need to go together soon. There is no more time."

"Simon, I don't know why you have become so obsessed with escape. We're all eager to get off this godforsaken island, but we just need to be patient. Eventually, we're going to be visited by someone, a fisherman, military, navy, someone."

Simon looks at me and jumps into a lecture, "That is exactly the point, Anders. We needed to leave Singapore because war was heating up. We needed to escape from an imperialistic Japanese army that was brutal to everyone and anyone who was in its path. Why would you think that if we do get a visit, it would not be from the Japanese? They are intent on controlling the entire region. No, we need to leave on our terms and, I fear, we need to do this as soon as possible." He continues to stare at me, his eyes boring through me, intent on controlling me.

Okay, maybe he's right. I'm sure we can figure out a way to float ourselves off this island. My concern is, what's next? Where do we go from here and how will we get there? For all I know, sea currents could pull us back to where we left, or worse, push us into the middle of the Pacific Ocean to die. My sailing experience is limited to the lakes in New York where we grew up and a couple charters in the Singapore Strait. They hardly prepared me for embarking into the Java or Flores Seas. Hell, we don't really know where we are. Simon's being foolhardy. We can't escape, so I need to stop him before he kills us.

To placate him, I lie. "Sure, Simon. We'll leave whenever you think we're ready."

Simon squints as if he has divined my deceit. "Anders, your friend Toothless_" I hate his sarcasm. "—can help us with the ocean currents so we will not get lost. And certainly, he has a good idea where we are. We just need to talk with him to figure out where that happens to be. If you do not feel comfortable talking with him, I will."

So, Simon thinks he has some great relation with Toothless that will somehow result in new learnings that can save us. What a prick. My brother must think he has a direct line to God or something. He refuses to recognize our predicament. And I used to think he was the pragmatist. He has lost touch with reality. I can't count on Simon being the objective brother any longer. Worse, relying on Toothless for information is bound to get us killed. If he knew where we were, he would have said something earlier. No, Simon's ignoring reality. We're stuck here until someone discovers us.

"Go ahead and try, my dear brother." I look at Toothless, who is in a deep sleep. Nodding in his direction, I continue, "He's just a grunt. You're kidding yourself if you think he's going to be able to give you some magical insight that will let us escape this place alive. Now, if you have some ideas beyond relying on Toothless, I'm all ears."

Simon looked back at the stars. "Never mind, Anders." He falls quiet.

This is typical for my brother; start a conversation and then end it when it doesn't go his way. I feel a need to keep talking, with him or anyone. "Simon?"

"Yes?"

"What did Toothless change with your traps? You guys pulled in a massive load of crab, our best catch yet."

"It was good, wasn't it? You know, I am not sure, but he left the traps in the water for the night so I suspect we will have a nice breakfast, too. I would welcome not having to worry about food for a day. We can pick some plants to supplement our diet on our way back from the spring tomorrow. It will be good to sleep without my stomach growling."

"Me, too."

Simon rolls over and pushes himself up off the sand to stand above me. Stretching, he tells me goodnight and wakes Ess to help her into the plane for the night's sleep. Instantly, the anger flares up in me again. He is taking Ess inside without asking me. Does he think she's his girl now just because he saved her? And what about Ess? She doesn't protest at all. In fact, she is leaning into him as they shuffle to the open hatch. I hate this man and I am beginning to hate Ess. How dare she? That bitch. I throw myself onto my other side to face away from the plane. Simon will never get the better of me. Tomorrow will be different.

CHAPTER 32
What Crabs Like to Eat

Day eleven—

Ouch, that is all I can think as I roll onto my back. The sand that was comfortable last night has become rock hard. That said, I slept late. I'm not the first to wake this morning. Pretending to still be asleep, I listen to the activity with my eyes closed.

First, there is Toothless. He is humming something. I vaguely recognize the melody, but don't recall where I have heard it before. It is refreshing to hear something besides the wind whispering through the trees or the tinkling noise of the water as it rubs against the sand. Who would have thought the sound of nature would become so monotonous that it would make me uneasy and anxious. It is thrilling to hear music coming from the mouth of man.

Then there is Ess. Her voice is so quiet, but just hearing it for the first time in more than two days makes me smile. A weight is lifted from my shoulders. I don't know why, but now I know she will make it through this ordeal. I forget my anger from last night and just want to throw my arms around her.

She is talking with Simon. "It hurts so bad, and I'm afraid to look at it. Will I live?"

There is a long pause before I hear the sand moving as someone walks closer. Then Simon says, "Ess, it is too early to know. It is good that you have not developed an infection yet, but it is too soon to say you are going to be all right. Here, open your mouth and put this between your teeth and gums. There is opium rubbed into the cloth. It will numb the pain."

I could not imagine before now that my Simon with his little opium-paste infused square of cloth rolled into a tube would be trying to seduce my Ess back into her drug induced stupor.

"No, I'll pass. I can't believe I even smoked the stuff. I think I can make it through; at least for now." There is a pause. "Why has this happened to me? To us?"

There is no answer from Simon, so I roll over to see to whom she asked the question. Simon has left the camp and is walking up the beach away from us. Ess is staring off into space, not looking at anyone. Does she think she's talking to God? If she is, she won't get an answer. I haven't, and I've asked the same question more times than I care to remember since we crashed on this turd of an island. Hopefully, God will have mercy on her and give her an answer, one that she can live with.

I get up from my sand bed and jog to join Simon. Once I catch up, I ask, "Did Ess sleep well last night, brother?"

"What is it to you? I did not think you were much interested in her anymore now that she is broken. That is how you put it, 'broken.' Right?"

"That isn't what I meant. She's my girl and always will be. I'll do anything for her."

"Anything? Anders, you did not even stick around to see if she lived when the pigs attacked us. You ran away. If that is your example of doing 'anything' for her, you and I have a radically different perspective of the meaning of that word. I think what you mean is that you would do anything as long as it is easy for you. You are lazy and a coward, face it."

I'm silent. What can one say when confronted with a truth you don't want to hear? There is nothing, so I silently walk alongside my brother. He's caught me in a lie. Well, not a lie. It's just that I can't be as good as I want to be and I sure as hell can't be as good as Simon. For all of Simon's faults, cowardice surely isn't one of them. Even as a kid, he always said and did what he thought was right. It's one of the reasons he always got into trouble. He was never mean, just very direct in how he approached every challenge. Every situation was either black or white. In his eyes, there was never room for gray. There were no dilemmas for Simon, just right or wrong; he never considered the consequences. Today was just like that. So, he sees me as a coward. Sure, it angers me, but that wasn't his objective. In this case, he is just stating fact as he sees it.

"So what if I'm a coward? It wasn't like I made a conscious decision to run. It just happened, but it won't happen again. I will show you. You'll be proud of me."

I won't discuss being lazy with Simon. I am guilty as charged. As a reporter, it was always easier to make something up rather than do the legwork to validate a story. Nobody ever questioned me when I referenced an "anonymous" source, especially if the article was "over-the-top" as they say in the reporting circles. It was even better if the story uncovered a salacious bit or two about someone famous. Everyone wanted to believe what I reported even when it wasn't true, which was typically the case. It didn't take long to realize hard work didn't pay off and the truth didn't matter. Being lazy became an asset.

We walked on in silence until Simon started talking again. "Anders, I can forgive you for what you did, but can Ess? Have you asked her? Are you even brave enough to ask?"

"I don't need to ask, Simon. She knows I love her. She knows that I would do anything for her." My brother won't stop prodding me, pushing me. Why is he doing this to me? I change the subject. "Why are we walking up the beach?"

Simon looks at me incredulously. "A better question might be, why you are walking up the beach? I am going to get the morning's catch. Remember, someone must feed us, and it has never been you."

Simon is more aggressive than I've ever recalled. It's as if he is trying to goad me into a battle. If he pushes much further, I will push back. I cannot recall when we have had a real fight, but we are getting close, and he is the one pushing me to it.

"Look, I just want to help. You can show me how you catch the crab and fish. Then you and Toothless won't be the only ones who can provide for us." As soon as the words leave my mouth, I am impressed by my own brilliance. Once he shows me how to fish, I won't need him anymore. If he gets in my way or steals Ess, I'll destroy him. He will be outwitted.

Simon looks at me quizzically, then turns back to the beach. "There is no magic to it. It just requires a box of some sort, your patience, and a little bait. You have patience, Anders?"

"Oh, I have patience. I've lived with you for how long?"

Simon smiles and laughs. "Too long, and me with you. Perhaps when we get home, I will get along on my own."

I have no choice but to laugh at this. "You betcha, Simon. Sounds good," I say, knowing Simon will never be able to function without me for support.

"Well, lookie there. I see what the first mate is using for bait. It looks as if those creepy crabs really like it," Simon says as he kneels into the shallow water, looking at their first trap.

I look in the box and vomit. Crabs are fighting over fingers, human fingers. My Ess' fingers. I yell. I can't help myself, and I turn and run toward camp. What the fuck was Toothless thinking? Why would he ever think this was okay? It is so wrong. My Ess, my Ess.

I storm into camp and fall into the sand, not knowing what to do. Ess looks at me with shocked eyes. I look at Toothless. His mouth is open in surprise. I can't help but look at the blood-stained log where my dear girl received her surgery, her terrible surgery. There's the axe, its head buried in the wood. I scramble up from the sand and grasp the handle. Looking at the ground on the other side of the log, Ess's arm is lying putrefied and rotting. Not the whole arm and hand; it is missing the fingers. That fuck chopped off her fingers, her beautiful fingers. I pull the axe free, swinging wildly, not thinking, just acting. I swing, and swing, and swing until the axe catches a purchase. I look down and see my victim. Toothless' eyes are lifeless now. The axe head bisects his forehead, cleaving all the way past his nose. I release my grip and fall to my knees. He will never have another chance to hurt my Ess. I told Simon I would not back down again.

Turning to face Ess, she is stunned and speechless. There is nothing for me to say. I stand up and return to our crab traps.

CHAPTER 33
Who Can I Trust?

There has not been a word uttered since I dispatched Toothless. Simon is cooking crab, but I doubt I can bring myself to eat one, knowing that in their bellies are morsels pulled from Ess's fingers. It makes me ill knowing we enjoyed eating this flesh last night.

What was Toothless thinking when he chose to use Ess's discarded members so disrespectfully? Didn't he think there would be consequences for his actions? Simon looks at me as if I'm crazy, but I'm not the one who took the time to chop the fingers from the hand and feed them to the fish. Toothless needed to be sent to Hell and I am fine being the dispatcher. May he rot and burn forever.

I want to take advantage of our abundant supply of opium, but I won't.

Simon stands and walks over to where Ess is sitting silently. She has not talked since I killed Toothless. Simon kneels beside her and whispers. I can't hear their private secret, and it infuriates me … at least until Ess whispers something in return and turns her face away from him. There are tears running down her face. Simon returns to sit next to me. He prods a crab with his green twig as it cooks in the flame. Silently, I laugh that he has been rebuffed by my girl. Good girl.

Simon speaks. "You were so wrong, Anders. I cannot believe you killed him. He was no danger to you or us. You murdered him in cold blood. We saw you. Neither Ess nor I will ever forgive you."

"Don't tell me what Ess will or won't do." I want to yell, but I keep my voice steady and measured. "You called me a coward, but you couldn't even kill that bastard, even after you saw what he did to my girl."

"You are still the coward. You took an axe to his head even though he could barely walk. He was trying to help save our lives and you took his. For what? To make you feel good and manly? You are hardly a man."

"You'll wish you could take back those words, Simon."

"Take them back? What are you going to do if I refuse? Are you going to take the axe to me, too? I think not. Hell, I am mad at myself. I thought if I kept the guns from you, the first mate might be safe for a while, but all you needed was an excuse and my stupidity to allow you to kill him. I knew you were intent on killing him the day you pinned that name on him. You hated him."

I was ready to strike at him until he continued with, "Did you know that he asked Ess first about the fingers?"

It struck me as if I had now been the one split by the axe. "What are you talking about?"

"Toothless asked her permission to use the fingers as bait while you slept. Fuck, you always sleep. Do you think the world stops when you close your eyes? It never has and it never will."

"You're lying," but I know he isn't when I look across the campfire to see Ess staring at the ground. She thinks I've ruined everything. Doesn't she know she should have told me? True, it wouldn't have stopped him from using the fingers, but I wouldn't have killed him. It's all her fault … and Simon's. They should have told me. Why can't they see that? They're to blame. Not me.

I fall on my side into the sand and close my eyes. I don't want to be here anymore. Please, just let me leave this place.

Simon leaves my side with the hot, steaming crab and goes to Ess. I can hear her reject his offer to feed her. Likewise, she rejects him when he offers her water. Good for her.

*

Simon stands and stretches out his arms. "Ess, if you do not eat, you are going to die."

"What do you care? We are going to die anyway. I'd just as soon go on my own terms, in my own way. If it means starving to death, so be it. At least then I'd be away from this place." Tears ran down her face as she talked.

"Do you want to try some of the opium to kill the pain at least?"

The question angers her. "No, not now, not ever. I'm going to get through this without it. That drug calls to me continuously and its hold on me scares me more than the pain. You might not know this, but I used to be a tough little lady, and I need to remember what that feels like." She spat the words out in defiance.

Simon stepped back away from her and looked at her face, glistening in the sunlight. Even in her anger, she was beautiful. He could understand why Anders was so taken with her. Anders just never really appreciated her. He thought she was a possession. Simon understood she could never be possessed.

He turned back to face Anders. His brother would not look at him. Instead he remained curled up on his side, lying in the sand with his back towards him. Simon shook his head and went to the airplane hatch. As he entered the hull that had been their home for the better part of two weeks, he called back over his shoulder, "It's about time we leave this place. I am packing us things to take. Yell if you have something you do not want me to forget." He paused, waiting for a response, any response. Getting none, he entered and set about preparing for his escape.

CHAPTER 34
Surprise

Day twelve—

It was a good night's sleep. I took great pleasure in sleeping in Toothless' hammock. I have won. His hammock is now my hammock. In fact, everything that was his is now mine. True, he hadn't possessed much. We have outlasted everyone and now Simon will figure out a way for us to escape. I know he will.

I lay silent for a while, listening for sleeping sounds of the remaining members of my tribe: Ess and Simon. There is nothing but silence. There is none of Simon's humming from the co-pilot's seat, no shallow, rapid breathing from Ess. Just quiet. I open my eyes and lay still until they adjust to the light that is now pouring in through the cabin windows. I sense I'm alone.

Throwing my legs over the edge of the hammock, I propel myself up to a sitting position and confirm that, yes, I am alone in the shell of the plane. I share the space with only boxes of opium and a couple discarded suitcases. The cabin door is closed tight and no light creeps in around its edges. I push myself out of the netting to stand upright, at least as upright as the fuselage allows. I push at the hatch to let myself out and find it impossible to move. The latch is fixed as if welded in place. How can this be? I panic and pound on the door. There is no response. This must be a dream. The door can't be locked from the outside. "Let me out!" I pound on the door again to no response.

Looking out the cabin windows, Simon and Ess are sitting in the sand just outside the door of the plane. If not for the skin of the fuselage, they are close enough for me to touch. They certainly can hear me. I pound on the window, but Simon ignores me; his attention is focused only on Ess. His eyes don't waver even when I scream at him. How can he do this to me? I yell out Ess's name, but she fails to respond, too. Her eyes are closed, and she sits with her back against that same blood-stained log. God, how I am beginning to hate that log. She looks as if she is dead. Yes, that must be it. She has died in the night and Simon is distraught, lost in his own world. It must be shocking to him to deal with this type of emotion for the first time in his life. I can understand. I'll sit and wait until he recovers enough to let me out of this piece of shit plane. Once I get out of here, I'll never set foot in here again.

*

Simon tried in vain to get Ess to speak. "Ess, I am sorry that Toothless is gone. It was terrible, I know."

Ess finally opened her eyes and whispered, "It was murder, just murder. It was horrific, and I can never forget. It haunts me every time I close my eyes. I see the axe head as clearly as if it were cleaving into me. It is terrifying, but still, I need to close my eyes to sleep. I am so tired, so tired." She closed her eyes and fell into what Simon could only assume was a fitful sleep, marked by short breaths and her head twitching to the side as if recoiling from the imaginary axe blows.

The murder of Toothless had unhinged her. Simon realized the damage of watching Anders bisect the first mate's forehead had done more harm to Ess than even the hungry pig that ruined her arm. Visions of the axe planted in Toothless' head would revisit her for the rest of her life. The only good thing was that her life might not be too long. Perhaps her hell would be forgotten when she took her last breath here on earth; at least he could pray for that. What a hell it must be knowing that a nightmare awaits you when you fall asleep. Death would be a welcome pardon.

Simon pulled a small fish he had been cooking from the flame and carried it to Ess. "Here, take this and eat. It will make you stronger. You need to get food into your stomach."

He tried to push a small bite between her chapped and cracking lips. She kept her eyes closed and clinched her mouth shut, making it impossible for Simon to insert even that small morsel into her mouth. He pushed the meat against her lips again, hoping his persistence would prevail and she would eventually open, allowing him to feed her. She turned her head to the side, knocking the fish from Simon's fingers.

He debated trying to place a little of the opium directly under her lip. As the numbing effect overtook her, he could then force her to eat a little food, and more importantly, take some water. Although he could force a small dab into her mouth, he knew that he was also taking the risk of killing her with an overdose. He had no idea how much would be too much. He feared even a small amount might overwhelm her body and stop her heart. Given how severely dehydrated she already was, the risk seemed reasonable. If he did not get some fluids into her soon, her heart was going to stop anyway. She was well on her way to ensuring she could never recover.

He pinched a small glob of the sticky opium and messaged it into a narrow strip of cloth. Then he folded the cloth into a small roll that he would attempt to insert between Ess's cheek and her teeth. He hoped she might choose to chew on the material just to get some saliva flowing. Once the drug started to kick in, he would force her to drink by pouring small amounts into her mouth. Hopefully, he could get enough into her system before she choked. The water was needed to keep her body from shutting down completely. She might hate him for saving her, but he would deal with that later. For now, his only desire was to save her for another day. Another day to seek her forgiveness for saving her.

He grabbed her face between his hands while holding the tacky roll of cloth with the thumb and index finger of his right hand. She struggled futilely against his grip. She was too weak to fight and quickly gave up resistance, and she allowed Simon to insert the cloth inside her cheek. He was shocked to find even the inside of her mouth was dry. The cloth stuck to the skin.

As soon as he removed his fingers, Ess began to fight again. Her tongue under her cheek worked to evacuate the pain-killing cloth from her mouth. Her lips and tongue worked frantically, but to no avail. He could not be sure if it was the lack of saliva that allowed the opium to stick like glue to the side of her mouth or just a lack of muscle coordination as her body began to fail.

The drug kicked in and Ess relaxed. Her breathing was shallow but remained steady. Simon took the opportunity to begin the arduous task of rehydrating her. Pulling apart her lips with his fingers on one hand, he used a cloth soaked with water to wet her mouth, droplet by droplet. After several drops of water fell behind her lips, he forced her mouth closed until he saw her throat move with the involuntary action of swallowing. Then repeating the process, he would open her lips for another round of several drops of the foul water. He feared his actions were already too late to save her, but he swore to himself he would not stop until her heart stopped beating. Maybe he had fallen in love with her or maybe he only wanted to give her a chance to forgive his brother. In forgiveness, Ess would be doing something he was unwilling to do himself. Anders was a murderer; he had done the unforgivable.

*

I've been sitting here for too long and it's getting hot. I need to get out. When is Simon going to open the door? I push myself up from the floor, sliding my back against the rounded aluminum skin of the fuselage. Looking out the window, I see my brother kneeling beside my Ess. He is holding a cloth above her face and squeezing a small stream of water into her mouth. That should be me and I bang on the window again. He ignores me. My God, I can help. Why won't he let me out of here to help?

I watch helplessly as Simon's actions become more frantic. He is pouring more water from one of our bottles onto the cloth and he's spilling most of it into the sand. *STOP*! I can't understand what he is trying to do. He squeezes water out of the cloth into her mouth again, but most of it just trickles out and runs down her face, soaking her blouse. He is just wasting the water now. Can't he see it? He never wastes anything, but now he is wasting everything.

There, finally, he's stopped with the squeezing. He drops the cloth and brings his hands up to his face and falls into the sand on top of the cloth. Why has he stopped? "Simon," I yell. He doesn't act like he hears me, but I know he does. He must.

I can't stay here any longer, so I look for something to pry open this fucking door. I know we had a toolbox in here behind the captain's seat. There must be something to free the latch on the door. I look to where the toolbox had been, but it's missing. Did Simon take it out when he played surgeon? I don't recall, but it's gone now. I look out through one of the fuselage windows and there is the box, lying in the sand next to where Simon had planted himself for the past several days as he played chef. It sits there, guarded by a dead Toothless, the axe still embedded in his skull. *Good work, Anders,* I congratulate myself.

The toolbox is open. Even through the hazy window, I can see pliers, a couple screwdrivers, and a hammer. What I wouldn't give to have that hammer now. I could pound my way through the aluminum skin, and then I could use that same hammer to pound some sense into my brother. How dare he lock me in here. I don't know how he did it, but he has. There is no one else capable of doing it.

I look back to Simon and Ess. Ess doesn't look well. Her skin has taken on a pallor. She is so pale she looks blue. No, she is blue; a grayish blue, as if she's dead. And Simon just lies there crying in the sand. Buck up, brother. Pull yourself together and let me out of here.

I yell to Simon again, "Let me the fuck out of here, Simon! And I mean now!"

Instead of obeying me, he pretends not to hear me. The asshole is ignoring me. I fall silent as he pulls himself up from the sand using the fallen tree to steady himself, but instead of coming to help me, he pulls Ess up from the ground, throwing her over his shoulder. I yell, but he continues to ignore me and walks away, carrying Ess down the beach. He leaves me here stuck in this oven. He disappears from my view as he walks south around the bend of the beach. What the fuck? She doesn't need rescuing; I do. Hell, she's dead. There's not a damn thing he can do for her now.

CHAPTER 35
Time To Be Alone

Ess seemed almost weightless as Simon walked with her draped across his shoulder. Tears flowed down his face as he trudged through the sand. He didn't know where to take her, but he was certain he would know once he got there. His eyes darted back and forth from the jungle to the sea and back again. He didn't want her final resting spot to be with the good captain, Preston, and Bradley; she deserved more. He walked past their makeshift graveyard. She never chose this trip, she was pressed into it, and she had paid with her life. It now seemed like they all would.

He continued to the far southernmost section of the island until he saw a grove of tall, large-leaved trees filled with intense pink flowers. He had seen these before, during his time in Singapore. They would soon be filled with a wonderful red fruit he knew as the Malay rose apple. He could think of no better place for Ess's final resting ground, so he laid her on the sand, and with his bare hands dug her grave under the shade of those beautiful trees.

He pulled out handfuls of sandy soil, deepening the hole until it began to fill with water, filtering in from the sea, and then he dug deeper. He would rather her body be swallowed by the sea than be torn apart by ants or, even worse, wild pigs. He was okay with the bugs and animals having their way with Toothless; after all, it was just a process of life and death. But for Ess, it didn't seem right.

His digging became futile as the hole's sides collapsed, replacing every handful of muck and sand he had thrown to the side. Slowly, the grave expanded both in depth and width until Simon found himself kneeling in the middle of an expanding puddle of gray water he couldn't empty. He gave up and stopped digging. After crawling out of the grave, he was disheartened that his effort had resulted not in a deep, protective grave, but a shallow crater that he feared would fail to deter the wild boars from digging up her body and the yellow ants from stripping her bones of tissue. He contemplated his options. His vision of ants crawling all over her body, tearing minute pieces of flesh a million times a day until only gleaming white bone remained tore him up. He realized he couldn't bury her here. It would be better to free her from the island prison.

He picked up the dead body that had already begun to stiffen with rigor and waded out into the sea. He continued until the water lapped at his chin and then he set her free, not caring if he was in danger from sharks. He was unconcerned for his own life. Death could be no worse than living forever alone, and he felt so alone.

Simon lost track of time as he sat on the beach, looking out to where he had released Ess. The sun had fallen into the sea long ago and now the water glistened silver from reflected moonlight. It was beautiful and peaceful. He could sit here forever if it would always be like this, but it wouldn't. Soon the sun would rise again on his left, making him squint with the light. The calming cool sand would become uncomfortably warm, even hot. The sun would burn his skin and remind him to seek shade. Another day would have passed, and he would be hungry and thirsty. He could remain here no longer. He got up to go home.

*

I see a shadow of a man approaching up the beach. He is nothing more than gray against the black of the water, but I can tell it's Simon. He's walking slow, as if time means nothing to him. I can tell this man thinks he's in complete control. This is Simon and he is about to learn that he's not in control. I am, and I always have been.

My nose presses against the window portal as he passes by without acknowledging me. That's okay; it is so dark in here he wouldn't be able to see me. Simon disappears from my view as he walks toward the front of our plane. I hear him as he climbs up the tree that had punched a hole through DC-3's windscreen. Although the window has been punched in, the tree branch all but filled the gap, preventing me from escaping. I know because I've spent most of the day trying to fit through the pierced windshield.

"Anders, are you in there?"

Of course, I'm in here; how could I not be? You locked me in, didn't you? "Yes, I'm here, Simon. When are you planning to let me out? You need to free me now. It's not fair that I need to wait for you to take care of me. I'm thirsty as hell, and I'm so hungry I could eat a horse. Are you trying to kill me? You are, aren't you?"

There is no response, but I see Simon's silhouette framed in the window. He's looking for me, but I doubt he can see me in the shadow of the fuselage. I enter the cockpit.

"Dammit, Simon, can't you hear me? Let me out."

"I can hear you just fine, Anders, but I cannot let you out anymore. You are too dangerous. You are a murderer. I am shocked you killed the first mate," he says to me, as if he hadn't wanted to kill him, too.

"How can you call that murder, dear brother? He hurt Ess, and from what I saw earlier today, it looks like she died. So he was the one who murdered. I just did what any jury would do; I executed him. That isn't murder. What I did was inflict justice on the bastard. He got exactly what he deserved."

Silence. And the shadow outside the window doesn't move. What type of game is Simon playing? "Simon, did you hear me?"

"So, you said you are hungry."

"Of course I am. I haven't had anything to eat all day. But I'll bet you stuffed your belly though. Didn't you? And I'll bet you didn't give a thought about me."

He seems to be unaffected by my accusation, but Simon responds calmly and quietly. It's unnerving to me.

"No, I did not eat or drink today, so I am hungry and thirsty, too. The only good thing about today is that Ess is not hungry anymore. I do not think she is in pain either. Did you even think of her today or have you just been preoccupied with your growling stomach? I want you to know, I couldn't care less about you. Do you get that? Am I clear?"

I'm shocked and frightened that Simon might be considering letting me die in here. "So, what are you going to do with me then?" I ask, not really knowing if I want to hear what he has to say.

"Anders, I am not going to do anything to you. I am not the monster. You are."

I struggle to understand what's happened to Simon. He's never tried to hurt me, but then again, he never speaks back to me. Until the past couple of days, he has never stood up to me, and yet, now he relishes being my jailor. He hates me. Has he always hated me? Isn't this the same man I've taken care of my whole life? Isn't he the one for whom I've shown nothing but love? How ungrateful he has become. I can't wait to get out of here. I will kill him.

"Simon, you need to let me out so I can help. It's going to be hard enough for you to take care of yourself, let alone getting me food and water." Shit, I just screwed up. What if he's planning to let me starve? What if that is what this is all about? True, I haven't made much effort to help with gathering food and water, or burying our dead, but that's not because I didn't want to help. I did. I just never got the chance. Someone always beat me to the punch. I can see now that they were being selfish. Simon, Toothless, Preston, Bradley, and even Ess, they did those good things just so they could say they did good things. Now Simon thinks that only they did good things. I now understand what Nietzsche meant by the "munificence of the magnanimous." People only want to appear to be generous and great. If they were really interested in doing good, they would've made me help. This is their fault, and Simon is the worst of them. I know he is going to use this as an excuse to let me die. He'll starve me.

I've been the only honest individual stranded on this island. I never tried to be someone I wasn't. Everyone else tried to be something they could never be, and they've died as a result. I have no intention of following behind them.

"Anders, you do not understand, do you? I may know you better than you know yourself. How can I ever let you out of there? Consider this your cell until I can trust you again. But, in case you are concerned, I will not leave you, and I will not let you starve. I am not like you."

It is as if Simon is reading my thoughts. I retreat back into the belly of the craft without saying anything more to him. It may only give him justification to leave me here until I am no more. I will sleep tonight and hope he regains his senses to let me out in the morning.

CHAPTER 36
Bonding Time

Day thirteen—

Sunlight streams in through the windows, throwing a yellow pall over my makeshift jail cell. The air is stagnant: hot and still. The light glistens off still dust particles suspended on nothing other than the weight of the micro-atmosphere of the cargo hold, cut off from the rest of the world. When I wave my hand, the little particles swirl as they float on the interrupted cloud of air, shining like little electric bulbs until they disappear into the shadows, belying their true nature. They have no innate light; they merely reflect that which is greater than them. I'm breathing this stuff. It can't be good for me.

I rise from an uncomfortable night sleeping on the steel bench seats and my back is stiff and sore. Why didn't I take advantage of one of the infinitely more comfortable hammocks? I have no idea. Looking toward the rear of the plane, I see the hammocks are missing anyway. My dear brother has been so kind as to steal them away in the night. I wonder what else my loving brother has been up to. The hatch door latch is still locked. Apparently, he hasn't had any change of heart.

Looking out through the windows, I see a vacant camp. Well, it isn't completely vacant; Toothless is still here, and the axe handle rises to my view through a couple windows. His body has been pushed up against the exterior of the cabin door. I can just make out his feet extending out from the plane. At least it's good to know the ass is still watching over things, but I'll bet he has a nasty case of split vision. I can't help laughing to myself at my joke. Still, it's bothersome that Simon has not moved the body away from camp. It won't be long before the ants find him and when they do, we'll all be just another meal. They won't care that we are still alive. At least Simon will be able to run, but where am I to go?

I move to the other side of the fuselage to look north and am comforted to find Simon working his little crates to catch us food. Funny, I don't feel so hungry this morning, but I must be famished. I know that I'll also need water soon.

I sit down on the foldout steel bench, waiting for Simon's return, and reach out with my feet to kick at the cardboard boxes that guard our opium. It must be worth a fortune. I'll need to remind Simon of its value before we escape this hell. It could set us up well wherever we end up. Certainly, we won't want to leave it here. As I look around, it strikes me how Simon has managed to clear everything of value from our little room. He must have been planning my incarceration for days. The two discarded suitcases he left lying on the floor with me are damaged and empty. He didn't even leave me a change of clothes.

I'm not sure what he intends me to do when I need to piss or crap. Certainly, he wouldn't expect his only brother to defecate in the same place he sleeps and lives. I know he doesn't trust me, but he's got to let me out to go to the bathroom; he must. I'd do the same for him. That's a lie, but I enjoy lying to myself. Just thinking about pissing has me now needing to urinate. Simon better show up soon or I'll be forced to piss on the floor. I guess that won't be the most terrible thing I could be forced to do. There are enough cracks in the seams of the plane to let it escape into the sand, but it will certainly stink. I hope he shows up soon.

I stand to watch Simon through the window. He's still wading in the water next to his traps. I'll bet he would stay there all day if I don't make noise. I pound on the window to see if I can catch his attention. He makes no notice of me. He needs to let me out to pee. My bladder is becoming uncomfortable. I move into the cockpit and yell his name through the broken windshield. Still no reaction from him. Either he is ignoring me, or the trees and breeze are sucking away the noise before it can reach him. He's ignoring me and enjoying it. Let him enjoy it for a moment; it will be the last time he'll be in this position of power. He will be sorry.

Giving up, I look for a crack in the skin of the plane through which I might piss. I open my pants to urinate, and … nothing. I know I need to urinate, but I can't. It must be dehydration. I need some food and water.

*

Simon nudged a final crab into the crate as he tipped it upright in the water, trapping the little creatures inside. He hated to use Ess' remaining stub of her severed arm as bait, but he also didn't think it quite right to waste it. He took some comfort believing that she wouldn't have wanted him to waste it either. Better to have it used to catch crabs than to leave it for the yellow ants.

The crate was full as he placed the top on it to keep the little beasts from escaping their hold. One or two should fill him for this morning's meal and perhaps one for Anders. He would return the crate to the shallow water to keep the rest of them alive and fresh for lunch and dinner.

The fire was still smoldering as he broke up some dry wood to rekindle the flame. He couldn't afford to break up any more of the crates for kindling. He had other plans for them, so he reminded himself that he would need to gather more firewood. The remaining intact crates and their captive scotch bottles were his only hope of floating off the island. Simon prodded at the coals with a stick and then knelt close to blow into the embers. They started to glow, first a dull red and then a bright orange just before the dry wood ignited to flame. He continued tending the baby flame until it grew hot enough and large enough to sustain itself. It was time to eat.

Reaching into the wooden box, he pulled out one of the carnivorous scavengers from Ess's arm. Having lost its purchase on the dead flesh, the creature refocused its pincers on trying to catch Simon, just nipping him as he dropped the creature into the flame. Although he couldn't be sure, he swore he heard the little animal scream as the flame licked at its shell, instantly beginning to turn it from an ugly brown to crimson. The crab froze and died. Simon turned it over and over in the flame with his stick before reaching back into the box to repeat the process with a second ten-legged beast.

The crab struggled against his grip. It was amazing how strong they were. It was as if they knew they were about to die, and this represented their last effort to escape. They didn't care that their lost freedom bought Simon time for his.

He slid the crabs from the flame onto the deformed "platter" of aluminum and set about stripping the meat from the shell. He was in no hurry. He had nothing else to do, so he took his time. Simon sensed Anders watching him from the windows. He wondered if Anders was hungry. He wondered if Anders felt fear that he might allow him to starve. Although Simon didn't relish making Anders suffer, he felt his brother needed to experience fear, some sort of punishment for his actions. No, he would not let Anders starve, but Anders didn't know that.

Simon forced himself to eat the meat even though he no longer had much of an appetite. Eating alone would always be a chore, not a pleasure. He washed the crab down with a gulp of cloudy spring water. It was funny how he was getting used to the water's taste. The same few ounces of purifying scotch they needed to make the water safe now made the water taste wonderful. Simon had not been much of a drinker before landing here, but now he understood the appeal of liquor. He found it interesting that the taste of dirt and mud in the water was repugnant, but the taste of peaty smoke in the scotch was good—no, better than good; it was wonderful.

No longer hungry, he took the remaining crab legs with their delicate white meat to his brother. He was sure Anders would be hungry, and he couldn't afford to waste anything. He climbed the nose of the plane and set the torn sheet of aluminum with the remaining food just inside the fractured window on a pillow of leaves.

"Anders, Anders, breakfast is served."

Just as he turned to slide down the smooth, rounded nose back into the growth that hid the cockpit, Anders called out, "Wait."

Simon looked back to see Anders' hand slip through the cracked window. "Please, Simon, you have to let me out of here. I can't stay here alone any longer. Please, just touch me, Simon. Hell, I'm your brother. I know I shouldn't have killed Toothless, but I can't turn back the clock. If I could, I would. You've got to believe me." Anders sounded as though he were sobbing.

The plea wrenched at feelings Simon had never felt before. He began to reach up to grasp the offered hand, if for no other reason than to have communion with another being. Anders was not the only one suffering from loneliness. Even though he was free from the fuselage, Simon felt just as much a captive as Anders was. He felt compassion for his brother, but, logically, he knew compassion could be dangerous when dealing with someone like Anders. His brother only wanted out and would say anything to get him to forgive and lower his guard. He wouldn't be taken in by Anders' pleading. He pulled back his hand as if repulsed before Anders could grasp it.

"I left you food to eat. You need to eat it."

"I'm not hungry," Anders snapped from the darkness of the cockpit. He sounded like a child on the verge of a temper tantrum.

"That is not my problem. If you want to starve yourself, that is your choice." Simon slid to the ground, but rather than leaving Anders, he continued talking with him. Leaning toward the broken shield, he asks, "Anders, why do you hate me? You know, the way I am?"

Simon's question quelled Anders' anger, "Why do you think I hate you?" Anders' voice floated out of the void. "I've spent my whole life looking after you, caring for you, loving you. How could you ever think I hate you?"

"You might think you have cared for me, but you have always been embarrassed because I was not like you."

"Well, of course, Simon. You couldn't cope with anything that seemed out of order. In the sea of life, you wanted the water surface to be glass smooth, a mirror that reflected your view of how things ought to be. You were compelled to change anything that didn't measure up to your view of perfection. Everything had to be perfect … and if it wasn't perfect you set about changing it. You pissed off everyone, but I was never mad at you. I never hated you. You just exasperated me."

"But you began to hate me, and now you thoroughly hate me, do you not?"

"Why would you say such a thing? It would be like… hating myself. I can't hate you."

Even though he couldn't see his face, Simon could sense Anders leering at him as he spoke. The bite of his voice contradicted his words. He could almost see the spittle flying from his mouth. His brother really did hate him.

"Anders, on the sea of life you like to refer to, why are you so intent on making waves? If you know I like the calm, why do you insist on splashing about with your arms to make random and continuous waves? You never once tried to help me. You would just make fun of me and pull me away from what I was trying to accomplish … and what did you ever accomplish? You made up stories to pad your pocketbook, even if they hurt others. I never hurt anyone. At least not on purpose."

"Are you kidding? What about Mom and Dad? Don't you think it hurt them each time you lost a job, each time you lost a friend? Don't tell me you never hurt anyone. Hell, you hurt me all the time. Every time I had to listen to you embarking on one of your dissertations, it tore at me. It tore at me just as much as it would have if I had been the one making a fool of myself. You make others cringe; don't you get it? It kills me to watch folks roll their eyes when you talk."

"Then why have you never stopped me? Why have you never told me? I could have changed. I would have changed." Tears rolled down Simon's cheeks as he poured his heart out to his brother. This was all new to him, but he was finding it a refreshing, rejuvenating experience. For the first time, he felt as though he was real, as though he could feel without fear of being mocked.

"Anders, you say you love me, but I am not sure you know what that means. Did you love Ess?"

Silence.

"Anders, did you hear me? Did you love Ess?"

Again silence. Simon thought he could hear footsteps from the cockpit moving away, back into the fuselage. Their conversation was done. He would try again when he brought water for his brother.

He returned to the campfire and sat next to Toothless. He knew he would need to move the body, but for some reason he procrastinated. If the body sat next to him, he could pretend he was not alone.

CHAPTER 37
Preparations

Leaving the island would be a huge challenge for Simon. Building his escape craft, nothing more than a conglomerate of wooden crates, wrapped tightly together with cargo netting and straps, seemed like a simple exercise, but launching it would mean a leap into the unknown. This was something that would have been difficult, if not impossible, for him prior to being stranded here on the island.

Even more disconcerting would be leaving alone. He no longer could see a path for taking Anders with him. He couldn't be trusted. In fact, he was sure Anders would do anything to undermine his attempt to leave. It didn't make sense, true, but Simon was convinced that this man who had been willing to try anything before they crashed here was now deathly afraid of leaving the island. He was convinced the fear was less the result of lost confidence and more the knowledge that his previous life no longer existed. It meant a return to a life in which he was not in charge; Simon could live on his own. Anders would come up with every reason why they had to wait for a rescue, even one that would never come. Faced with the ultimatum that Simon was leaving him, he would stoop to sabotage. If that failed, Anders could be counted on to kill again. Anders had to win; he had to be the boss. But Simon was now the boss.

Simon began laying out the wooden crates he would eventually fill with empty scotch bottles. They would be strapped together to form his raft. It had seemed so simple to construct the craft, but he had to admit the thin wooden crates hardly seemed durable enough to build anything that might be considered seaworthy. True, if everything worked well, the empty bottles would provide buoyancy and the crates would provide the superstructure, but that would only work so long as the waters remained calm. A big wave and the crates would crack, releasing their glass floats, and lose their ability to carry him above water level. If there was any rough sea, he would be doomed unless he could swim to another one of the many uninhabited islands that dotted this part of the ocean. But a new island would mean being completely alone, potentially without any fresh water, questionable food, and NO ONE to be with. He would really be alone.

No sooner had he started laying out the building blocks that would eventually be his raft than he realized a major shortcoming; he had no way to guide the craft. Without a sail to catch the wind and propel it through the water, he would be completely at the whim of the currents. If they carried him close enough to an inhabited piece of land, great; he would be saved. If not, he would be adrift in more than a hundred thousand square miles of nothing but aqua blue. He would float until his boat fell apart or he died from a lack of water and exposure. The raft and a little luck would be the only things standing between life and death. But for Simon, staying here would be the same thing as death. It was worth the risk.

He was in no hurry to complete the raft. Leaving his brother was something he didn't look forward to. Dawdling on with the design and the fabrication provided an excuse to spend more time with Anders. It also provided him hope that he might invent a means to guide the boat. Certainly, a sail would prove beneficial if he could figure a way to fashion some type of mast that could hold up under a reasonable wind. The sail itself would be a separate challenge, but he soon realized they had been sitting on the solution from day one. The canvas pillows, if one could really call them pillows, were really nothing more than folded canvas. Cut a couple seams and, voila, instant sail. It wouldn't be large, but it would work.

As he laid out the parts that would eventually become his escape craft, Simon occasionally glimpsed a shadowy face peering out at him from the silver trunk of aluminum and steel that was his brother's prison. Each time, the face dropped from view, only to be followed by his brother crying out to him from the broken windshield. He tried to ignore the pleading, but eventually surrendered. He grabbed up a bottle of water, took a swig, and carried it with him to the nose of the DC-3 to speak with Anders.

"Okay, Anders, I am here. What is your problem? What could I have that you need?"

"Oh, stop pretending to be innocent, you prick. I see what you're doing. You're building a boat. What in the hell are you thinking? You're going to kill us. Once we set out to sea, we'll have no way to control where we go. Hell, we'll just float out to the middle of the Java Sea to die. We'll be just another meal for a bunch of sharks. I'm not going to go with you."

"I did not ask you to go. You can stay here if you want. In fact, I think I want you to stay here, You will stay here."

Anders clambered over the tree branch occupying the pilot's seat in the cockpit, the same branch that had pinioned the captain. He stuck his face against the hole. "You little fuck, you are not going to leave me here alone. It's wrong and it's not fair. Even if you don't drown out there, you can't survive without me and you know it."

"Seriously, Anders. Do you even listen to yourself? In one breath you say you will not leave, then in the next you say you refuse to be left alone." Simon paused to gather his confidence. "I can only say that I will leave this island. I will not stay to die as our friends have. By the way, you never answered me; did you love Ess?"

"Why should I answer such a stupid question? What even gives you the right to ask me that?" Anders snapped.

“I have every right. It was me who rescued her from the wild boars. I cut her damaged arm from her body. I held her while she breathed her last breath. I have every right to ask if you loved her.”

Anders wouldn’t or couldn’t answer the question. Simon could see the hatred in his brother’s face, but it was meaningless. Simon was now in control of everything.

Anders finally offered a response. “I don’t know.”

“What do you mean, you don’t know? How could you pull her away from Singapore, her job, her entire life, if you did not love her?”

“Look, I thought I loved her. Hell, I tried to save her.”

“Tried? Tell me, Anders, what does it feel like to ‘try?’ You either did or you did not save her. You failed and you did not even ask for her forgiveness. You may have thought it, but you never did it. You let her die without ever telling her you were sorry. You never loved her.”

“Screw you, Simon. How would you know anything about love? The only things you love are facts and figures. Anything that falls outside of your definition of logic just doesn’t compute. It doesn’t register with you at all. You know nothing at all of love, so stop preaching to me.”

“I love you.”

Anders offered only silence in response.

*

I know what he is doing, but why he’s doing it is a mystery to me. I mean I get that he is building a raft, but it looks as though it would crash apart at the first contact with a wave. He’s smart. He must realize the futility of his effort and yet he continues as if there is no other option for him. It keeps him busy. I understand that. I wish I had something to do. I am going crazy cooped up in here.

The food Simon has left me remains sitting where he left it, perched precariously in the branches just inside the broken windshield. He left it sitting on this little piece-of-shit beaten sheet metal. He thinks that if he serves me the food, I'll eat it. Fuck him. I'm not going to eat or drink anything until I'm free again. I laugh at how I am going to outsmart my brother with my hunger strike. He can't bear to let me starve. It is only a matter of time before he opens the door of my cell and grants me my freedom. I need my freedom.

Even though I've already scoured every square inch of my dark home time and time again, looking for an escape, I start my hunt all over again. I begin at the tail of the plane. There are minute cracks in the fuselage I hadn't noticed before. They cede their presence through the almost infinitesimal fingers of light that manage to intrude on my darkness. How could I have missed these? I push against the hull in a futile attempt to enlarge the cracks.

Even with these little spider webs of light leaking through the fractured aluminum and steel and the small window portals, my cell seems perpetually draped in shadow. The light is all sucked up before reaching the floor of the cabin. I drop to my knees and crawl around the floor, blindly feeling with my hands for something, anything, that might enable me to enlarge the small cracks that already exist in the fuselage's skin. A screwdriver, a hammer, anything that I could use to pry at the torn metal would at least give me hope of escape. I have time, too much time. Just the effort would allow me to break the monotony.

So far, I have found nothing to help me. As I mentioned before, Simon has even removed the two net hammocks that had hooked to the steel skeleton of the fuselage. He is making my time of incarceration inhumane. I move forward on my knees, constantly feeling where the floor meets the curved wall, hoping to find a purchase of some sort on which I can pull, something that might surrender some hidden, secret compartment that I have missed before, something in the floor, a stash of tools, anything that might serve to help me escape. Or something I can use to negotiate with Simon? Perhaps I might find something he could use, something he needs, to build his tiny ship. Something that will make Simon have to release me. I know it's not likely Simon has missed anything in here, but I can hope. I need to hope.

Crawling and groping accomplishes nothing more than getting my hands cut and dirty. Although it is difficult in the dark to see the blood seeping from my cuts, I feel it; the warm, sticky liquid. I hold my hands up into the light to see the crimson liquid running down my arms. Its metallic smell excites my hunger, so I stick my bloodied fingers in my mouth to sup on the thick fluid. I know the cuts on my fingers will get infected if I don't clean them. My saliva will have to do.

I drop back on to my hands and knees to search the floor because, well, I have nothing else to do. I stop only when I have reached the bulkhead. Here the flow of the curved wall is abruptly interrupted by a wooden partition bolted to the floor and so far, I have found nothing of use. I repeat the process on the other side of the cabin, taking additional time to feel around the base of the hatch door to see if I might discern how Simon has fixed the door so that it can't be pushed open. I try to force the door. I push and pull on the handle, but I have no success in making even the slightest of movement. I have no idea how Simon fastened the door.

Giving up, I lay on the steel bench seats. I am crying. I can't help myself. It is embarrassing because I never cry. Does Simon know how terrible a punishment he is inflicting on me? He's keeping me in solitary confinement. He's imprisoning me without any trial, without any witnesses, without any law. Simon must feel he is now the law, the jury, and the judge. I suppose he considers himself a benevolent dictator. He has become a dictator, but he is hardly benevolent. Isn't that what history would tell us, all dictators eventually become malevolent and self-serving. Simon certainly has become nothing more than self-serving. He will only allow my freedom if he thinks it is to his benefit. I need to find a reason for him to release me. Then, I'll be the king and he'll be my subject. I will make him beg for my forgiveness.

CHAPTER 38
How Could You Know Me?

Simon peered into the darkened cockpit to ensure it was vacant before reaching through the hole in the window to retrieve the little makeshift tray. He was disheartened to see the food was untouched. "Anders, why have you not eaten your food? You must be hungry. I ate all of mine and I am still starving."

There was no answer, but he could hear the breathing of a creature coming from the dark depths of the plane. The sound was ominous, louder than he would have expected from a mere human being. He could almost imagine the noise emanating from a lion or a bear. Suddenly, he was afraid of what he had really imprisoned inside.

"Anders, come here into cockpit so I can see you when I talk to you."

"Simon, is that you?" Anders' weak voice was a striking contrast to the heavy breathing from only a moment before. "I feel ill, real ill. I'm afraid I might be dying. Can you bring me some water? I am so parched."

Although the voice was weak, Simon could discern a powerful evil hidden in each word. It was an act, and it was a poor, uncompelling performance. Anders was a poor actor. He would fool nobody other than himself.

Simon responded to Anders's begging, "I cannot come in to help you, brother, but I can bring you some more food and a dish of water if you can come into the cockpit. I will need you to come up here into the light so I can see you."

There was no response. Even the heavy breathing fell silent. Then there was a crash as Anders flew into the cockpit. Simon recoiled from the window and slid down from the plane's nose, falling to the ground, as his brother reached frantically through the hole in the window to grasp his brother. He was screaming incoherently while his arm flailed wildly outside the plane trying to get a hold of Simon.

Eventually, the arm tired and slowed only to retreat into the cockpit. Then quietly, "You can't leave me in here. I'll die. I am dying."

Unwilling to climb back onto his perch to look into the cockpit, Simon replied, "Let's talk of death then. How do you want to be remembered, Anders? Have you ever thought about your legacy? What is it you want out of life?"

"My legacy? You've got to be kidding. I'm trapped in here on an island nobody knows about or cares about, and you want to embark on a philosophical discussion that has no purpose, no meaning?

"You need to get your head on straight, Simon. You're nothing without me; you never have been. My legacy? You are my legacy whether you want it or not. Your life is important only because I will it to be important. You can't understand that? You think you're important because of some sort of innate set of values you possess or because you are blessed with a unique intellect. You aren't. None of us are. We're important only as a comparison to others; that's the measure. I can't allow you to grow, because for you to grow means I diminish. I can't let that happen."

"So, you think your value is only relative?" Simon asks.

"Not just mine, all of ours. I'm important because you aren't. If you're more important, I must be less so. If you think you are valuable to society, you must think I have little value. Face it, Simon, our life is meaningless outside of how we might be better or worse than others. Success itself is only an abstract measure of how my life is better than yours."

"Funny logic, Anders. You treat an individual's worth as finite, something that is dependent on others. Something that cannot be developed without threatening the status quo. You live in a nihilistic world where life has little innate value. But I do not agree with you. We all have value independent of each other. Now I understand why you cannot be happy that I am finally growing. I have stepped into my manhood. I no longer need to live the contrived, constrained life that you created for me, afraid of failure, afraid of imperfection. You are a sad lot, and I pity you."

"How dare you pity me," Anders spat back. "I've sacrificed for you. I did everything for you."

"You did nothing for me. You kept me afraid so that you could be my hero. Were you not thrilled pretending to be my savior? You did nothing altruistically. You did everything with an expectation you would be enriched, maybe not financially, but certainly to fuel your feeling of self-worth. You were happy seeing me as an emotional vacuum with you being the very air that would fill me up. I can no longer live that way.

"You need to make some decisions, and you better make them quick. Can you live without me? Because I am quite sure I can live without you. I will bring you some more food and water. It will be your choice if you want to partake in it. I will not force you to eat; how could I? But if you do not eat the next meal, you will not get another. I cannot afford to waste my time and effort just for you to throw it away." Simon left to return to the campsite that now seemed a world away. He left the gloom of the forest and the cancerous mind of his brother to return to the sunlight.

*

Simon hasn't come back since leaving me the tray of fish and green ferns. I assume the ferns are edible. I doubt he would try to poison me, but after our last talk, it's clear he despises me. Beside the food is a piece of aluminum that he has hammered into a small bowl that is filled with water. If I shake the branch, the food and drink will fall to the floor.

I now know Simon doesn't feel any obligation to me even after all the years I have taken care of him. Hell, I deserve a medal for all I've had to put up with. He doesn't comprehend how much he's benefited from me. And to think he can survive without me in the future. No way!

I sit here in silence in the copilot's seat staring at the uneaten food. I won't touch it even though I feel both hunger and thirst. Simon's right that I must decide, but the decision is different than the one he proposed. You see, I think he's bluffing. He won't let me starve. I'll sit here without moving until he returns. I'm not going to move until he opens that fucking door and frees me.

The day is beginning to wane and what little sunlight I can see through the canopy of trees is diminishing. I think I'll sleep here tonight. The seat is comfortable, and the windows provide a view of the outside. I know why Simon slept here. I can also hear the noises of the evening. It's amazing how the world comes alive after the lights go out. Our little empty island is anything but empty; it's filled with life. I must have been blind. I close my eyes, just for a bit.

CHAPTER 39
Ready? Set? …

Day fourteen—

Simon stood to look at his construction effort. He had been optimistic that a seaworthy craft would be simple to build, but that was turning out not to be the case. In fact, he was beginning to consider whether his brother had been right, that this effort would just be an exercise in futility. While the idea of using the scotch empties as buoys locked inside crates that could then be held together with cargo netting sounded good, he was now concerned the thin wood slats could split and splinter as the raft twisted and flexed in the water. If the boxes split, the precious glass floats would be released or, worse, would break and he would be left treading water in the middle of nowhere.

His second concern was that of guiding the craft. He had been so proud to have happened on such a simple solution for a sail, but now, when faced with adding a mast that could hold up under the wind, he was stymied. If the wooden crates were potentially too weak to hold up under the basic undulations of the water, how could they work as a foundation to which he might affix a mast? Even if he could come up with a solution to fly the sail, he would also need some type of rudder to work in conjunction with the sail or he would be at the whim of the currents of wind or water. Luck would be paramount in his navigation to safety.

For an individual that was comfortable living in the world of the known, always acting rationally and logically, Simon was embarking in a region he had rarely visited: the unknown. This was a land governed more by faith than known solutions. He accepted that solutions would make themselves apparent as he progressed with the construction.

He laid out the cargo netting in the sand. It would be the glue that held the raft together. If it failed, the boat failed. On top of the net, he interlaced the first layer of crating. Each of these crates would be filled with a mix of full and empty scotch bottles. The hope was that the full bottles might provide ballast to the craft, helping to control its pitch and roll as it moved over the swells in the sea. Although he really could not attest to the validity of his theory, it sounded plausible and it did give him an excuse to not waste all the scotch, pouring it into the sand. He thought it funny that, although Anders had been the drinker, he had now developed a taste for the nectar. He held up one of the bottles to admire the rich amber color. It was as if the sun had married the moon just before dropping into the ocean for the night and this was the resulting child.

After reattaching the top of each crate to provide strength and to ensure the bottles could not float away, he wrapped cargo straps around the entire layer, cinching them tightly together as a single structure. He then wrapped it in the netting and pulled the raft's substructure into the shallow water. If he added a second level of crates while the craft was on dry sand, he doubted he would have the strength to drag the raft to the water. Placing a second level of crates on the partially floating and moving first level would be difficult, but necessary. This second level of boxes was significantly lighter, filled almost entirely with empty bottles; this would be the primary source of buoyance for his sea craft. The only exceptions were reserved for the water bottles that were his only potable water supply and one crate that would hold his limited cargo of food, clothes, and, most importantly, Bradley's leather briefcase with its £110,000 hidden in its secret compartment. If he survived the escape, this would set him up for good.

Simon cinched the second layer of crates together with the cargo straps before pulling the netting loose of the first level and rewrapping it around both layers. He closed the netting by weaving another cargo strap through the mesh and pulling it taut. He sat back in the sand to admire his boat before pushing it further into the water to see how it would float.

Pushing the raft out to the sea was both frightening and exhilarating. Frightening in that to test the craft, he would need to float out further into the sea than he had gone before. He had no idea where the sea floor would fall away to a point that he would no longer be able to stand. If he fell off the edge, this would no longer be a rehearsal; it would be the real performance. If the boat fell apart, there would be no way to recover. The exhilaration came from knowing that if the test were a success, he would be leaving tomorrow.

True, he had no rudder or mast, but if the boat held together, he had a chance. He was convinced staying provided no certainty other than he would serve out his final days as a slave to his brother. He would not allow himself to fall into that trap.

*

What the hell is he doing? From my vantage point I can only see the corner of his raft, but it looks too small. Certainly, it's too small for both of us. If we get hit by a wave, it'll topple us into the sea. What's he thinking? Simon is pushing his raft out into the water. He moves beyond the edge of the window, and I lose sight of him. All I know is the boat looked to be floating fine. I fly to the other side of the cabin to see if I can get a better view. I place my face tight against the glass. I just want a glimpse as to where Simon has gone. I can't see anything. Damn it, Simon's left me. He hasn't even bothered to release me. I'll die in here.

I return to my original window and stare outside, squishing my face against the glass surface to improve my angle of view. There is nothing to see but sand and water. I wait and watch. I will wait and watch until he returns. He must return, but he has already been gone too long.

*

Simon smiles as he sits atop his creation. It was floating and it was stable, better than he had anticipated even though it sat lower in the water than he had hoped. He slid off the edge into the waist-deep water to pull his raft back to shore. Sure, right now it had shortcomings as boats go, but at least he could count on the vessel staying above water if the sea remained calm. A storm the likes of the one that delivered them here would transform his ship into kindling and broken glass. Maybe a prayer, if he knew how to pray, would be in order before he set sail.

Pulling the boat back to the beach was tougher than he expected, a lot tougher. The boat sat so low in the water that the invisible current, although slow, had taken a massive grip on the craft, trying to tug it out to sea. Had he stayed on the raft another ten minutes or so, he would have been pulled to a point of no return and his journey would have already started. After fighting the current and winning, he managed to get the vessel nestled snuggly onto the sand in shallow water. He made a mental note that he would need to attach some type of leash to his raft to ensure it did not float away on the tide this evening.

His test, although successful, pointed out the need to add some means to hang his sail just to ensure that he would not be completely at the whim of the sea current; it was more formidable than he could have imagined. A rudder was also critical if he were to have any hope of truly navigating his craft, but the sail was a necessity no matter what.

Before tackling the problem of mounting his sail, getting a good meal and some water in his belly needed to take priority. He had no idea how long it might be before he would be able to consume some significant calories again, so he would fill himself today. He would also take Anders' share of the food. Although it hurt to acknowledge the inevitable, Anders had decided to waste food for the last time. It was not a luxury he could afford. It was difficult enough to feed himself, let alone take care of another. He didn't know if letting Anders die was the right thing to do, but he felt that if there were a God, he would understand that he would either let one die or they both would die. How could he hold it against an individual for letting another die to save oneself? Perhaps the real test was that of the soul, that this life meant little and what really counted was beyond this physical life. If that's the case, Simon would need forgiveness for what he would do tomorrow.

CHAPTER 40
Goodbyes

Day fifteen—

Simon rolled over in the already warm sand. Even after fighting the sand fleas all night, he slept better than he had in what seemed forever. Had the sun not started to beat down on him, he would have been glad to have slept the day away. Pushing himself up to his knees, he paused just long enough to brush away the loose sand from his arms and face. He stood up and then ran into the water, diving in headfirst, rinsing off the grains that had refused to be casually brushed away. The cool salt water knocked him wide awake and served to quell the itching from what seemed hundreds of tiny welts from the flea bites. He cupped his hands to pull the sea water to his face and hair, rinsing and cleansing himself in the briny water. It was refreshing. He was energized and anxious for this day, the first day of his new life.

Walking from the water, he couldn't help but smile. He could feel the muscles in his cheeks cramping, but he was still unable to quit. Even seeing Anders's solemn face through a cabin window couldn't dampen his spirit. He felt joyous. Anders had been right; for him to grow, Anders must diminish. Certainly, as Simon became happier, Anders became sadder.

Last night he'd completed his preparations for his trip, packing food and some clothes in his cargo hold along with his water supply. He decided to sacrifice one bottle of water, instead using the bottle to hold the bank notes to keep them dry. Even his two design shortcomings that had become apparent in his test float were no longer issues. He still did not have a rudder, but he had added a bag of sand as ballast that would hang from one corner of his raft. He hoped it would function much like the tail of a child's kite fluttering in the wind. The bag, made from the tied-off legs of a pair of Toothless' pants, would be dropped into the water when he used the sail.

The sail took more work to fabricate than he had anticipated, but, here, too, he happened on a solution that, although flawed, would provide him some ability to navigate his barge. He laced several thin branches onto the canvas fabric using the same wire he had used to make sutures. Through perforating the canvas with the wire and then wrapping the wire around the branches, he had constructed a light frame to keep the long horizontal sail standing upright on the surface of his raft. The entire sail would be held in place by one of the hammocks he had stolen from the plane. At one end, the sail was hooked to the same corner as his ballast bag. The other end would be held and controlled by him. Shortening or lengthening the amount of sail that could catch the wind allowed him to manage the direction that the air pressure would push the craft. If it got too windy to hold, he would merely lay the sail down on the deck and use it as a pad to lie upon. He had an overwhelming sense of pride; it was a feeling new to him. It was a feeling Anders had never let him experience.

He proceeded to pick up a last bottle of water from the sand. The other bottles had already been loaded into the cargo hold of his raft the night before. He disappeared into the edge of jungle that hid the cockpit from view. He took a sip from the bottle before calling to his brother. "Anders, come to the window. I have something important for you."

He knew that Anders had been watching like a sentry from his post in the cabin, but he heard no response. Anders was continuing his poker game, calling what he thought to be a bluff regarding his food, but he was wrong. There was no bluff and, quite frankly, there was no poker game. Anders was playing a game of solitaire and had lost long ago; he just didn't know it.

Simon expected Anders to stay committed to his fiction long after he had sailed away, but he no longer cared.

Simon climbed up the nose of the plane using a tree for assistance. Looking into the dim aluminum and steel cave, he could see nothing, "Anders," he called again. "I have water for you. I will stick it in the tree branch. It will take care of you for a while if you conserve it. I want you to know I love you."

"Bullshit!" Anders screamed as his face slammed against the inside of the glass. Simon recoiled, pulling his hand from the bottle in fear that his brother would grab him and never let go. He imagined a terrible end to their lives, one on either side of a metal wall engaged in a death grip, a grip that would only be relinquished when one or both died.

Anders had changed. He had come to grasp, finally, that he would never leave his cell. His face was one of anguish. Spittle sprayed from his mouth with each angry breath.

Simon slid from the nose to the safety of the ground. Although he had not looked forward to saying a final goodbye to Anders, his anxiety diminished instantaneously once he recognized that Anders gave him no choice. His brother could not be trusted. He was a killer.

"Anders, goodbye. I pray that God takes care of you. You've been my shadow forever, but I cannot take you with me." And with that, Simon left.

*

What has he done? I push my face against the glass trying to get a glimpse of where fucking Simon has gone.

"Simon, don't say goodbye. You can't leave me. You need me and you always will." There is no answer, but I know he is still there, standing in the shadows just below the sill of my window. I can't see him, but I'll wait here until he speaks again. I'm afraid to return to the cave of the cargo hold behind me. It's dark there, and in darkness, shadows disappear.

CHAPTER 41
Landings

Day fifty-six—

"Ashley, why are we slowing?" asks Landry to the ship's steward, who had just brought his aperitif of chilled vermouth along with a small selection of cheeses to stimulate his appetite. He appreciated the extravagance, but it was difficult getting excited about more food and drink. He had done little but eat and drink since their seaborne escape from Singapore a week ago. This trip, that had started so hurriedly out of fear of being trapped by the invading Imperial Japanese Navy had turned into a vacation.

He and his family had delayed their escape so long that they could see the war ships with their smoking guns in the distance. The sound of pounding cannon punched through the air, the concussions pressing against their faces as the engines pushed their yacht away from the battle. They had thought they waited too long to run, but now that they moved as far south as the Java Sea, and the boat had slowed to a leisurely crawl to conserve fuel, the sense of urgency waned. The Landry family was now intent on enjoying the benefits of their family boat. In truth, it was hardly a boat; their yacht was just over a hundred feet in length and manned by ten full-time crew members who attended to their every need and whim.

Their escape was now nothing more than a relaxed sea cruise, one that Landry felt more fitting for an individual of his pedigree and wealth. International trade had been very kind to him and his family. He traded in all sorts of commodities: some legal, some not so legal, but all profitable. They had accumulated enough wealth to enable multiple generations of his family to live in luxury, and the Landry wealth would continue to grow if those Japanese buggers didn't screw things up with this war they started.

Now confident that they were safely away from the impending battles, Landry desired to make their passage one of memories and enjoyment. He had even asked his captain this morning to consider deviating from their course to provide his family the luxury of some sightseeing. Given that they had escaped the devilish Japanese, they could afford to take their time on the way to their second home in Brisbane.

The steward approached Landry. "Sir, the captain suggested we might drop anchor to allow your family to visit one of the small islands in this area. We can use the dinghy, and he thought he might accompany you to do a little exploring and get a little exercise. Based on your request this morning, he thought this might meet with your desires?"

"I think that would be fabulous, but is it safe?" Landry asks.

"Of course, sir, and if you don't mind a suggestion, perhaps you and your family might desire to delay lunch so that we might set it up for you on land?"

"Again, that sounds like a wonderful idea. Please ask the captain what the appropriate attire for our little foray into the local peoples might be."

"Sir, I will be glad to inquire, but I suspect anything comfortable would be appropriate. You see, for the most part, these tiny islands are uninhabited; they are only visited by the occasional fisherman. You should have the island all to yourselves."

Approaching the steward and Landry, the captain interrupted, "I can see that Steward Ashley has already informed you of our little surprise. I hope it will meet with your expectations?"

"Captain Mathews, of course. Quite frankly, I am hardly hungry after our late breakfast. I think I can speak for the entire family in that delaying lunch a bit would hardly be an imposition. In fact, it would be welcome. Ashley tells me these islands are uninhabited. Is this true?"

"Well, if you ignore the wild boars, bats, and the monkeys, they are. They do receive the occasional visitor, however, typically just for the day. I was hoping you might consider letting the crew pull together a cookout on the beach of one of these picturesque atolls followed by some napping in the warmth of the sun, and then cap it off with a stroll around the island before heading back to the ship. I think it wise to spend the night in the safety of our vessel."

"I think you're right. That sounds a hell of a lot better than sleeping with boars and bats. I can't imagine Matilda getting excited about sleeping in the wilderness. It might prove traumatic when she needs to visit the loo."

The captain smiled at Landry's subtle dig at his spouse. Landry's wife would find fault with everything on this excursion: the sand would be too white, the sun too hot, the water too cool, the vibrant colors too intense. There really was no pleasing Matilda when it came to nature. If dinner were not served on bone china with a place setting that included a minimum of five pieces of flatware, she would consider the meal uncouth and unworthy of her graces. It could prove comical watching her pout and complain over the informality of a cookout, but a sleepout under the stars would pitch her into a bout of bitchiness and his crew would end up being the target. The captain was relieved that Landry supported spending the evening on the boat.

Landry took a sip of his aperitif and placed it back on the table without touching the cheese before excusing himself. "Gentlemen, let me round up the family so that we can change in preparation for our trip into the wild. Any idea as to when we can plan to disembark?"

The captain replied, “Well, I think the first officer has already chosen an excellent island that should prove wonderful. Apparently, he has visited several of these islands in the past, and this one has left him with fond memories due to the shallow waters and the abundant colorful fish you can see while wading. We’ll bring swimming shoes. You won’t want to cut your feet on the coral. We also have a couple pairs of swim goggles if the children would like to see the fish up close and personal. Before I turned over the bridge to him, the first officer already had the island in sight, and we should be there in half an hour. I’ll tell the crew to be ready to disembark within the hour, if that meets with your approval?”

“That will be fine, Captain. I’ll look forward to it, as will my kids. And Matilda, well, she needs a touch of informality. It will be good for her.”

As Landry left for his stateroom, the captain turned to Steward Ashley. “Ashley, join me along with the second mate and the cook on the bridge to discuss the status of our preparations. I think this should be fun.”

An hour later, Mr. Landry, his wife, Matilda, and their two boys, Gregory and Jerry, along with the captain and second mate, were slicing through the placid turquoise water to an emerald island. The boys sat in the bow with huge smiles as the breeze tousled their hair. For them, the island was paradise. Landry, on one side of the dinghy, grinned at the boys’ excitement. This was a wonderful break from the monotony of the yacht. Matilda, sitting across from Landry, found the outing less than enjoyable. With her stoic face, her hair wrapped in a scarf and her eyes covered with sunglasses, she looked like more like a starlet feigning a desire not to recognized than a mother enjoying an afternoon outing with her family. Landry glanced at his wife in sadness that she seemed so incapable of having fun.

Sliding up onto the beach, the captain hopped out of the boat first and grabbed the mooring rope to steady the boat as the Landry family climbed out. The captain was excited to warm his feet in the sand as was the family.

This was the second landing for the dinghy. Previously it had delivered food, cooking supplies, lanterns, towels, deck chairs along with the cook and Steward Ashley. By the time the family arrived, the site was already set up for comfort with a couple small propane cook stoves to fry up steaks and shrimp for their lunch. The cook was busy prepping the food while Ashley was making drinks: gin martini for Landry, Tom Collins for Matilda, and lemonade for the boys.

Landry grabbed his martini and plopped down in one of the deck chairs. "Marvelous. Matilda, we should build a house here. What do you think?" he says smiling, knowing full well this would likely be the last place on Earth that would appeal to her. She had a need to be important and to be seen with other important people. A life of seclusion was hardly something she could ever endure. It would only be a matter of time before she would push to leave Brisbane and relocate to someplace like New York City.

Landry couldn't care less where he lived. He was important and no longer needed the recognition from others. Living out his days in Brisbane seemed perfect. He should send Matilda to New York on her own. He and the boys could visit her whenever they wanted, which was never. He drained his martini and held up his glass as Ashley poured another for him. Landry would be drunk by this evening, but he didn't care. The captain would take care of him. They had been together for years and when out of earshot of others, called each other by only their names, scuttling any reference to title. Captain Philip Mathews became just Phil and Mr. Landry was Landry. Nobody ever used Landry's first name. Even to his wife, he had always been Landry.

CHAPTER 42
Discoveries

After lunch, Matilda pulled her deck chair to the water's edge and sacrificed just a little of her indifference to soak her feet in the cool water. In one hand she held her third Tom Collins of the day, in the other the book *For Whom the Bell Tolls* by Ernest Hemingway. She wasn't enjoying the book. She hadn't been aware it was a story about war when it had first been recommended to her as a "fine read." Now that she had started, she felt compelled to complete it even though she hated it. She had no idea if it was a character flaw or blessing to have to complete things she started. Well, today, at least the gin was making the reading more palatable. Of course, she probably wouldn't remember anything she read and would need to reread these pages when sober.

The boys had finished seconds of their lunches and were now crawling through the water with their goggles to see the colorful fish. The second mate stayed within a few feet of them, continuously checking for danger. Although most of the fish the boys would encounter would be harmless, they shared these waters with sea snakes, jellyfish, and even the occasional and intriguing blue-ringed octopus—a tiny, innocuous creature that would certainly attract the boys' attention … and kill if it bit one of them.

The captain and Landry had taken the opportunity to walk around the island before evening set in. The captain carried a pistol as protection. Although they were friends, the captain had no misunderstanding as to his obligations. He was an employee and was charged with ensuring Landry and his family would arrive safely to their destination. He took his obligation seriously and would sacrifice his life for the family if necessary.

"Phil," Landry started, "why bring the gun? There isn't another person for miles. We are safe."

"Hardly, Landry. I don't know if there are any wild pigs here, but I sure as hell don't want to take a chance on running into one of those bastards without my friend here." He patted his holster with its large revolver. "Have you ever seen them? They're huge and as vicious as any rabid dog. They'll attack anything.

"You know, I've heard the pigs swim from island to island. It hardly seems possible, but I'd rather not chance it."

"What about the kids? Are they safe then?"

"Absolutely, the mate and the cook are carrying pistols, too, and they're both better shots than me." He smiled and added, "The kids are safe, but Matilda, I don't know."

Landry laughed. "Shit, Phil, there's not a pig alive that would want to take on Matilda. One bite and they'd die of frostbite."

They continued in silence, walking clockwise around the island, first heading east for a short while before bending to the south for a much longer stretch, disappearing into a haze. They moved their walking path closer to the water to take advantage of the firm wet sand and the better footing. Landry broke the silence, "Phil, do you still think this place is uninhabited? I keep getting this feeling that we're being watched. It seems weird."

"I know what you mean, but I think it's just the quiet. There's no way this tiny place could support people. We're going to be to the southern tip in just a few minutes. You can see where the jungle ends up there, that's it." He pointed to a point where the trees disappeared and the sea seemed to extend forever. "From there we'll bend around to the north and head back to camp. I can't imagine the whole walk being more than a few miles. This place is way too small for people. We will be back in an hour or so and then we can pack things up and return to the boat. Hey, but if you want, we can turn around now."

"Heck, no. If I did, you'd never let me forget it. You'd call me chicken."

This time, Phil laughed. "Hell, Landry, I already do. I say you are scared to death of your wife. The only problem is nobody laughs. She frightens the crew, too. Ashley has nightmares about her."

"Seriously?"

"No, I'm just kidding you. She's not so bad, just cold, real cold."

"You know, she wasn't always like that. She just needs a shock, something to shake her up."

The first shock on the island was not for Matilda, but for Landry and the captain. As they reached the southern point of the island, Landry tripped on a stick protruding up from the sand, but it wasn't a stick; it was a bone. They discovered a body. The stick was part of a human leg, the foot had been torn away and the flesh had been eaten; the bone gleamed white. Given the size of the bone, they thought it might have belonged to a small woman or a child. They didn't know it, but the sea hadn't wanted Ess and had given her back to the island.

Phil was first to speak as he pulled his gun from his holster. "It looks like I might have been wrong. We might not be alone after all. Let's get back to your family." The captain started to retreat the way they had come, until Landry called him back.

"Let's keep going this way, the sun is setting so it's going to be darker on that side of the island. I know it feels creepy, but let's hustle." He continued around the point and bent northward up the west side of the island.

They were almost jogging when they came upon the "graveyard" Toothless had created, only it wasn't really a graveyard. The pigs and ants had combined their talents and appetites to turn three bodies into scattered bones. For the captain and Landry, it was difficult to really determine how many dead people lay there, but they only found three skulls. Someone had placed these bodies here, meaning they might still be here, and with the number of bodies they had already found, that someone might not be good.

"Phil, are you really good with that thing?" Landry asks, pointing at the pistol in his hand.

"You bet. I had a lot of training with this when I was in the Royal Navy. I was just kidding when I said the cook and mate were better shots. But I'm starting to feel like we should gather our group and get off this place."

"Agreed," and they began to jog again, continuing north.

Sometimes surprises are fun, sometimes they're troublesome, unwanted, and come in bunches. Today was like that. The final surprise came just around the bend and answered a lot of questions. They saw the silver tail protruding out from the trees before seeing anything else. As they approached, they could make out a fuselage and a wing while the rest of the plane disappeared into the jungle. It was as if it had been swallowed by darkness. All was silent.

"Well, I'll be damned. Phil, I know that plane and the guy that flies it."

"You're kidding? How can you tell?"

"Let's just say that when I have questionable cargo, this was the guy I would call. He was small time, but he was always on schedule and could be trusted, two very important traits when you are dealing in real valuable stuff, stuff that you can't afford to lose."

"What's his name?"

"Normally, I wouldn't share it, but it looks as though it doesn't matter anymore. His name was Robert, and he had a sidekick named Thompson. I only met Thompson once. What a crusty old fart. Now it looks like I am going to have to find another carrier."

Landry and Phil entered what had been a campsite, Phil leading the way with his gun cocked and pointed forward. His head darted from the trees to the plane and back to the trees. "Shhh, you hear anything?" he asks Landry.

"Nothing, but the rippling water and breeze blowing through the trees. I think that if anyone survived, they are long gone now."

"All except for the dead sob's we found down the beach and that poor ass someone left guarding the plane." Phil pointed his gun to a skeleton that sat propped up against the cargo door. An axe blade was embedded in the silent sentry's skull. "Well, whoever this guy is; he really must have pissed someone off. He didn't die from natural causes."

Landry laughed, "No shit, Phil, how could you tell?"

Landry stepped up to the corpse and grabbed the axe handle to pull it from the skull. It just seemed wrong to leave the poor bastard sitting there with his murder weapon suck between the two voids that used to hold his eyeballs. He pulled the handle and the man's torso collapsed to the sand.

"Holy shit, he stinks," the captain whispered as he brought his hand up to cover his mouth. Bugs, interrupted from their eating, spewed out the corpse's clothing only to scuttle about in search of another access to what little rotting tissue still clung to the skeleton. The skull, covered with only bits of gray hair, stared blankly into the sun. They would not have to worry about being haunted by the eyes of this dead man, they had been eaten out long ago. One might imagine this body having been here as little as a week or as long as a couple of months.

"You want to check to see if he has any identification or anything?" Landry asks.

"Hell, no. I am not going to touch him, but I am going into that plane. Somebody killed that guy. No way he planted that axe in himself," and he moved to the closed cabin door.

"You want to open it, or do you want me to pull on it?" the captain asks.

"You stay there with the gun ready to shoot and I'll pull it open. Ready?"

Thinking that if someone were hiding inside, they would have the door locked; Landry expected the door not to move. Instead, as he pulled back the latch, the door slid open effortlessly. There was no noise, no sign of movement from inside the hold. He stood still, waiting for his eyes to adjust to the shadow inside the fuselage. He half expected this thing to be filled with more bodies, and he had no desire to walk in and surprise the dead. They could have the place to their own for eternity as far as he was concerned. There was no odor other than a musky smell, so no dead people. The dark fuselage looked to be empty.

The captain crept inside keeping his gun up, ready to fire. He was shaking. He had overstated his prowess with the weapon. True, he had been a good shot when he was in the navy, but that had been a long time ago, and he had never shot a gun at a person. Hell, he had never shot at any living thing. He didn't know if he could pull the trigger if he needed to. He debated backing out of the plane and handing the gun over to Landry. Unfortunately, Landry might think that an act of cowardice rather than Phil's self-doubt in his ability to take another's life. He shook his head and proceeded forward to the cockpit. It was empty save for a large, encroaching tree branch and a small sheet of metal that sat in its leaves, covered with what looked to be old crab shells and bird dung. There was a square bottle that looked to be full of dirty water cradled in the branches. Other than those, the cockpit was empty. The cargo hold was likewise empty except for a stack of cardboard boxes filled with bags of a thick viscous brown stuff. He thought he knew what the gooey stuff was, but he had no desire to stay in the dark to look at it closer. He grabbed one of the bags and made for his exit, returning to the light of day.

"Landry, nobody there. It's empty except for a whole lot of this stuff. Any idea what it is?

"Of course, this is the stuff Captain Robert was famous for. That, my friend, is raw opium." He caught a look of disgust on Phil's face. "Hey, don't act so holy. That stuff helps pay your salary."

"Crap, Landry, I really don't want to know."

"Well, then pitch that little cellophane bag back in the hull and let's get out of here. I don't want to be here when the owner comes looking for it."

The captain looked at Landry, "If it's as valuable as you say, you sure you don't want to pack it up with us? As you said, it could pay a lot of bills and there is a ton of it in there."

"No way. It's not mine and I don't want it on my boat. If it ends up going to Australia with us, probably the best thing that would happen would be losing my yacht. More likely, we could end up spending the rest of our lives in some jail. Even worse, we could end up like that guy." He pointed to Toothless. "Best leave the cargo of the dead with the dead.

"Let's just get back to the family and get out of here. There is nothing any of us can do for Captain Robert or his crew. They are all dead."

Landry and Captain Mathews were back at the family picnic after walking no more than a hundred yards further up the beach. Had they chosen to go around the island counterclockwise, they would have discovered the plane wreck within minutes of starting and they would have avoided being introduced to the entire crew and passenger list, save one, of a DC-3 flight from two months earlier. Captain Mathews was right, though; the island was uninhabited, at least with any living souls.

EPILOGUE
Endings and Beginnings

Anders is gone forever and I don't miss him. I don't think anyone ever found our plane. When I close my eyes, I can still imagine it sitting there with its aluminum tail sticking out from the jungle that hides so many secrets. There is no joy in thinking about those two weeks, but occasionally I find myself drifting back in time to wonder how things might have been different.

In one respect, I am thankful for my time on the island. It allowed me to grow so much. It forced me to discover myself and that made me brave and daring. Before the crash, I would never have considered floating off into the sea on a raft built of nothing more than kindling and bottles.

Oh, the bottles. They saved me. Their golden liquor purified and cleansed, and their glass floated me away to a new life. They are with me even today. I never had a sip of scotch before my time stranded on the island, but today I have one or two glasses each evening after my dinner. Without the drink my memories drift back to the terrible things Anders did on the island, the death he caused. The golden liquor numbs me and forgives me. My housekeeper tells me that at my age I shouldn't drink anymore, but she's so naïve. She doesn't understand I need it to forget the bad things. I have done this ever since my escape some fifty years or so ago.

It has been a long time. Not all my recollections are bad. It seems like yesterday that I crawled onto a new beach, soaked and sunburnt, to fall into the arms of a tiny fisherman. His family took care of me for days until I could care for myself. That very day I thanked him and left the islands forever, taking only my little bag of clothes and the £110,000 in banknotes.

Back then, £110,000 was a lot of money, a small fortune. It was enough for me to go back to the States. I landed in Los Angeles and then went south to San Diego and decided to stay there. I spent most of the money buying up land on the coast just north of the tiny city. Back then the land was cheap, extremely cheap. It was good that Bradley's money wasn't wasted and could make someone happy. I am happy.

Believe it or not, I decided to become a real journalist, but I did it straight, no made-up stories, and I wrote under my full name, Simon Anders Cartwright. I was a good writer, even if my stories were less than exciting. At least they were honest. It was good to be whole again.

I did eventually marry. Even though part of me cared deeply for Ess, the other part of me cared for no one. It took me a long time to understand what love was. Ess and I were never truly made for each other. We were just thrown together by circumstance, and I mistook that for love. I know better now. I found the love of my life shortly after making San Diego my home and we ended up having a little baby boy a year later.

That little boy grew up and became a journalist, a husband, and a father, but I outlived my son. He was killed in Vietnam on a stupid assignment for a television station out of LA. His only son was born a week later. My grandson never got to see his dad. I know is sounds harsh, but I don't feel sorry for my son, Simon Junior; he died doing what he loved. Only the lucky get to do that. But I do feel sorry for myself. I never got to see him develop as a father. And I never shared with him anything about my time on the island.

My grandson has become a journalist, too. He is one of those handsome guys you see on TV. I don't think he likes to get his hands dirty digging out a story, but he will learn. I hope he never needs an Anders.

Acknowledgements

My Brother's Keeper and its characters are purely fiction. Although you will get to know the persons in this story, and a couple are alluded to in my other novels, they are alive only in my mind … and now yours.

Please note that the Japanese Imperial Army invasion of Singapore and their subsequent occupation was real. Sixty-two thousand Allied soldiers ended up as prisoners of war with more than half dying as prisoners. Estimates of Singaporeans who perished during the occupation vary wildly, even today, from five thousand to fifty thousand. It was a dangerous time for those trapped. Unlike the characters in *My Brother's Keeper*, those who escaped were lucky.

I thank my wife, Caylor, and my children, Shelby, Nick, and Tom for their endless support and encouragement with this endeavor. And this would never have been possible without the feedback and input from my dear friends and early readers, Bruce Jenkins, Stacy Allen, and Hal Mortier for their direct and honest feedback. Their suggestions have contributed to making this book what it is; their comments made it better.

Lastly, I would be extremely remiss without providing a heartfelt thank you to my publisher, Carly McCracken at Crimson Cloak Publishing and their wonderful editors, Kate McCracken and Denna Holm. Without them, this book wouldn't exist.

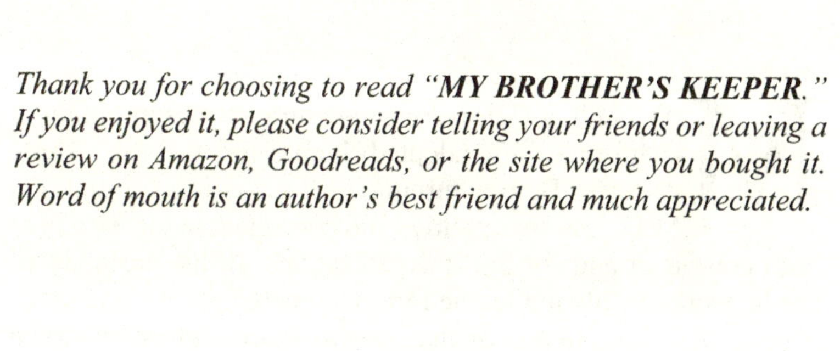

*Thank you for choosing to read "**MY BROTHER'S KEEPER**." If you enjoyed it, please consider telling your friends or leaving a review on Amazon, Goodreads, or the site where you bought it. Word of mouth is an author's best friend and much appreciated.*

ABOUT THE AUTHOR

M.D. Nuth, a Colorado native, now resides in Southern California, his adopted home for the past three decades. Before turning to his passion for writing, M.D. was an executive and consultant in the worlds of both non-profit and for-profit organizations. In his professional life he worked with and learned from an incredibly diverse set of people, from the poorest of the poor to successful international business leaders. Throughout his life he has remained grounded though family, faith, music, and writing.

Life experience gives M.D. a unique perspective and knack for storytelling, providing him insight to illustrate the human factors that affect all of us. His writing transcends socio-economic status while speaking to each of his readers on a personal level, unifying them through life events in which we all can relate. "My Brother's Keeper" is his fourth novel.

https://www.mdnuth.com

Also by M.D. Nuth

Novels:

Countenance of Man
Nails
The Day Before Tomorrow (coming soon)

Poetry:

Davis
Wyatt
Most Important Job
Unnamed
What's Real with You Today?
Man
Sometimes It Rains

Made in the USA
Las Vegas, NV
07 March 2024